Dan Jacobson was born in South A
parents. He has worked as a scho
journalist in South Africa and als
kibbutz in Israel. He moved to Englai   ... many
years he pursued a career as a freelance writer of fiction and
essays. He then entered academic life and eventually became
professor of English Literature at University College London.
He also held visiting professorships and fellowships at
universities in the United States and Australia. Since his
retirement from University College he has resumed working as
a full-time writer. His novels and stories are strikingly various
in nature and set in many countries – among them South Africa,
England, ancient Palestine and the Republic of Sarmeda, a
country of his own invention.

BY THE SAME AUTHOR
ALL PUBLISHED BY HOUSE OF STRATUS

INKLINGS: SELECTED STORIES

Dan Jacobson

HOUSE OF
STRATUS

Copyright © 1973, 2001 Dan Jacobson

All rights reserved. No part of this publication may be reproduced, stored in a retrieval system, or transmitted, in any form, or by any means (electronic, mechanical, photocopying, recording, or otherwise), without the prior permission of the publisher. Any person who does any unauthorised act in relation to this publication may be liable to criminal prosecution and civil claims for damages.

The right of Dan Jacobson to be identified as the author of this work has been asserted in accordance with sections 77 and 78 of the Copyright, Designs and Patents Act 1988.

This edition published in 2001 by House of Stratus, an imprint of Stratus Holdings plc, 24c Old Burlington Street, London, W1X 1RL, UK.

www.houseofstratus.com

Typeset, printed and bound by House of Stratus.

A catalogue record for this book is available from the British Library.

ISBN 1-84232-137-4

This book is sold subject to the condition that it shall not be lent, resold, hired out, or otherwise circulated without the publisher's express prior consent in any form of binding, or cover, other than the original as herein published and without a similar condition being imposed on any subsequent purchaser, or bona fide possessor.

This is a fictional work and all characters are drawn from the author's imagination. Any resemblance or similarities are entirely coincidental.

CONTENTS

THE BOX

My brother and I kept homing pigeons for many years. We had a *hok* at the bottom of the backyard, and were members of the Lyndhurst Junior Homing Pigeon Society. We used to send our birds south to Winterton and Dors River, and farther, deep into the Karroo, to Mirredal and Platkops Siding. Sometimes all the birds came back, sometimes only a few; in the Society's races we were in the first three only once, I think. But we watched the pigeons assiduously, watched their mating, their breeding, their performances, and their personal characteristics too.

In the season in which our enthusiasm reached its peak, we even infected Jan Louw, the coloured houseboy. He used to laugh at our affection for the birds, but he was interested in them himself and followed their performances keenly. 'That one is going to come back,' he would say, pointing at Brighteyes, the blue-bar hen, 'but that one is going to get lost.' Sleepy, the one pointed at, nibbled unconcernedly at her feathers. He was often as wrong as he was right in his prophecies: he went too much simply by size. A big pigeon was a good one, for him. When he was wrong, we teased him about it of course. 'You will see, I'll be right next time,' he said, smiling. He was a smooth-skinned, yellow-skinned young man, with a small European nose that he wrinkled when he smiled, in a rather boyish way. But otherwise, if anything, he was older in habit and appearance than he ought to have been.

He was already getting plump: the work about the house was not very heavy, and as my father so often said about the servants, 'Where they came from, they've never seen food of the kind that we give them.' Fitting his plumpness Jan had a fat little sense of complacency that nothing could shake. If he had said that a bird would not come back, and it did, he was not at all abashed. 'It will get lost next time.' In the same way, if we asked him to mend a puncture in our bicycle tube and he didn't do it, he would never make excuses or apologies. He would simply smile that fat youthful smile of his and suggest that we walk to school. It was only when my father ordered him to do the job that he would take the bicycle and the tube of solution and a basin of water and fix the puncture, on the back stoep. While he worked, he told us stories. He told us about the *koggelmander* that snatched at people walking through the veld, about how he had once seen a man stabbed at a dance, about Gong-Gong and the diamond diggings where he had been born, and how they had tried to trap him with Illicit Diamond Buying when he had been only sixteen years old. He was not really a good storyteller; he wasn't sufficiently interested in his own stories. The tube slithered in his hand as he passed it through the basin, he pulled it taut and a jet of tiny bubbles rose to the surface. '*Daar's hy. Ons het hom nou.*' He spoke a curious mixture of Afrikaans and English, both strongly marked with the high sharp notes of the Cape Coloured intonation.

He was much more interested in gossip than he was in telling stories. Particularly in gossip about ourselves, about his three young masters: Master Dandy, Master Hitch, and Master Yoshwa, as our names became in his mouth. It was all gossip in the future tense, for he wasn't very interested in our immediate lives, I think because they were too far out of his ken. School successes or defeats, rugby matches, dressing up for the Jewish Holidays – these did not interest him very much, not to talk about. But about our futures he could let himself go. In the

2

same way in which he would confidently predict this or that bird's return, so he mapped out our careers. Master Dandy was going to go into *die politiek*, you could see how much he liked himself. Master Yoshwa was going to be too busy running after the girls to worry about that. Master Hitch was going to make lots of money and become the richest man in Lyndhurst. His eyes narrowed against the sun in which we were sitting, his face glistening in the light, squatting on his haunches with one surprisingly tender spot of brown skin showing through a tear in his trousers, his teeth white and nose wrinkled, he smiled at us, on the back stoep, in the backyard, the front garden, 'Ja Master Yoshwa you'll be running after the girls. *Ek kan sien hoe jy van die meisiemense hou.* I can see already how you like the girls.' We used to contest his prophecies hotly.

He had a few songs too, that he used to sing as he worked, or at our request. One was his own version of a hit tune of the day: 'I am sitting, On the topping, Of the *wêreld.*' But there was a pleasant Afrikaans one, that went as far as I can remember it, and as far as I could make out his pronunciation:

> *Daar onder in die pampas vlei*
> *Daar sny hul die waatlemoen.*
> *So rooi soos bloed, so suikersoet*
> *Dit lyk net soos gesteelde goed.*

Which could be translated: 'There in the flat valley, they cut the watermelon. As red as blood, as sweet as sugar, it looks like stolen fruit.'

He did his work quite well. There was not so much for him to do. He pottered about in the garden, but growing a garden in Lyndhurst is an almost hopeless business, and ours consisted of a young wilderness of coarse kikiyu grass and a few beds of petunias. He made all the beds and polished all the floors, all the shoes, the bathroom. The cooking was done by Dora, who

3

was his aunt. In the afternoon they both repaired to their rooms and slept through the heat, until about half-past three when we came back from school, clamouring for sandwiches and milk.

But the relationship between the servants and ourselves was a completely casual one, at least from our side; for the most part, if we had better things to do we simply disregarded them. So when I saw Jan busy with one of the butter boxes we used as mating nests for the birds, I took no notice of what he was doing. I remember him busy the whole afternoon, banging away at the box, singing to himself, but I didn't go up to him and ask him what he was making. Something for his room probably – the room that we all shrank from entering, with its cheap furniture and iron bedstead and bright calendar pin-up stuck to the wall, all impregnated with Jan's smell, with what we thought simply of as the Kaffir smell.

That evening when I came back from cricket in the piece of veld behind the lane – my ears still ringing with the sounds of our shouts and my eyes dim with the twilight into which we had strained our sight to get in the last possible hit at the ball that swung so suddenly out of the gloom and on to the bat – Jan was waiting for me on the back stoep.

'Look, Master Dandy, you must come with me,' he said, and beckoned me into the yard.

'What is it, Jan?'

But he was being mysterious and just went on walking into the depths of the backyard. I followed him impatiently.

'Look, Master, I made it for the pigeons.' He held up a box for me. I couldn't see it in the darkness, so we went on to the back stoep again, and looked at what he had made in the light that came through the open kitchen door.

My impatience gave way to embarrassment. The box was no good for the pigeons. Obviously he had put a lot of work into it: there was a little front step, then a tiny room, a doorway into another room which was split horizontally into two levels, upstairs and downstairs. The other half of the box was given over to one larger room, with a little shelf round it. The whole thing was very well done, but useless; there would be no room in it for the breeding bowls, and besides the pigeons would simply have no use for all the partitions. It was a foolishness that Jan had made, I felt, but I didn't want to tell him that. I said, 'It's very nice, Jan,' and looked at it a bit more. He was smiling at me, proudly, with the pride of a craftsman in his work.

'Master Dandy didn't know that I could make such a clever thing?'

'No, I didn't know.'

'I showed it to Master Yoshwa, and he said that it is very clever. *Kyk, Master Dandy, die duif kan hier inklim, en as hy moeg van die kamer is dan kan hy maar hier deurloop. En kyk die trappies.*' He explained the box to me eagerly, showing me with his hand how the pigeon could go through the doorway, and rest here, and his hand rested, and if it wanted to fly out it could do so, and his hand flew out of the box.

'It's very nice, Jan. It's a very nice box.' I was hungry and went inside.

The next day was Saturday, and free of school. I went out to the pigeon coop early to see whether the squeaker we were expecting had pecked its way out of the egg on which Brighteyes was nervously sitting. I let the pigeons out for an early morning flight, and round and round they circled, their wings beating sweetly in the air. They were flying low that day, though it was a clear day, clear blue sky with a promise of heat later in the day, and just a hint of the meagre Karroo spring in the air. I had been planning to make a nest for a pair of birds which we were mating. I went into the woodshed and looked about there among the coal and lumber, but there was no box that was suitable. Jan's box, the box he had worked on, was on the stoep, where he had shown it to me the previous night. I was a little sorry to do it, but I had felt all along that the box was an absurdity, so I took it and knocked out the partitions and the shelves and everything else that he had made, and fixed it up like all the other mating boxes, and put it in the *hok*. Later when the birds came down and had been shepherded into the *hok*, I locked up the two birds that were to be mated in their new austere home. The rest of the day was like any other Saturday: long hours to run loose in about the flat streets of the town and the veld behind the houses, where lizards flickered on the rocks.

That night Jan asked me what had happened to his box.

'I put it in the *hok*.'

'Is it in the *hok*? Let me go and see.' He came back to me soon. 'I don't see it in the *hok*, Master Dandy.'

'Yes, it is there. I locked the pigeons up in it.'

'Oh, the closed one ... But that isn't my box, Master Dandy.'

'Yes, it is. But I took out all the bits and pieces you'd put in. They were no good for the pigeons.'

His mouth had fallen open. For the first time since we had started talking I began to feel that I had done something wrong. 'It was no good for the pigeons,' I said again.

'*Hoe kan die kleinbaas?*' he started speaking, then walked away suddenly. It was twilight again, and again we were in the backyard. He walked to the *hok* at the end of the yard, and I heard him go in. I heard the pigeons flap their wings, and call, disturbed. I wondered what he was doing, and ran down the yard to see. He came out of the *hok*, holding his box in his hand.

'What have you done?' I shouted at him. 'I put the pigeons in there.'

'What have I done?' he asked me. 'What have you done?' He lifted the box towards me. 'Look at my box.' He thrust it closer to me.

'Look at my box,' he repeated, and he began to cry. At first I was more surprised than anything else. I had never seen a grown-up cry before, and I just watched the strange wrinkling of his face, his nose wrinkling as it did when he laughed, the tears running slowly down his cheeks. He sniffed. He did not move. He stood and cried, holding the box in his hand.

There was nothing I could do. I said 'I'm sorry,' but it didn't help him. Anyway, though I was sorry, terribly sorry, my surprise was still stronger than my remorse. I couldn't understand his grief, it was beyond my understanding that he should have had such grief for something of his making. I suppose my attitude was simple enough, in the end: I didn't know that they felt like that. And *they* were all the coloured and African people that I passed every day, taking for granted their serf status and their ragged clothes and everything else about them. They were a strange, twilight people to me; I liked some and was afraid of others, but they were beyond an uncrossable barrier, even when we played with them or listened to them talking. The barrier was simply that they didn't feel. They had emotions; I had seen them angry or laughing or subdued under a white man's curse. But somehow they weren't real emotions; my emotions; they were black emotions, different to my own. Now Jan had crossed the barrier. He was crying as I might cry. There was no difference between us at all. He was human, and he was crying.

'Stop crying, Jan. You can make another box.' But I could not touch him, I could not put my arm around him. He was still black. 'Oh, Jan, you can make another box,' I cried, louder for my later betrayal.

He walked away from me, carrying his box. I followed him a little way, calling out to him, but he didn't reply. He went to his room and shut the door. I knocked at the door but he did not answer me, and I left off knocking, and went back to the house.

Jan and I were soon friends again of course, but my relationship with him was different to what it had been before. We had both

7

lost, or gained, something – I think in him there lurked throughout some remnant of his hurt and anger; I became self-conscious for the first time towards him, hesitant, aware that there were things about him and others that I had to learn, worlds of feeling which I had somehow managed to regard at a distance before, and which now came close and stood next to me.

But he left our service shortly afterwards anyway, and joined the army. The war had broken out, and he joined the Cape Coloured Corps, and was posted away from Lyndhurst. He came to the house once. How we had grown! He himself looked fit in his uniform, and he was very proud of it too. By chance, my eldest brother, who was also in the army by then, was down on leave, and Jan was very happy about that. 'We are both in Jan Smuts' army,' he said, and everyone laughed. He looked older too.

Though in the long run, we were saved that sad, stock, embarrassing situation, in which the servant comes back, and comes back, and the children are grown, and the gap has grown too great to be crossed by anything but uneasy smiles and a talk of memories that embarrass as one is reminded of them. Unthinking and unfeeling the childhood contact may have been, but it was at least free of that self-consciousness which colour can become – not merely a screen through which one observes the other's reaction, but a chain around one's limbs without which one might feel mother-naked and ashamed. As I say, we were saved that in Jan's case, because he was killed at El Adhem, near Tobruk, in the fighting against the Germans in the Western Desert. We heard the news from Dora. She still comes, though she has long left our service; she has grown almost blind from the cataracts that are covering her eyes, and we buy off pity and guilt with five shillings every visit, and perhaps a blanket, a blouse of my sister's, a pound of sugar.

A DAY IN THE COUNTRY

We had spent the day on the farm, as we usually did every Sunday. Rather a dull day it had been, I remember, in April; it was too cold to go swimming in the river, and there had been nothing much else to do except sit in the car and watch my father as he helped the boys round up the cattle driven down from the veld, and then walk through them, stick in hand, prodding their sides, stopping to discuss at length what to do about the heifer who was going blind in one eye, or what a pity it was that this miserable beast should be in calf again when what it needed was a long rest. He could spend hours like that, perfectly happy among the slow red cows and oxen, with the African herd boy who knew each head of cattle as an individual and respected it as such. He prodded, leaned against his stick, screwed his face up against the sun, listened to the herd boy's comments, and twisted his ankle on one of the rocks that littered the piece of veld where the cattle were gathered.

Once he had ricked his ankle, my father had had enough. He got back into the car and we set off home, with the herd boy's children riding with us on the back bumper, as far as the gate. At the gate they climbed off and opened it for us; we passed through, they waved, and we waved back. Now there was just the thirty-mile run home, through Rietpan, bypassing Dors River, meeting the tarred road to take us to the Boer War Memorial – and so home. My brother was driving, my father and mother sat in front with him, and my sister and I were in the back seat. The first stretch of road was really bad, not a road at all, but a cart track across Rietpan Commonage, a piece of veld that had been grazed to complete nudity by the donkeys of the villagers. A few donkeys, a cow or two, one or two goats: those were generally the sole possessions of the Rietpan villagers, together with a mud-walled house and five irrigated acres. But though Rietpan was poor, it had its 'location', even poorer, where the black-skinned inhabitants of the village lived. They were conducting some sort of religious rite as we passed the location, and a man held up a cross of plaited twigs towards us. He was wearing a blue cowl on his head. The wind blew all their clothes in bright fluttering rags as they walked behind the leader. The sun shone bare upon them through the wind.

Inside the car it was dull and dusty, with the Sunday newspapers in a mess on the floor. My sister was knitting. We passed through Rietpan quickly, in a cloud of dust, with a greeting for Major le Roy on his front stoep and a pause to give way for someone's sheep. The road between Rietpan and Dors River was better, and my brother increased his speed.

My father looked up from the comic he was reading. He read it with an air of absolute puzzlement: 'Who reads these things?' he asked. Then: 'Oh, oh, oh, boy, slow down.' He placed a hand on my brother's arm. There was a car standing in the middle of the road, and a group of people at the side of the road, looking down at something.

We thought it was an accident. It looked like an accident. We prepared ourselves for something horrible and warily our car crept up to the other, then drove past it and stopped.

'What is it?' my sister said shrilly.

'I don't know.' We couldn't see. The other car was blocking our view of what the little group was seeing. Our car went forward a few feet. Dear God, it was an accident. The group stood over a small African child, a group of white men and women. A few Africans stood some way off, looking at what was going on, and saying nothing. The white people were talking to one another. They seemed quite unmoved, almost lighthearted, but the black child lay still on the ground. I could see its spindly legs like the winter branches of a tree.

'What is it?' my father called out through the window of the car, and as he did so, one of the white men stooped and picked the child up. The black legs kicked wildly, and a shriek went up from the child. I saw one of the Africans take a pace forward, then fall back. The group turned to their car, one man still carrying the child. Then I saw a strange thing. They were laughing, all of them were laughing. The child still screamed and kicked, and then writhed over in the man's arms, away from the motorcar, butting its head into the broad grey-shirted chest, as a child turns into its mother's arms for protection. We saw white face after face, all bared in smiles, and their laughter surrounded the thin screams of the child, until one could no longer believe that what one heard was truly a scream of fear.

'What is it?' my father called again. But no one took any notice. One of the men ran forward and opened the bonnet of the car. We heard him say in Afrikaans, 'Come on, put him in,' and the child screamed again, awfully.

But we knew now. It wasn't an accident, it was a game. I don't know whether we felt more relief or disgust. One of the grinning men saw us watching them, and still with his grin, he waved to us that we could go on. They didn't need our help; it wasn't an accident. None of us grinned back at him. I think he saw that we weren't amused at his game for he looked away.

'For God's sake let's go.'

'I've had enough of this.'

My brother started the car. As we drove off I said, 'What dirty swine.' I looked through the back window of the car. They had put the child back on the road, one of the men was standing half-way in his car, the bonnet down. Apparently the game was breaking up. We hoped that it was our condemnation that had broken it up. Yet there was the taste of guilt in each of our mouths that we had just looked our condemnation and not said anything to them, not made a protest in the name of humanity. But we were used to that sort of scene and that sort of guilt. Together they almost make up a way of life.

We had driven on only a short distance when with a roar of wind and a cloud of dust the car passed us. As it whipped past, one of the men in it leaned his head, half his body, out of the window, and shouted something at us. None of us heard what he was shouting, it was lost in the wind and the dust. All we saw was a white shirt and a white face and a pair of bright red lips opening and closing grotesquely.

My brother and I swore at the billows of dust which followed their car. But my father, in a moment, was trembling with rage.

'Chase them,' he shouted.

'Don't be mad,' my brother said.

'Then stop the car.'

'Why? What for?'

'I'll show you why. Stop the car.' My brother didn't, so my father leaned over and switched off the ignition key.

My brother lost his temper as the car slowed down and stopped. 'All right, take your bloody car,' he said and got out and came in the back, slamming the door behind him.

'Michael, what are you going to do?' my mother asked. My brother and I were both yelling at my father to leave it, cut it out, forget the whole business and he was saying, 'No one shouts at me like that. No one shouts at me like that,' as we tore along the road. We could see the other car ahead of us, still raising dust. But we were catching up with it. Soon we were in the car's cloud of dust. Small stones struck against the windscreen, and we could see very little through the grey murk.

'Michael, you're going to have an accident.'

'I'm not going to have an accident.'

'For God's sake, Dad, let's not have a scene.'

'What do you mean let's not have a scene, when they shout at me like that?'

'You don't even know what he shouted.'

'I know well enough what he shouted.'

'What did he shout?'

'No one shouts at me like that.'

We came to the crossroads of the main road to Lyndhurst and the Rietpan-Dors River road. The front car went towards Dors River, so we went that way too, still at a dangerously high speed.

'Michael, you're going to have an accident.'

Dors River was about us. J. Wassenaar *Algemene Handelaar*/General Dealer. There was the station. The road passed J. Wassenaar and then turned a corner at the low, iron-roofed, gauze-netted hotel, the Savoy, with two petrol pumps in front of it. Then there was a house, another, a piece of veld, two more houses, and a last shop. In front of the last shop stood the black Dodge we had been chasing. The people were climbing out of it. One of them, the man in the white shirt, the one who had shouted, saw us coming and stood looking at us with his mouth open.

Again we drew level with the car. Inside ours, everyone with the exception of my father was dreading the scene that we knew was about to follow.

We stopped. My father said: 'How dare you shout at me like that.'

Now they were all out of their car. There were six of them, three men and three women. They stood at various points around their car, looking at us.

The young man in the grey shirt said, 'What's the matter with you?' He was the one who had been carrying the child. He wore a broad-brimmed hat on the back of his head, and it made his face look round and flabby, under the circling rim of his hat. But he was big and strong, with enormous bare arms folded on his chest. I knew that if it did come to a fight he would be the one to give us the most trouble; the one who would probably beat us at that. He walked over to our car, arms still folded, contemptuously, and said again: 'What's the matter with you?'

But he was speaking English. Was that already a victory for us? He was speaking our language, we weren't speaking his. But he was big, much bigger than any of us as he stood at the driver's window of the car and said: 'What's the matter with you?'

My father suddenly blazed out at him. 'What sort of a person are you? First you torture a child that's done nothing to you, and then you scream at someone you're passing on the road. Well, let me tell you that I'm not a little Kaffir piccanin. You can't do what you like with me. I'll teach you manners before I'm finished with you.'

The man said, 'How?' He added: 'You're too old.' And it was true, pitifully true, my father was too old to fight him. He could have killed the old man.

This was the cue for my brother and myself. We climbed out of the car and walked round. The big man wheeled to face us. I saw his muscles tighten under the hair of his arms and I knew that if we were to win this argument it wouldn't be by force. But we stared at each other as though we weren't frightened. He probably wasn't.

My father said: 'You people make me sick. You've got no idea how to behave. But if you think you can go round bullying everybody like you bullied that Kaffir child, you're mistaken.' He opened the door of the car as though to come out, and quickly the man darted at it, to slam it on him. With me a little way behind him my brother moved towards the man. My brother said: 'No you don't.' He was panting as he spoke, as if he had been running in a race.

Now, if there was to be a fight, it would be now. But there was no fight, and I did not understand why, as the old man, apparently the father of the two younger ones, came up and said, 'You've got no right to talk like that about my people. We weren't doing anything to the piccanin.' He gestured, almost appealingly.

We stared at him. He said again, 'You've got no right to talk like that about my people' – and then I realized that our fear – the fear that we would be called 'Bloody Jews', the fear which perhaps had kept our mouths closed when we had seen the piccanin being tortured – was his fear too. He, the Afrikaner who spoke English to us, felt that my father was sitting in his car and despising him for the race he belonged to, and judging him and his race by what we had seen on the road; and I realized, with what relief, that the father did not want to be judged by that act, and did not want his son to fight us, for even if we should fight and his son should beat us, our original and damning judgement would remain, would even be confirmed. He didn't want to beat us, he wanted us to think well of his race, and how could he do that while the piccanin screamed with terror and kicked helplessly against his son's arms? He stayed his son's arm, and said, 'It was only a bit of fun and you had no right to swear at us.'

'Swear at you?' my father asked.

'Yes, swear at us,' the other son said, coming up. I saw then why his lips were so red. It was lipstick on his mouth. It must have come from the lips of one of the girls who were leaning against the mudguards of the other car, watching the scene. Like his father, this son did not want to fight. He said, 'We heard you swearing as you drove off.'

'You were the one,' my father said, interrupting him. 'You were the one who leaned out of the car and shouted.' My father looked at him.

He wiped his mouth with his hand. There was another smear of lipstick on his cheekbone. He said, 'I shouted at you to mind your own business.'

'But we said nothing to you. We didn't like what you were doing, but we didn't say anything to you.'

'You said "bloody swine".'

'That's simply not true,' my father said.

I said nothing.

'I heard you,' the man repeated.

'You couldn't have heard it because no one said it.'

Despite this foolish wrangling, the tension remained where it had been all along, where it had been when it had looked as though there was to be a physical fight. The unspoken words lay heavily on our tongues: *Dutchmen, Jews*. But they were never used. Racial tensions usually aggravate brawls, but this time they didn't, for they were too widely shared. Our fear was theirs: it was almost as though we co-operated with one another to keep the significance of the argument hidden, yet never for a moment forgot it. Had we not been Jews, we might have reproved them more strongly for what they did to the piccanin – for kinship in oppression, or fear of oppression, has two sides, one less noble than the other. Had they not been Afrikaners who believed their reputation to be one of brutality and uncouthness – all of which they had confirmed, they feared – they might simply have fought us off. But we were all prevented from fighting, and prevented from peace.

I remember the father saying, 'Do you think we would have done anything to that piccanin? We aren't mad people. It was just a bit of fun among ourselves.'

And the younger son, who did not want to fight, spoke earnestly to me. 'You see, this little native child ran right across our car, in front of our car, and I had to brake like hell not to knock him over. So we thought we'd give him a lesson he'll remember. It's for his own good too, you know. He'll be a damn sight more careful now. He'll look what's going on before he runs across the road. Perhaps he'll live longer that way?' Tentatively he smiled at me.

The father was saying, 'You see that boy there, he goes to university. In Pretoria. Already he's in his second-year studies. A university student. Do you think that people like that, university students, gentlemen, educated people, are going to do anything that they'll be ashamed of afterwards?'

I said, 'You made a mistake. No one shouted "bloody swine".' What I said was true, but it was a lie too. In all that squalor it hardly mattered, but I had to add: 'But we didn't like what you were doing.'

'All right, then I shouldn't have shouted at you from my car. But it was our business what we were doing with that piccanin, especially as we weren't going to hurt him. It was only a bit of sport.'

'Not a very nice sport,' my mother called out. We seemed to be winning all the way down the line. The big son had moved away and was being ignored by everybody. The other two continued their laboured explanations, struggling for English words to express themselves in. Once the father veered towards an aggressive tone, and then, as though remembering the faces in the car, closed and hostile, with the struggling black body in his son's arms, as guilty as blood, he became defensive again.

So a sort of peace did come, and we got back into the car. No one shook hands with anyone, there had been no reconciliation to warrant that. But no blows had been struck, and no one had called anyone a bloody Dutchman or a bloody Jew, so everything was as well as could be expected. Better really, for us, because we still despised them. We despised that family: it is not our fault they misinterpreted it. And they should have

17

known that we were as frightened of them as they were of us. We left them there, outside their whitewashed shop with the house behind it, that looked across the sand road to the railway line and the railway paddock where one chestnut horse was growing thin in transit between two lost farms.

It was a quiet journey home. Everyone was feeling depressed and beaten, though, as I have explained, the victory was ours. But we had all lost, so much, somewhere, farther back, along that dusty road.

THE ZULU AND THE ZEIDE

Old man Grossman was worse than a nuisance. He was a source of constant anxiety and irritation; he was a menace to himself and to the passing motorists into whose path he would step, to the children in the streets whose games he would break up, sending them flying, to the householders who at night would approach him with clubs in their hands, fearing him a burglar; he was a butt and a jest to the African servants who would tease him on street corners.

It was impossible to keep him in the house. He would take any opportunity to slip out – a door left open meant that he was on the streets, a window unlatched was a challenge to his agility, a walk in the park was as much a game of hide-and-seek as a walk. The old man's health was good, physically; he was quite spry, and he could walk far, and he could jump and duck if he had to. All his physical activity was put to only one purpose: to running away. It was a passion for freedom that the old man might have been said to have, could anyone have seen what joy there could have been for him in wandering aimlessly about the streets, in sitting footsore on pavements, in entering other people's homes, in stumbling behind advertisement hoardings that fenced undeveloped building plots, in toiling up the stairs of fifteen-storey blocks of flats in which he had no business, in being brought home by large young policemen who winked at Harry Grossman, the old man's son, as they gently hauled his father out of their flying-squad cars.

'He's always been like this,' Harry would say, when people asked him about his father. And when they smiled and said: 'Always?' Harry would say, 'Always. I know what I'm talking about. He's my father, and I know what he's like. He gave my mother enough grey hairs before her time. All he knew was to run away.'

Harry's reward would come when the visitors would say: 'Well, at least you're being as dutiful to him as anyone can be.'

It was a reward that Harry always refused. 'Dutiful? What can you do? There's nothing else you can do.' Harry Grossman knew that there was nothing else he could do. Dutifulness had been his habit of life; it had had to be, having the sort of father he had, and the strain of duty had made him abrupt and begrudging. He even carried his thick, powerful shoulders curved inwards, to keep what he had to himself. He was a thick-set, bunch-faced man, with large bones, and short, jabbing gestures; he was in the prime of life, and he would point at the father from whom he had inherited his strength, and on whom the largeness of bone showed now only as so much extra leanness that the clothing had to cover, and say: 'You see him? Do you know what he once did? My poor mother saved enough money to send him from the old country to South Africa: she bought clothes for him, and a ticket, and she sent him to her brother, who was already here. He was going to make enough money to bring me out, and my mother and my brother, all of us. But on the boat from Bremen to London he met some other Jews who were going to South America, and they said to him: "Why are you going to South Africa? It's a wild country, the blacks there will eat you. Come to South America and you'll make a fortune." So in London he exchanges his ticket. And we don't hear from him for six months. Six months later he gets a friend to write to my mother asking her please to send him enough money to pay for his ticket back to the old country – he's dying in the Argentine, the Spaniards are killing him, he says, and he must come home. So my mother borrows from her brother to bring him back again. Instead of a fortune he brought her a new debt, and that was all.'

But Harry was dutiful, how dutiful his friends had reason to see again when they would urge him to try sending the old man to a home for the aged. 'No,' Harry would reply, his features moving heavily and reluctantly to a frown, a pout, as he showed how little the suggestion appealed to him. 'I don't like the idea. Maybe one day when he needs medical attention all the time I'll feel differently about it, but not now, not now. He wouldn't like it, he'd be unhappy. We'll look after him as long as we can. It's a job. It's something you've got to do.'

More eagerly Harry would go back to a recital of the old man's past. 'He couldn't even pay for his own passage out. I had to pay the loan back. We came out together – my mother wouldn't let him go by himself again, and I had to pay off her brother who advanced the money for us. I was a boy – what was I? – sixteen, seventeen, but I paid for his passage, and my own, and my mother's and then my brother's. It took me a long time, let me tell you. And then my troubles with him weren't over.' Harry even reproached his father for his myopia; he could clearly enough remember his chagrin when shortly after their arrival in South Africa, after it had become clear that Harry would be able to make his way in the world and be a support to the whole family, the old man – who at that time had not really been so old – had suddenly, almost dramatically, grown so short-sighted that he had been almost blind without the glasses which Harry had had to buy for him. And Harry could remember too how he had then made a practice of losing the glasses or breaking them with the greatest frequency, until it had been made clear to him that he was no longer expected to do any work. 'He doesn't do that any more. When he wants to run away now he sees to it that he's wearing his glasses. That's how he's always been. Sometimes he recognizes me, at other times, when he doesn't want to, he just doesn't know who I am.'

What Harry said was true. Sometimes the old man would call out to his son, when he would see him at the end of a passage, 'Who are you?' Or he would come upon Harry in a room and demand of him, 'What do you want in my house?'

'Your house?' Harry would say, when he felt like teasing the old man. 'Your house?'

'Out of my house!' the old man would shout back.

'Your house? Do you call this your house?' Harry would reply, smiling at the old man's fury.

Harry was the only one in the house who talked to the old man, and then he did not so much talk to him, as talk of him to others. Harry's wife was a dim and silent woman, crowded out by her husband and the large-boned sons like himself that she had borne him, and she would gladly have seen the old man in an old-age home. But her husband had said no, so she put up with the old man, though for herself she could see no possible better end for him than a period of residence in a home for aged Jews which she had once visited, and which had impressed her most favourably with its glass and yellow brick, the noiseless rubber tiles in its corridors, its secluded grassed grounds, and the uniforms worn by the attendants to the establishment. But she put up with the old man; she did not talk to him. The grandchildren had nothing to do with their grandfather – they were busy at school, playing rugby and cricket, they could hardly speak Yiddish, and they were embarrassed by him in front of their friends; when the grandfather did take notice of them it was only to call them Boers and *goyim* and *shkotzim* in sudden quavering rages which did not disturb them at all.

The house itself – a big single-storied place of brick, with a corrugated iron roof above and a wide stoep all around – Harry Grossman had bought years before. In the continual rebuilding the suburb was undergoing it was beginning to look old-fashioned. But it was solid and prosperous, and indoors curiously masculine in appearance, like the house of a widower. The furniture was of the heaviest African woods, dark, and built to last, the passages were lined with bare linoleum, and the few pictures on the walls, big brown and grey mezzotints in heavy frames, had not been looked at for years. The servants were both men, large ignored Zulus who did their work and kept up the brown gleam of the furniture.

It was from this house that old man Grossman tried to escape. He fled through the doors and the windows and into the wide sunlit streets of the town in Africa, where the blocks of flats were encroaching upon the single-storied houses behind their gardens. In these streets he wandered until he was found.

It was Johannes, one of the Zulu servants, who suggested a way of dealing with old man Grossman. He brought to the house one afternoon Paulus, whom he described as his 'brother'. Harry Grossman knew enough to know that 'brother' in this context could mean anything from the son of one's mother to a friend from a neighbouring *kraal*, but by the speech that Johannes made on Paulus' behalf he might indeed have been the latter's brother. Johannes had to speak for Paulus, for Paulus knew no English. Paulus was a 'raw boy', as raw as a boy could possibly come. He was a muscular, moustached and bearded African, with pendulous ear lobes showing the slits in which the tribal plugs had once hung; on his feet he wore sandals, the soles of which were cut from old motorcar tyres, the thongs from red inner tubing. He wore neither hat nor socks, but he did have a pair of khaki shorts which were too small for him, and a shirt without any buttons; buttons would in any case have been of no use for the shirt could never have closed over his chest. He swelled magnificently out of his clothing, and above there was a head carried well back, so that his beard, which had been trained to grow in two sharp points from his chin, bristled ferociously forward under his melancholy and almost mandarin-like moustache. When he smiled, as he did once or twice during Johannes' speech, he showed his white, even teeth, but for the most part he stood looking rather shyly to the side of Harry Grossman's head, with his hands behind his back and his bare knees bent a little forward, as if to show how little he was asserting himself, no matter what his 'brother' might have been saying about him.

His expression did not change when Harry said that it seemed hopeless, that Paulus was too raw, and Johannes explained what the baas had just said. He nodded agreement when Johannes explained to him that the baas said that it was a pity that he knew no English. But whenever Harry looked at him, he smiled, not ingratiatingly, but simply smiling above his beard, as though saying: 'Try me.' Then he looked grave again as Johannes expatiated on his virtues. Johannes pleaded for his 'brother'. He said that the baas knew that he, Johannes, was a good boy. Would he, then, recommend to the baas a boy who was not a good boy too? The baas could see for himself, Johannes said, that Paulus was not one of these town boys, these street loafers: he was a good boy, come straight from the *kraal*. He was not a thief or a drinker. He was strong, he was a hard worker, he was clean, and he could be as gentle as a woman. If he, Johannes, were not telling the truth about all these things, then he deserved to be chased away. If Paulus failed in any single respect, then he, Johannes, would voluntarily leave the service of the baas, because he had said untrue things to the baas. But if the baas believed him, and gave Paulus his chance, then he, Johannes, would teach Paulus all the things of the house and the garden, so that Paulus would be useful to the baas in ways other than the particular task for which he was asking the baas to hire him. And, rather daringly, Johannes said that it did not matter so much if Paulus knew no English, because the old baas, the *oubaas*, knew no English either.

It was as something in the nature of a joke – almost a joke against his father – that Harry Grossman gave Paulus his chance. He was given a room in the servants' quarters in the backyard, into which he brought a tin trunk painted red and black, a roll of blankets, and a guitar with a picture of a cowboy on the back. He was given a houseboy's outfit of blue denim blouse and shorts, with red piping round the edges, into which he fitted, with his beard and his physique, like a king in exile in some pantomime. He was given his food three times a day, after the white people had eaten, a bar of soap every week, cast-off clothing at odd intervals, and the sum of one pound five shillings per week, five shillings of which he took, the rest being left at his request, with the baas, as savings. He had a free afternoon once a week, and he was allowed to entertain not more than two friends at any one time in his room. In all the particulars that Johannes had enumerated, Johannes was proved reliable. Paulus was not one of these town boys, these street loafers. He did not steal or drink, he was clean and he was honest and hard-working. And he could be as gentle as a woman.

It took Paulus some time to settle down to his job; he had to conquer not only his own shyness and strangeness in the new house filled with strange people – let alone the city, which, since taking occupation of his room, he had hardly dared to enter – but also the hostility of old man Grossman, who took immediate fright at Paulus and redoubled his efforts to get away from the house upon Paulus' entry into it. As it happened, the first result of this persistence on the part of the old man was that Paulus was able to get the measure of the job, for he came to it with a willingness of spirit that the old man could not vanquish, but could only teach. Paulus had been given no instructions, he had merely been told to see that the old man did not get himself into trouble, and after a few days of bewilderment Paulus found his way. He simply went along with the old man.

At first he did so cautiously, following the old man at a distance, for he knew the other did not trust him. But later he was able to follow the old man openly; still later he was able to walk side by side with him, and the old man did not try to escape from him. When old man Grossman went out, Paulus went too, and there was no longer any need for the doors and windows to be watched, or the police to be telephoned. The young bearded Zulu and the old bearded Jew from Lithuania walked together in the streets of the town that was strange to them both; together they looked over the fences of the large gardens and into the shining foyers of the blocks of flats; together they stood on the pavements of the main arterial roads and watched the cars and trucks rush between the tall buildings; together they walked in the small, sandy parks, and when the old man was tired Paulus saw to it that he sat on a bench and rested. They could not sit on the bench together, for only whites were allowed to sit on the benches, but Paulus would squat on the ground at the old man's feet and wait until he judged the old man had rested long enough, before moving on again. Together they stared into the windows of the suburban shops, and though neither of them could read the signs outside the shops, the advertisements on billboards, the traffic signs at the side of the road, Paulus learned to wait for the traffic lights to change from red to green before crossing a street, and together they stared at the Coca-Cola girls and the advertisements for beer and the cinema posters. On a piece of cardboard which Paulus carried in the pocket of his blouse Harry had had one of his sons print the old man's name and address, and whenever Paulus was uncertain of the way home, he would approach an African or a friendly-looking white man and show him the card, and try his best to follow the instructions, or at least the gesticulations which were all of the answers of the white men that meant anything to him. But there were enough Africans to be found, usually, who were more sophisticated than himself, and though they teased him for his 'rawness' and for holding the sort of job he had, they helped him too. Neither Paulus nor old man Grossman were aware that when they crossed a street hand in hand, as they sometimes did when the traffic was particularly heavy, there were people who averted their eyes from the sight of this degradation, which could come upon a man when he was senile and dependent.

Paulus knew only Zulu, the old man knew only Yiddish, so there was no language in which they could talk to one another. But they talked all the same: they both commented on or complained to each other of the things they saw around them, and often they agreed with one another, smiling and nodding their heads and explaining again with their hands what each happened to be talking about. They both seemed to believe that they were talking about the same things, and often they undoubtedly were, when they lifted their heads sharply to see an aeroplane cross the blue sky between two buildings, or when they reached the top of a steep road and turned to look back the way they had come, and saw below them the clean impervious towers of the city thrust nakedly against the sky in brand-new piles of concrete and glass and facebrick. Then down they would go again, among the houses and the gardens where the beneficent climate encouraged both palms and oak trees to grow indiscriminately among each other – as they did in the garden of the house to which, in the evenings, Paulus and old man Grossman would eventually return.

In and about the house Paulus soon became as indispensable to the old man as he was on their expeditions out of it. Paulus dressed him and bathed him and trimmed his beard, and when the old man woke distressed in the middle of the night it would be for Paulus that he would call – '*Der schwarzer*,' he would shout (for he never learned Paulus' name), '*vo's der schwarzer*' – and Paulus would change his sheets and pyjamas and put him back to bed again. '*Baas Zeide*,' Paulus called the old man, picking up the Yiddish word for grandfather from the children of the house.

That was something that Harry Grossman told everyone of. For Harry persisted in regarding the arrangement as a kind of joke, and the more the arrangement succeeded the more determinedly did he try to turn it into a joke not only against his father but against Paulus too. It had been a joke that his father should be looked after by a raw Zulu: it was going to be a joke that the Zulu was successful at it. '*Baas Zeide!* That's what *der schzwarzer* calls him – have you ever heard the like of it? And you should see the two of them, walking about in the streets hand in hand like two schoolgirls. Two clever ones, *der schwarzer* and my father going for a promenade, and between them I tell you you wouldn't be able to find out what day of the week or what time of day it is.'

And when people said, 'Still that Paulus seems a very good boy,' Harry would reply:

'Why shouldn't he be? With all his knowledge, are there so many better jobs that he'd be able to find? He keeps the old man happy – very good, very nice, but don't forget that that's what he's paid to do. What does he know any better to do, a simple kaffir from the *kraal*? He knows he's got a good job, and he'd be a fool if he threw it away. Do you think,' Harry would say, and this too would insistently be part of the joke, 'if I had nothing else to do with my time I wouldn't be able to make the old man happy?' Harry would look about his sitting room, where the floorboards bore the weight of his furniture, or when they sat on the stoep he would measure with his glance the spacious garden aloof from the street beyond the hedge. 'I've got other things to do. And I had other things to do, plenty of them, all my life, and not only for myself.' The thought of them would send him back to his joke. 'No, I think the old man has just about found his level in *der schwarzer* – and I don't think *der schwarzer* could cope with anything else.'

Harry teased the old man to his face too, about his 'black friend', and he would ask him what he would do if Paulus went away; once he jokingly threatened to send the Zulu away. But the old man didn't believe the threat, for Paulus was in his room at the time, and the old man simply left Harry and went straight to Paulus, and sat in the room with him. Harry did not follow him: he would never have gone into any of his servants' rooms, least of all that of Paulus. For though he made a joke of him to others, to Paulus himself he always spoke gruffly, unjokingly, with no patience. On that day he had merely shouted after the old man, 'Another time he won't be there.'

Yet it was strange to see how Harry Grossman would always be drawn to the room in which he knew his father and Paulus to be. Night after night he came into the old man's bedroom when Paulus was dressing or undressing the old man; almost as often Harry stood in the steamy, untidy bathroom when the old man was being bathed. At these times he hardly spoke, he offered no explanation of his presence. He stood dourly and silently in the room, in his customary powerful, begrudging stance, with one hand clasping the wrist of the other and both supporting his waist, and he watched Paulus at work. The backs of Paulus' hands were smooth and hairless, they were paler on the palms and at the fingernails, and they worked deftly about the body of the old man, who was submissive under their ministrations. At first Paulus had sometimes smiled at Harry while he worked, with his straightforward, even smile in which there was no invitation to a complicity in patronage, but rather an encouragement to Harry to draw forward. After the first few evenings Paulus no longer smiled at his master, but he could not restrain himself, even under Harry's stare, from talking in a soft, continuous flow of Zulu, to encourage the old man and to exhort him to be helpful and to express his pleasure in how well the work was going. When Paulus at last wiped the gleaming soapsuds from his hands he would occasionally, when the old man was tired, stoop low and with a laugh pick him up and carry him easily down the passage to his bedroom. Harry would follow; he would stand in the passage and watch the burdened, barefooted Zulu until the door of his father's room closed behind them both.

Only once did Harry wait on such an evening for Paulus to reappear from his father's room. Paulus had already come out, had passed him in the narrow passage, and had already subduedly said: 'Goodnight, baas,' before Harry called suddenly:

'Hey! Wait!'

'Baas,' Paulus said, turning his head. Then he came quickly to Harry. 'Baas,' he said again, puzzled to know why his baas, who so rarely spoke to him, should suddenly have called him like this, when his work was over.

Harry waited again before speaking, waited long enough for Paulus to say: 'Baas?' once more, to move a little closer, and to lift his head for a moment before lowering it respectfully.

'The *oubaas* was tired tonight,' Harry said. 'Where did you take him? What did you do with him?'

'Baas?'

'You heard what I said. What did you do with him that he looked so tired?'

'Baas – I –' Paulus was flustered, and his hands beat in the air, but with care, so that he would not touch his baas. 'Please baas.' He brought both hands to his mouth, closing it forcibly.

30

He flung his hands away. 'Johannes,' he said with relief, and he had already taken the first step down the passage to call his interpreter.

'No!' Harry called. 'You mean you don't understand what I say? I know you don't,' Harry shouted, though in fact he had forgotten until Paulus had reminded him. The sight of Paulus' puzzled and guilty face before him filled him with a lust to see this man, this nurse with the face and the figure of a warrior, look more puzzled and guilty yet; and Harry knew that it could so easily be done, it could be done simply by talking to him in the language he could not understand. 'You're a fool,' Harry said. 'You're like a child. You understand nothing, and it's just as well for you that you need nothing. You'll always be where you are, running to do what the white baas tells you to do. Look how you stand! Do you think I understood English when I came here?' Then with contempt, using one of the few Zulu words he knew: '*Hamba!* Go! Do you think I want to see you?'

'*Au* baas!' Paulus exclaimed in distress. He could not remonstrate; he could only open his hands in a gesture to show that he understood neither the words Harry used, nor in what he had been remiss that Harry should have spoken in such angry tones to him. But Harry gestured him away, and had the satisfaction of seeing Paulus shuffle off like a schoolboy.

Harry was the only person who knew that he and his father had quarrelled shortly before the accident that ended the old man's life. That was one story about his father he was never to repeat.

Late in the afternoon they quarrelled, after Harry had come back from the shop in which he made his living. He came back to find his father wandering about the house, shouting for *der schwarzer*, and his wife complaining that she had already told the old man at least five times that *der schwarzer* was not in the house: it was Paulus' afternoon off.

31

Harry went to his father, and he too told him, '*Der schwarzer's* not here.' The old man turned away and continued going from room to room, peering in through the doors. '*Der schwarzer's* not here,' Harry repeated. 'What do you want him for?'

Still the old man ignored him. He went down the passage towards the bedrooms. 'What do you want?' Harry called after him.

The old man went into every bedroom, still shouting for *der schwarzer*. Only when he was in his own bare bedroom did he look at Harry. 'Where's *der schwarzer*?'

'I've told you ten times I don't know where he is. What do you want him for?'

'I want *der schwarzer*.'

'I know you want him. But he isn't here.'

'I want *der schwarzer*.'

'Do you think I haven't heard you? He isn't here.'

'Bring him to me,' the old man said.

'I can't bring him to you. I don't know where he is.' Harry steadied himself against his own anger. He said quietly: 'Tell me what you want. I'll do it for you. I'm here, I can do what *der schwarzer* can do for you.'

'Where's *der schwarzer*?'

'I've told you he isn't here,' Harry shouted. 'Why don't you tell me what you want? What's the matter with me – can't you tell me what you want?'

'I want *der schwarzer*.'

'Please,' Harry said. He threw out his arms towards his father, but the gesture was abrupt, almost as though he were thrusting him away. 'Why can't you ask me? You can ask me – haven't I done enough for you already? Do you want to go for a walk? – I'll take you for a walk. What do you want? Do you want – do you want –?' Harry could not think what his father might want. 'I'll do it,' he said. 'You don't need *der schwarzer*.'

Then Harry saw that his father was weeping. His eyes were hidden behind the thick glasses that he had to wear: his glasses and beard made of his face a mask of age. But Harry knew when the old man was weeping – he had seen him crying too often before, when they had found him at the end of a street after he had wandered away, or even, years earlier, when he had lost another of the miserable jobs that seemed to be the only ones he could find in a country in which his son had, later, prospered.

'Father,' Harry asked, 'what have I done? Do you think I've sent *der schwarzer* away?' His father turned away, between the narrow bed and the narrow wardrobe. 'He's coming –' Harry said, but he could not look at his father's back, at his hollowed neck, on which the hairs that Paulus had clipped glistened above the pale brown discolorations of age – Harry could not look at the neck turned stiffly away from him while he had to try to promise the return of the Zulu. He dropped his hands and walked out of the room.

No one knew how the old man managed to get out of the house and through the front gate without having been seen. But he did manage it, and in the road he was struck down by a man on a bicycle. It was enough. He died a few days later in the hospital.

Harry's wife wept, even the grandsons wept; Paulus wept. Harry himself was stony, and his bunched, protuberant features were immovable; they seemed locked upon the bones of his face. A few days after the funeral he called Paulus and Johannes into the kitchen and said to Johannes: 'Tell him he must go. His work is finished.'

Johannes translated for Paulus, and then, after Paulus had spoken, he turned to Harry. 'He says, yes baas.' Paulus kept his eyes on the ground; he did not look up even when Harry looked directly at him. Harry knew that this was not out of fear or shyness, but out of courtesy for his master's grief – which was what they could not but be talking of, when they talked of his work.

'Here's his pay.' Harry thrust a few notes towards Paulus, who took them in his cupped hands, and retreated.

Harry waited for them to go, but Paulus stayed in the room, and consulted with Johannes in a low voice. Johannes turned to his master. 'He says, baas, that the baas still has his savings.'

Harry had forgotten about Paulus' savings. He told Johannes that he had forgotten, and that he did not have enough money at the moment, but would bring the money the next day. Johannes translated and Paulus nodded gratefully. Both he and Johannes were subdued by the death there had been in the house.

Harry's dealings with Paulus were over. He took what was to have been his last look at Paulus, but this look stirred him once more against the Zulu. As harshly as he told Paulus that he had to go, so now, implacably, seeing Paulus in the mockery and simplicity of his houseboy's clothing, feeding his anger to the very end, Harry said: 'Ask him what he's been saving for. What's he going to do with the fortune he's made?'

Johannes spoke to Paulus and came back with a reply. 'He says, baas, that he is saving to bring his wife and children from Zululand to Johannesburg. He is saving, baas,' Johannes said, for Harry had not seemed to understand, 'to bring his family to this town also.'

The two Zulus were bewildered to know why it was then that Harry Grossman's clenched, fist-like features should have fallen from one another, or why he stared with such guilt and despair at Paulus, while he cried, 'What else could I have done? I did my best!' before the first tears came.

THE LITTLE PET

They put the rabbit hutch at the bottom of the garden, in a sheltered position between the back fence and a bank of tall lupins that grew across the bottom of the lawn. The weather was warm and summery, and it had been like that for weeks, with only an occasional thundercloud passing overhead at night and letting fall a little rain, so that their enclosed back garden was heavy every morning with the smell of growth and bright with the glittering of water on grass. Into a leafy, clean-smelling corner went the rabbit hutch, and the pregnant rabbit within it.

'Poor thing, she doesn't know what's happening to her.'

Martha kneeled on the ground to have a closer look at the rabbit, and her husband leaned over her, propping himself on a corner of the hutch with one hand. His movements were all quick and angular, and he made too many of them; the eye of an onlooker might have been tempted to skip the lightly-dressed, light-coloured husband, and rest on the wife. She could comfortably have taken the scrutiny, for she was small, dark and pretty enough, with her broad brow and wide brown eyes. But she too – like her husband – had the strained and guilty air of the perpetually well-intentioned. It was their laugh that betrayed them: only two people who had lived together for some years and were very keen on meeting each other at all points could have laughed so much like each other. It was a practised, accommodating, nervous laugh that they both had, a laugh that never lasted long but was always quick to come again, with a rattle in their throats and a chatter between their teeth. It was a pity that little Francis, their only son, who was standing silently by, did not join in their laughter too.

'She'll soon get used to being here,' Martha said to the boy, 'and then you'll be able to play with her.'

'Yes,' the little boy said.

'You'll love playing with her,' Martha said.

'Yes,' the little boy said.

'Oh, see what she's doing now,' Francis senior said. He and Martha were standing arm in arm, so he could easily wheel her round to see. The boy stepped forward carefully to see too, and his parents, together, made way for him, grateful for the interest he was showing. The rabbit had been bought for him, after all, and they let him stand in front of them and look. They could see easily enough, over his head.

The rabbit had been bought for little Francis, and how the parents worked in the next few weeks at the fun that the rabbit was going to provide him. How assiduously they cleaned out the hutch every day and saw to it that there was fresh water for the rabbit to drink and fresh grass for the rabbit to lie on. When it rained they brought the hutch into the kitchen and kept it there, though it was quite a job for Francis to bring the clumsy contraption of wood and wire netting through the door without scratching the paint on the doorposts, and Martha found it very much in the way when she was cooking. They fed the rabbit lettuce and carrots and cabbage leaves, even though carrots, particularly, were dishearteningly expensive that season. And they watched the rabbit, talked to the rabbit, put their fingers through the wire and waved them at the rabbit, tried to get the rabbit to answer their calls, invented names for the rabbit, discarded these names and invented better ones. They said the rabbit looked like a grandmother, so they called it Granny; they said the rabbit looked like the villain in a western, so they called it Pardner; sometimes it simply looked sweet, they said, like a bunny that had something to do with an Easter egg or a cold little bunny on a Christmas card, and then they admitted, laughing rapidly and leaning against one another, that they didn't know what they should call it except a darling of a bunny br'er rabbit. To this joy they added the joy of thinking of names for the little ones the rabbit was at any time due to have. Irresponsibly they prophesied that the rabbit would have at least seven little bunnies, at least ten little bunnies, twenty.

'What'll we do if it has twenty?' Francis asked, mockingly aghast.

'We'll declare it a public holiday,' Martha replied. And then to the little boy: 'Wouldn't you like twenty little bunnies to play with? *Twenty*. What a lot of bunnies.'

'Do rabbits ever have twenty babbies?' the boy asked.

The parents looked at one another, and their laugh went no lower than their throats. 'I don't think we know.'

'Then why did you say it will?'

'We didn't say it will, darling. We were just hoping. Wouldn't you like twenty little bunnies to play with?'

Little Francis considered carefully for a moment before he flatly replied, 'Yes.' His watchfulness upset his parents; they had hoped that more of it would have been directed upon the rabbit and less of it upon themselves.

But they persisted. They persisted with the rabbit even though the rabbit was no more responsive to their humour than their son. The rabbit never really looked like a grandmother or a villain in a western or a bunny on a Christmas card, and it never responded to their names and their games: the rabbit ate the food they gave it and went about its rabbity business in the little space it had. Loudly and laughingly, Martha and Francis insisted on how very amusing it was to have a rabbit in their back garden, how cleverly the rabbit's ears moved, how handsomely its fur lay, how intelligent its eyes were – but neither of them was keen on actually handling the rabbit, for fear of fleas, and even for fear of being bitten, for the rabbit had the look of a rabbit that would bite if it felt like it.

And really, Martha and Francis could not help thinking sometimes, a rabbit was a strange-looking animal. Its face was so strange, with that squared, prominent shape of the central bone, cut sharply downwards, almost hammer-like, like one of those sledgehammers that men use to break rocks. And then, a long way below the eyes, below the crown of that hammer-like bone, there was the rest of the face: the flat, almost indistinguishable nose, with the rifts of the nostrils concealed unless they were active; and below that secretive nose the mouth, with its upper lip that split so horribly in two when the animal ate, revealing shamelessly pink flesh, gaping like some kind of wound. While above all, mysteriously independent of the rest, the tall ears swung forward or lay back flat or half-turned, pivoting in some crafty hollow in the skull. The rabbit was black in colour, but not entirely, for many of the hairs were tipped at the end with a strange rusty colour, a kind of red, the colour of dried blood. These tips glowed, when they caught the sunlight, so that the crouching animal looked like a drop that would be scorching to hold in the hand – a little ball of fire for which Martha and Francis had too lightly assumed responsibility. But when the sun was gone from it, the rabbit in its hutch looked no more than nondescript. Only its eyes were bright and mobile then, though sometimes the whiskers and half-secret nostrils would tremble with apprehensions that Martha's or Francis' grosser faculties could not respond to, in their green garden, behind the fence of palings.

The catastrophes with the rabbit came quickly upon one another, the second within a day of the first. When the rabbit finally gave birth Francis came down one morning and found one tiny mouse-like creature crawling blindly around its mother. It had grey fur, still darkly matted, and it seemed quite blind, and the mother rabbit showed no interest in it. Confidently the adults prophesied to one another that during the day it would give birth to more, to more than one; but in the evening when Francis came back from work it was to find that no more little rabbits had been produced. 'She's hiding the little one,' Martha said. 'She hasn't moved.'

'How is the little one?'

'I don't know,' Martha said. 'I've only seen it once, and it looked so feeble. Do you know what a little rabbit is supposed to look like?' she asked her husband. 'This one looks so awful, like a kind of worm. Are they supposed to be blind? Like kittens – kittens are born blind, aren't they?'

Francis laughed, but his wife did not join him. 'And little Francis?' he asked.

'He's in the garden. He's playing. I haven't seen him watching her much.'

'And he wouldn't have seen much if he had been watching her?'

'No.'

'One little rabbit. I hope Francis doesn't remember what we promised him.'

'I hope the little rabbit is all right.'

'Oh, it is,' Francis assured his wife.

When Francis went out before supper the little rabbit was hidden under its mother. Francis junior was playing quietly in the garden; he was as quiet as ever, and as neat, with the comb marks in his hair still showing from where his mother had combed it after lunch. He too told his father that he hadn't seen the little rabbit since the morning.

The next morning, when Francis came down early to make the coffee and put on the toast, there was still no sign of the little rabbit. But Martha's first question on waking had been about it; disturbed by his wife's anxiety, Francis was determined now to see it – to see if it were really the grey, blind bundle of feeble movement that he remembered it to be. He tempted the mother rabbit forward with some wet grass that he plucked at his feet, but she did not move; he went back into the kitchen and brought some lettuce leaves out of the larder and offered them to her, but still she did not move. He snapped his fingers, he called her – not by any of the names they had given her, but simply saying, 'Come here, come here,' but she did not come forward. So in a petulant little anger he pulled out a cane from one of the flower beds and prodded her with it. The cane slid for a moment on the rabbit's close-packed fur and the loose skin beneath, before it found a hold on the haunch. Francis jabbed, he struck upwards, and the rabbit slowly came forward. Francis stared, with the stick in his hand. There was nothing under the rabbit.

He stared, and for a moment he turned and looked up at the window of the bedroom where Francis junior slept. Had the boy taken the little rabbit out? Had Martha? But that was madness, and his heels slipped on the wet grass as he turned and stared again at the point of his stick, where the little rabbit should have been. There was nothing there.

Then Francis saw that there was something there. There were a few hairs and a few droppings, but Francis gingerly moved the stick past these, and carefully turned over a small ball of hair, and saw the dark clots of blood within it, and in the next that he turned over, and the last. They were all that was left of the little rabbit.

Francis dropped his stick. 'Martha!' he shouted. 'Martha!' He met her in the kitchen, and together they rushed to inspect what Francis had told her of. But they had time only to stare for a moment into the hutch before Francis junior appeared through the kitchen door. 'He mustn't see it,' Martha said. 'He mustn't know. Take him away, Francis, quickly!'

'Breakfast,' Francis cheerfully called and picked up the little boy and carried him back indoors, with Martha following them both. While she was giving little Francis his breakfast, the father went outside and cleared up the mess. He did not speak to the mother rabbit, nor did he look at her. Only once, when she got in his way, did he give her a fierce unwarranted jab in the ribs with the garden trowel he was using for the job.

After breakfast the little boy was sent into the garden, and then Martha, who had been very calm and stiff during breakfast, fell upon her husband. 'I will not have that animal in my house for another single day. I can't bear it. I don't want it. You must take it to the pet shop at once.'

'But, darling, I'll be late for work.'

'I don't care if you'll be late for work. You must take it away. I will not have it here.' Martha was small and fierce, like a little fighter, and Francis could not argue with her.

'All right, darling,' he said. 'I'll take it in the car.'

'Do it at once.'

'All right, darling.'

He went to the garden, and for the last time picked up the clumsy hutch. But little Francis followed him.

'Where are you taking it? Where are you taking the bunny?'

'Back to the pet shop.'

'Why?'

'He has to, darling,' Martha said. 'The bunny's sick.'

'No it's not,' the boy said, turning to his mother. He was dressed, as always, with great neatness, in a white T-shirt and a pair of khaki shorts; he was not a boy whose features anyone remembered particularly, but Martha saw to it that his clothes were always spotless.

'It is sick, darling.'

'No it's not.'

If Martha had not been so upset she would simply have ordered her husband to get on with what he was doing. Now she brought her hands to her mouth and from behind her knuckles she asked, 'Francis, do you know why we're taking the bunny to the pet shop?'

'Yes,' the child replied.

Martha half-dropped one hand, the other remaining at her mouth. Francis senior could not move, though he stood with his arms spreadeagled, carrying the hutch. Then Martha moved, grabbing the child by the wrist. 'Why?' she demanded, and shook his arm. 'Why?'

'I think it's because she killed the little bunny.'

'So you *know!*' Martha shrieked.

'Yes.'

'And you didn't say anything about it!' The parents looked with horror at their child. But he met their gaze.

When eventually he spoke he did not seem to be in any way excusing himself. Rather he seemed to want to help his parents by explaining, 'I saw the little bits.'

'Francis!' Martha exclaimed. Francis senior could say nothing. He could only put the hutch down, and sit on it, and get his arms akimbo. Underneath him the disturbed rabbit was scurrying, as if seeking for a foothold.

Martha bent towards the child again. 'But why didn't you tell us?'

The child looked down at the hutch. 'Because I thought you'd take the bunny away if I told you.'

Francis senior spoke at last, with a jerk of his head and a jerk of his arms. 'And you're right. We aren't having it here for another day.' To silence the scurrying rabbit he gave a vicious little back-kick at the hutch beneath him. The scurrying increased in violence.

'There you are,' said the little boy.

He seemed acquiescent enough, but Martha straightened herself and moved to her husband, and took him by the arm.

'Wait,' she said. At the sound of her voice Francis rose to meet her. Husband and wife stood closely together. 'Francis,' Martha said softly, as if the word she had to speak might break in her mouth if she said it carelessly, 'do you love the bunny?'

She could not meet the clear grey stare the child gave her. He looked straight at her, and did not open his mouth to answer her question, like someone who would not admit that he knew the meaning of the word.

Martha dropped her husband's arm and began to walk away. 'Let it stay,' she said. 'Let him have it.'

'But –'

'Let it stay,' Martha said from a few yards off, without looking back, still walking towards the kitchen.

'All right then,' Francis senior said, giving the hutch a parting kick. 'But you'll have to feed it and give it water and everything else.' He began to walk after his wife. He left the hutch in the middle of their lawn.

'Yes,' the little boy said.

He waited until his father had gone into the house, then he went on his knees in front of the hutch. He put his finger through the wire netting. 'Come here,' he said to the rabbit. 'I'm not cross with you. I knew you didn't like your baby.'

THE GAME

Roger Merrit was the one who organized the expedition. At the age of seventeen Roger Merrit was a tall blond fellow with a high-pitched voice and a gangling stride that left his torso hanging just a little behind his legs. Roger was a contemporary and a close friend of my elder brother's; and the three of us made up the hunting party on my father's farm.

My father's farm was merely seventeen hundred morgen of veld in the Northern Cape, on which the only building was the mud-walled, iron-roofed hut of the African herd boy. Across the seventeen hundred morgen there grazed a herd of cattle, some sheep, and a few horses, all of which were supposed to be fattening up for the summer, when they would be sold at the sales. My father had bought the farm after one of the wettest years we could remember in Lyndhurst; he had come to it at the end of summer, when the slopes of the veld were covered in grass that was knee-high, green at the stems, and beginning to go to a silvery-blue seed at the tips. Clouds moved across the sky; and the light, when it fell to the earth, seemed to be taken in by the grass and subdued there. The veld was wide and so gentle one could hardly understand why it should have been empty of people, why from a single point only on the farm it was possible to see just one neighbouring farmhouse, miles away.

But the afternoon we went hunting, eighteen months later, it was difficult to know why anyone – ourselves included – should have been there. The single barbed-wire fence along the side of the farm where we walked was something remarkable, a sign of lonely human endeavour – it seemed so strange that anyone should ever have bothered to survey this place, to mark off one section of it from another. The fence was like a monument. The whole sky seemed to glare down at us, and as we walked our feet struck against ground that was hard and cracked, or sank into drifts of loose sand; from both the loose sand and the crust-like earth shoots of yellow grass started up here and there, as stiffly as sticks. The few bushes, which a season before had merged gently into the grass around them, now stood out, the only dark things to be seen. The other colours were all pale, the colours of drought, each one like something scraped across the eyeball: a scrape of yellow, a scrape of brown, a scrape of white, the dark scrape of the bushes. We walked with big hats over our heads, and took turns at carrying the rifle, and heard the grass cracking under our feet.

Roger Merrit carried the rifle like a soldier, slung easy over his shoulder; my brother had it slung across his back like a Boer on Commando; and I carried it in both hands, in front of me, like a street fighter in the war films that we were at that time – during the Second World War – seeing so regularly. My brother and Roger Merrit were both in their last year at school, and both of them were going to join the army at the end of the year; or so they both said. I was only thirteen, and had no hope that the war would go on until I was old enough to join the army, so I took a vicarious pride in the intentions of my brother and his friend who, when I yielded the rifle to them, seemed to me already to be marching not across the peaceful desert of South Africa, but across the terrible desert of North Africa. There in the north there were places like Tobruk, El Alamein, Bardia,

Mersa Matruh, that seemed to me, when the older ones took the rifle, just beyond the horizon that encircled us in a whitish glare of heat. We walked, we took turns with the rifle; the soles of our shoes seemed to burn upwards with every step we took, and the rims of our hats cut into our brows, as if they had been made of steel.

'Where are those buck you're talking about?' my brother asked Roger Merrit, complainingly.

Roger shook his loose shoulders. 'It's your farm, not mine.'

'I'd exchange all of it for a Coca-Cola right now.'

I was a little ashamed of my brother. He seemed to me to lack the right gravity of spirit for an outing of this sort.

'You said you saw some buck when you were riding,' Roger said to me.

I had said this, and I had told the truth: that had been the germ of the expedition. When we came out with my father over the weekends we used to take one or two of the farm's few horses and go riding, aimlessly, in any direction, for miles, until the loneliness of the veld and its silence would begin to frighten us a little, and we would turn back. More than once on these rides we had seen a few head of buck. Because my father did not allow any of the neighbours to shoot on the farm, these buck were more curious and less frightened of us than they should have been. They were pale brown, and swift when they ran; but they could halt in an instant, and would stand with their heads turned, watching us, before fleeing again. I had mentioned this to Roger one day; a week or two later he had told us that he had managed to get hold of a rifle, and thought that we should ask my father to let us go on just one afternoon's hunt. My father was reluctant, but consented, and gave us the car to drive to the farm.

'I have seen them,' I assured Roger. 'Lots of times.'

'Perhaps they were sheep,' my brother suggested.

'Don't be funny. You saw them too,' I said.

'And who'd take a sheep for a buck?' Roger asked.

'I don't know – someone who's short-sighted, or excited, or hasn't had the differences pointed out to him.'

'Funny!'

Roger breathed whistlingly through his small nose when he was tired. My brother sweated freely; he said that any buck who couldn't smell him coming deserved to get a bullet through its head. My head was aching; and every footstep now was so much heat shaped like a shoe sole. But I wanted us to see a buck, at least one, after what I had said.

Later my brother said: 'I just don't get the point of this.' We had halted on the crest of a rise, and from where we were the world seemed to go only downwards, beyond the farm boundary, beyond the boundary of the next farm, for miles and miles. It was not until the horizon that the veld lifted in the sudden blue humps of a few isolated koppies.

'You'll get the point of it all right, when we see something,' Roger said. Roger seemed to me in every way a more satisfactory hunting companion than my brother. Not only was he taller than my brother; not only did he carry the rifle in finer style; but he was serious and determined as well. He had not complained once about the heat or the distance we had walked, or the inhospitability and dullness of the veld. Constantly his eyes had scanned the veld in front and behind him – whereas my brother had pulled his hat so low over his eyes that he looked like a clown and could not see anything more than ten yards in front of him.

Then, to cap it all, my brother walked to the shade of the nearest thorn tree and sat down on the ground. 'You walk on,' he said. 'When you come back, I'll be waiting here for you.'

Roger looked angry; I felt I was being put to shame.

'Come on,' I said, and gave my brother a gentle kick.

'No, man,' he said comfortably.

Roger stood a yard or two away, in the sun. My brother propped himself against the tree trunk, and pushed his hat still lower over his eyes. Beyond, the veld burned yellow, burned brown, burned white, sloping down from us, for as many miles as we could see.

'Of all the damn –' Roger said. 'Honestly –'

'You go on,' my brother said. 'You don't need me.'

I laughed and said to Roger, 'Come on. If we go on, you'll see he'll follow.' But I said it with more certainty than I felt.

Roger and I began to walk on. The veld was quiet. When we looked back, my brother had sunk even lower against the narrow black trunk of the tree.

'Why did he come, if that was what he was going to do?' Roger asked me.

'I don't know.'

'That's sportsmanship!'

I said nothing. We walked on, but not for more than a few minutes. Then Roger hesitated, looked up at the sun, looked back at my brother, looked at the veld that lay ahead of us.

'Let's go back,' Roger said. And we turned and went back without another word.

My brother watched us coming. 'Did you get anything?' he shouted, when we were still a long way off.

'Joke!' I shouted back.

But we had no sooner rejoined my brother – we were standing accusingly over him – than we saw two head of buck coming out of a ragged line of bushes a few hundred yards from us. They were low, not much higher than the grass, but a little darker in colour; they moved cautiously, with their small triangular heads turned to us. In a moment Roger had raised the rifle, and was taking aim; he fired, and a cloud of dust rose where the buck had been standing. I saw one buck running low, and Roger fired again at it; another cloud of dust went up, but from the place where we had first seen them. The one that was running kept moving, and I lost it in the grass. Then, from the same place as before, silently, a third cloud of dust rose from the ground, to a height of perhaps three feet, and we saw it begin to drift, over the pale grass.

We started running, all three of us. When we were about a hundred yards away from it, we saw what was making the dust go up. The buck rose in the air, its small body twisting, arching in mid-air, almost fish-like. It was curved, brown, a dust-brown; we saw it fall, and the dust went up again.

'Kill it,' my brother said, as he ran. We dropped, and waited, feeling under our hands and knees the hot sand and the sharpness of the grass, hearing our own panting. We waited for the buck, and at last we saw it rise, slowly this time, and stand. Roger took careful aim, and fired, and the buck simply fell, with almost no dust going up. It was dead when we came to it, a little stembuck, in height not much taller than a fair-sized dog, but slender in the shoulders, haunches and muzzle; most slender in the legs. One of the legs dangled by a ligament a few inches above the hoof. The first shot had snapped its leg; the second had gone through its chest. The leg was almost bloodless, only clean bone and severed skin showing, but some dark blood was oozing out of the body.

Roger said, 'There's another,' and we looked up, and saw a buck standing – perhaps the one we had seen before, perhaps another. As we turned it began running.

'It's your turn,' Roger shouted, thrusting the rifle at my brother. My brother lifted the rifle, and fired.

'You missed,' Roger said, for the buck ran still. We watched it go; Roger took the rifle from my brother. Then, to our astonishment, we saw the buck stop, turn its head, stand clearly outlined against the darkness of a bush as it looked at us. Roger lifted the rifle; I was standing next to my brother, and I heard him muttering. I had been unnerved by the sight of the little buck leaping in agony, and now lying dead and ignominiously smeared in dust behind us; but I was more unnerved when I heard what my brother was saying. He did not know that I was listening; his attention was all on the buck, and he was talking to it. 'Run!' he was saying. 'Go on, run!' Roger fired; and the buck ran. Its light brown body was lost in an instant on the pale veld.

Then we went back to our prize, and had a long talk about how we were to bring it to the car. 'I'll carry it,' Roger said boastfully. He picked up the buck and slung it over his shoulders, as he had seen hunters do in the pictures. And we set out. But Roger was soon staggering. Though the buck was small, it was a considerable dead weight to carry over the rough surface of the veld, under that sun. We took turns at carrying it, but even then we tired; eventually we put it under a thorn tree, and Roger and my brother went ahead to fetch the car: they would simply drive it over the veld and pick up me and the buck.

I waited with the dead buck, in the veld, where nothing moved, not even any birds. I tried to remember the mood with which we had set out; I tried to think of El Alamein, and Bardia, of Mersa Matruh and Tobruk; but I could not put out of my mind my brother's rapt face, his lips moving, the hat over his eyes, as he prayed for the life of the buck. I was ashamed of him; yet I knew that his feeling was my own. And I really did not know, then, whose cowardice was the greater: his in admitting his own feeling, and giving it speech, or mine in trying to deny it, even with the shame I felt.

We loaded the buck into the boot of the car, when Roger and my brother returned.

But young though I was, I sensed a kind of covert logic in Roger Merrit's sudden shamefaced admission that afternoon, when we were driving home, that his father had refused to give him permission to join the army. There was no conscription in South

Africa during the war, and without his father's permission, Roger, at the age of seventeen, could not serve.

My brother said, 'My father's already given me his permission.'

'You'll be in the army next year,' Roger said.

'Yes, I will,' my brother said. Then, 'You're the lucky one,' he broke out, almost angrily.

Roger thought my brother was joking; but a little later he said; quietly, 'Perhaps you're right' – as if he too had realized that afternoon how little time they had to play at being men. On the main tarred road across the veld, the car rushed northwards.

A WAY OF LIFE

Lena, her employers admitted, looked awful. She had two long yellow teeth in the middle of her mouth, and no other teeth at all; the rest of her face was shrunken and wrinkled. Her eyes were bloodshot; her hair was thin; painfully she had dragged her peppercorns into a series of tiny topknots, bound together by strips of cloth. She wore her mistress's cast-off clothes; but even when she was given a dress in reasonable condition it looked bedraggled and old-fashioned immediately she put it on. Partly this was because Lena was so much smaller than her mistress, though Annette Capon was not herself a large woman, so that the dresses all trailed about Lena's ankles, with an odd missionary look. Seeing Lena one might have expected the worst: slovenliness and illiteracy, servility, dishonesty, and shiftlessness.

In fact, you found nothing of the kind. Lena spoke a good English and wrote a clear hand; she was punctual, she was honest, she was loyal, she was clean. She never complained; she laughed often, showing her two teeth; and she was devoted to little Adam, the Capons' three-year-old son. Where, how, had Lena learned her honesty, punctuality and loyalty, her cheerfulness and cleanliness? It was impossible to say. Her qualities, her virtues, seemed to be simply there – in her, part of her, like her teeth or her hair or the tiny red veins in her eyes. She had not known her father at all; her mother had been a washerwoman, who had gone in every week with bundles of clean washing to the white suburbs of Johannesburg, and had brought back dirty bundles to be boiled on the stove and hand-pressed in the single room which was shared by Lena, her mother, her sister, her aunt and a fierce uncle. Lena had gone for a few years to a school run by a mission; but the school had been so crowded that it took in batches of children for only three hours a day. The rest of the time Lena had just wandered about the dusty streets of the 'location'. As soon as she had been old enough, she had begun to help her mother with the washing, in addition to attending the school; then her mother had died of TB, and her aunt had left the location with 'another man'. Lena had been fourteen, then, she thought, but she wasn't sure; her sister had been a year younger. As for her sister: 'Soon,' Lena had told the Capons, in her plaintive creaking voice, 'she died also, from having a baby.' Lena herself had been more fortunate; she had managed to get taken on as a domestic servant with a white family almost immediately after the death of her mother; and a domestic servant she had remained ever since, for the last forty years.

During that time she had had positions with innumerable families; she had also had three children by three different men. She now knew the whereabouts of the two surviving children, but of none of the men. She was, she announced gladly to the Capons, 'too old to get married now'. Lena had no tribal loyalties (she did not even know to which tribe her father had belonged); she had no religious beliefs; she had never been legally married; her 'papers' were in a state of chronic disorder; and though she had been born in Johannesburg, she was convinced that she was liable to instant deportation if she were ever caught by a policeman or a clerk in the Native Affairs Department vengeful or conscientious enough to follow up her case.

She had been with the Capons for four years, ever since she had been brought to Annette Capon by another servant in the block of flats who had known that Annette was looking for a 'girl'. Annette, who was working in town during the day, had been desperate for someone to look after the flat; and had taken Lena on as a stopgap merely until she found someone more presentable. But that day had never come. The Capons had been glad to keep her on. They gave her clothes to wear, newspapers to read, and a wage larger than that earned by most of the other 'girls' who worked in the same block of flats. Lena's employers respected her; they were amused by her; they trusted her. And Lena trusted them. She had a good job with a 'good baas' and a 'good missus', and she was content.

Every morning she came down from the servants' dormitory on the top floor of the block, made coffee, and brought it into the Capons' bedroom, together with the newspaper. Then she went into the next room and dressed Adam; while the Capons drank their coffee and dressed, and Leslie Capon glanced at the paper's headlines, they heard Lena and Adam talking and laughing next door. Often Lena sang to Adam, garbled nursery rhymes or hit tunes, and Adam sometimes joined in. Their voices both sounded pure – the one pure with youth, the other with age. When Adam ran into his parents' room, Lena went back into the kitchen and made the porridge, and fried the eggs. After breakfast, Leslie Capon went off to work; Annette stayed a little longer, before taking Adam to the nursery school and going on to her own work. For the next few hours Lena washed dishes, made the beds, prepared lunch for herself and Adam, peeled vegetables for dinner; sometimes she went shopping, presenting to the grocer and butcher the lists which Annette wrote out for her. She talked to the other 'girls' in the block of flats, and to the 'boys' who polished the floors and the bathroom in each of the flats, and the corridors outside. At twelve o'clock she went to fetch Adam from his nursery school, and she and the little white boy walked home together, through the sunlit streets, Lena carrying Adam's tiny school satchel. Their lunch they ate in the kitchen; Lena usually had her own mess of rice and 'soup meat' cooking on the stove, and Adam ate the food which his mother had put out for him. Soon Annette Capon came back from town (she had a mornings-only job), and then, unless there was something she particularly wanted Lena to do, Lena took a couple of hours 'off'. Later in the afternoon she helped Annette with making dinner, or did the washing and ironing; she served dinner, and ate her own meal among the unwashed pots and plates in the kitchen. She had a special white overall and cap which she put on to serve the dinner; this was the smartest of her outfits, and hid most of the trailing garments she wore underneath. After washing up, she left the flat quietly, to go upstairs to her dormitory. She walked up the six flights, because she was nervous of the lift.

On alternate Sundays she took a whole day off to visit her daughter in Alexandra Township; and she had twice gone down with the Capons to the sea, when they had taken their holidays.

Then Lena fell ill – or rather, the Capons found out that she had been ill for some time. She had been feeling dizzy in the mornings; she had had funny feelings in her chest and arms; sometimes she had difficulty in breathing. The Capons found out about it only when Lena fell down in the kitchen one morning; they heard a crash of crockery, and when Annette Capon rushed into the room she found Lena trying to get up from the floor, but unable to do so. Pieces of plates lay on the floor around her, together with slices of bread that she had been about to put in the toaster.

'Lena! What's the matter?'

The servant's mouth opened and closed for a moment, before she replied in a whisper, 'Madam.'

'Have you hurt yourself?'

Again Lena tried to speak. On her second attempt she managed to say, 'Sorry, Madam.'

Annette was in her dressing gown; her blonde hair was in disorder, and on her lips there was some pale lipstick which she had not washed off before going to bed the previous night. She seemed very quick and firm, plump and young, next to Lena, as she helped the old woman to her feet. Lena stood against the sink, her head hanging over it. Her ears were filled with sound; the white sink seemed to jump with every beat of her heart, though she could feel its hardness and coldness, as if from a distance, between her fingers. So far as she was conscious of anything, Lena was ashamed – ashamed of having been found on the floor, of the dishes she had broken, even of the way she was feeling. 'It's nothing, madam,' she said, 'it comes like this sometimes.'

'Like what?'

'Like funny,' Lena said eventually.

'Lena, are you sick? How long have you been sick?'

'I don't know, madam.'

'Why didn't you tell me? We must call the doctor.' Annette couldn't help wondering whether Lena's illness was infectious; she also wondered what she would do about fetching Adam from nursery school. Yet her concern was genuine.

'No, madam, it is nothing.'

'Are you sure?'

'Yes, madam.'

Slowly Annette took her arm away from Lena's shoulder; she stared doubtfully at Lena's bent back. 'Do you want to lie down?'

'No, madam, I will be all right in a minute.'

Annette filled a glass of water and held it to Lena's lips. 'Drink this, it'll make you feel better.' Lena took two sips at the water. Suddenly she clutched hard at the sink; she would have fallen again if Annette had not taken hold of her. Annette staggered as she led Lena to a chair, surprised by the sudden dead weight of her, though she was so small. Leaving Lena sitting at the table, Annette ran through to ask her husband to go and fetch Dr Kantner, who lived in one of the flats on the same floor.

Dr Kantner came in with his shirt neatly buttoned, his chin freshly shaved, but with slippers on his feet and no tie around his collar. He examined Lena carefully, in Annette's presence, undoing without distaste the various layers of blouse and vest which Lena wore under her dress. The examination abashed Lena anew, especially as she was feeling better again; but she answered the doctor's questions as well as she could. When he had finished his examination, the doctor went into the next room and told Annette and Leslie Capon that he didn't like the look of it – her heart beat was not what it should be, her blood pressure was high, she would have to rest. He suspected that she would have to rest for a long time, he added. He would have another look at her later, when he could better spare the time; in the meantime, she must go back to bed. Then he went back into the kitchen and said jovially and loudly, 'You're a naughty girl, Lena. You've got no business to upset everyone like this. From now on you must look after yourself, do you hear?'

'Yes, master,' Lena said in complete, subdued acquiescence. She was ashamed of having upset everyone; she felt particularly guilty when she saw the doctor's felt slippers on his feet.

The Capons were left staring at each other. There was no breakfast, the kitchen was in a mess, Adam was shouting from his bedroom, Leslie would be late for work, and Annette would have to get off early to fetch Adam from his nursery school. And what would they do tomorrow? And the day after?

When they went into the kitchen, they found that Lena had swept up the broken crockery, and was now, with trembling hands, trying to lay the table for breakfast. 'No, you must come with me!' Annette shouted crossly, upset by the confusion of the morning, and by the pity she felt at seeing Lena attempting to carry on with her work. She led Lena out of the flat, and went with her in the lift to the top floor. The servants' dormitory was right on the roof of the building, and they had to climb up a flight of steps after the lift had gone as far as it could. On the flat roof, in the open, there were numbers of washing lines, a couple of galvanized iron pressure tanks, the stack of the building's central-heating plant, two lavatories, and two low rooms of raw brick, with a single window of frosted glass let in at the end of each. One room was for the 'boys'; the other for the 'girls'. Inside the 'girls' room, the beds stood in two rows, with a passageway between the rows, and about two feet of free space to the sides of each bed. Though it was a bright day outside, very little light came in through the window. A naked bulb was burning in the middle of the room, and its rays showed up the grey patched blankets on the beds, and the tin trunks which gleamed from under some of them. The room smelled faintly but distinctly of food and sweat.

Here Annette left Lena, and here Lena remained for a week, getting up only to go to the women's lavatory at the other end of the roof. Once a day Annette came up to visit her, though she hated the room, and was embarrassed when any of the other African 'girls' who happened to be off duty were sitting or lying there; and though Annette hated, too, the sight of Lena lying in her bed, like a dark shred of illness and pain, only her yellow teeth and her sunken eyes reflecting any light, Annette felt guilty about her own repugnances; Lena, for her part, felt guilty for her illness and idleness, whenever her mistress was with her. But when Annette was not there Lena lay in a reverie, only half-aware of what was around her; she had vivid dreams sometimes, and called out in her sleep. She was not afraid of death; but she was frightened of losing her job.

The doctor examined her several times, and told the Capons firmly that Lena should not go back to work – not for a couple of months at least; if she did, he would not be responsible for her. When Annette broke the news to her, Lena wept, for the first time since she had come to work for the Capons. She made no sound, but her head shook from side to side on her ticking-covered pillow, and the tears ran down the sides of her drawn black cheeks. Annette promised Lena that she would let her have the job again as soon as she was better. 'You can find me another girl, or your daughter can, and you can explain to her that she can have the job only while you're gone.' But Lena cried that she was quite well again, that she could work for the missus if only the missus would let her. 'If I go, the missus will forget me,' Lena cried. 'Let me do my work, madam.'

'The doctor says you mustn't.'

'And how will I live without work? Where will I sleep?'

'We'll give you a little money, and you can stay with your daughter.'

Lena's daughter was a plump, sly young woman, much lighter-skinned and much more smartly dressed than her mother. She came to fetch Lena after a message had been sent to her through one of the other 'girls' who worked in the block; she came in a taxi, which Leslie Capon had agreed to pay for, and she brought with her the girl who was to take Lena's place – a very young, clean girl, wearing a pinafore dress, like a school gym tunic, and a black beret on her head. This girl's name was Frances, and she had a tiny, humble voice, and downcast eyes. Lena was helped out of the dormitory, and the new girl moved in with her tin trunk and blanket roll. 'The madam will forget me,' Lena said, without tears now, as she was being helped into the taxi; but Annette assured her that she would do no such thing. Though the day was bright and warm, Lena was wearing her coat, and she held its lapel over her mouth, as if she were suffering from toothache. She looked very old, even older than she had before her illness. Annette had given her a few pounds, and told her to send a message through her daughter if she needed more. Then the taxi – an enormous, decrepit, black Buick, with a sign *African Taxi : Non-Europeans Only* above the number plate – drove off. Lena was sitting on the back seat, but as it drove off Annette could not see Lena's head through the rear window.

A week later, Lena appeared at the door of the flat. 'You shouldn't be here,' Annette scolded her, though she was pleased to see her. 'How are you, Lena?'

'Very well, madam.'

She did seem much better; she spoke more firmly, and she clapped her hands with delight when she saw Adam. 'Little master, how big you grow!' she cried out. She had come to ask for her job. 'I can't live with that girl,' she told Annette – 'that girl' being her daughter. 'She complains to me, whatever I do, madam. I take up too much space. I eat too much food. I make work for her. And her husband, he is even worse. He took my money, madam, the money that the madam gave me. And he teaches the children to be cheeky to me. Please, madam, please take me back. The madam will see that I can still do all the work. I can't go back to that place.'

Annette was distressed – not only to hear Lena's tale, but to have the whole problem of Lena's life thrust upon her once again. She pleaded with Lena to go back; she told her that she would speak to Lena's daughter and tell her to be kind to her mother; she asked Lena if she didn't know of some other woman with whom she could stay.

'Every woman will want too much money, madam, and I have no money.'

'But we can give you some.'

'Not enough, madam. How can the madam pay for me to live with another woman, and to buy my food, when madam is already paying for one girl here?'

Annette had no answer: what Lena had just said had been worrying Annette and her husband too. The Capons only just managed to come out each month; they couldn't afford to pay indefinitely for two servants, one of whom did no work. 'But it will be for only a few weeks, Lena.'

Lena shook her head. 'And if at the end the doctor says I am still not strong enough to work? How can the madam still pay for me? Then all I can do is to look for work with another missus, who does not know that I'm sick.' Lena had been sitting forward over the kitchen table; she leaned back, as if to show herself to Annette. 'Madam can see that I'm getting sick and old, but she can see also that I must still live.'

Annette frowned. 'No,' she said. 'I can't take on the responsibility. We'll help you, Lena, for the next few weeks, we'll give you money, and then the doctor will look at you again.'

'And then, madam?'

'Then we'll see.'

Lena went back to her daughter; the new girl, Frances, stayed on in the flat and continued to do the work that Lena had done. At the end of six weeks Lena came back to the flat, and the doctor examined her again. His report was discouraging. She was better than she had been; but she was far from well. She should still be resting in bed, not thinking of starting work again. On the other hand, she was not really sick enough to be given a bed in one of the African hospitals, which were all impossibly overcrowded, and which had to use their beds for those who required continuous attention, not those who merely needed to rest a strained heart. 'It's tough,' the doctor said as he packed his bag; and as a friend he added, 'But you can't let yourself get too involved, you know. And I suppose she'll be able to draw some kind of sickness benefit – I'll write out anything she needs for that, if she applies.' Then he went out; and the Capons were again left with their problem.

'You know what her benefit would be, more or less,' Capon said to his wife. 'About five shillings a week. Sixty pennies. Think of that.'

Annette said, 'Besides she'd never go to claim it. She wouldn't go near any Government office, you can bet.'

'No.'

'She'll take another job, that's what she'll do.'

'Yes.'

What were they to do? The Capons were decent people, who conscientiously voted for the most liberal candidate at elections, and who talked, frequently, of getting out of South Africa altogether, the whole racial set-up was so distasteful to them. Not that their getting out would help people like Lena. Poor bloody Lena. What could they do with her? They couldn't pay for her upkeep indefinitely; they just couldn't afford it. And as long as Annette worked (and it was only because Annette worked that they were able to come out each month), they *had* to have a servant, and one they could rely on, too – not one who would be sick, on and off. But to send Lena away, to turn her out of doors, and tell her to go to the dreaded Native Affairs Department to claim her sixty pennies a week, or to send her trudging the streets looking for another job – that was impossible too.

'We'll just have to keep her,' Annette said, 'and put up with whatever happens. And see that she takes care of herself.'

Gloomily, her husband agreed. 'I just don't want to have her fainting all over the place all the time, that's all.'

'Nor do I, believe me.'

Frances was called into the sitting room, and was told that Lena was better now, and she would have to go. The girl received the news submissively and silently, as she had received every order given to her since she had come into the flat. She went out of the room, and Lena was called in.

'We've spoken to the doctor, Lena.'

'Yes, madam.' Lena waited quietly, clutching at the skirt of her dress with one hand, the other hand lifted to her flat bosom. She looked at neither of her employers.

'He says you're still sick, Lena. You are better, but you still aren't well. Do you understand?'

'Yes, madam.'

'Do you still want to work for us?' Annette did not know why she asked the question; only later did she realize that it was an attempt to shift the responsibility for the arrangement from her shoulders on to Lena's.

'Yes, madam, I do want to work.'

'Even though the doctor says you mustn't?'

'The doctor doesn't say how I can live if I do no work, madam.'

'No.' Hurriedly Annette went on, 'That's why we've decided you can stay with us, Lena. But you mustn't work too hard. You must be careful with yourself.' She stopped, for Lena had bowed her head and covered her face with both hands.

When she took her hands away, Lena's face was grave, her eyelids were lowered. 'I am sorry that the madam has to take me,' she said. She raised her eyes to look directly at her employers. 'The madam must not worry. If anything happens to me, it will not be the madam's fault.'

'Whose fault will it be?' Leslie Capon called out suddenly, urgently, as if Lena might answer him. But none of them could answer the question.

The next day, Lena made the coffee and brought it in with the newspaper; she dressed Adam, and sang to him; she made the breakfast and washed up after breakfast. At noon she went to fetch Adam from the nursery school, and carried his little satchel for him. Annette found them happily together when she came back from work. She sent Lena upstairs for her rest; and the only change was that now, timorously, Lena got into the lift and travelled up with it as far as it could go. Then slowly she climbed the last flight of steps to the dormitory.

BEGGAR MY NEIGHBOUR

Michael saw them for the first time when he was coming home from school one day. One moment the street had been empty, glittering in the light from the sun behind his back, with no traffic on the roadway and apparently no pedestrians on the broad sandy pavement; the next moment these two were before him, their faces raised to his. They seemed to emerge directly in front of him, as if the light and shade of the glaring street had suddenly condensed itself into two little piccanins with large eyes set in their round, black faces.

'*Stukkie brood*?' the elder, a boy, said in a plaintive voice. A piece of bread. At Michael's school the slang term for any African child was just that: *stukkie brood*. That was what African children were always begging for.

'*Stukkie brood*?' the little girl said. She was wearing a soiled white dress that was so short it barely covered her loins; there seemed to be nothing at all beneath the dress. She wore no socks, no shoes, no cardigan, no cap or hat. She must have been about ten years old. The boy, who was dressed in a torn khaki shirt and a pair of grey shorts much too large for him, was about Michael's age, about twelve, though he was a little smaller than the white boy. Like the girl, he was barefoot. Their limbs were painfully thin; their wrists and ankles stood out in knobs, and the skin over these protruding bones was rougher than elsewhere. The dirt on their skin showed up as a faint greyness against the black.

'I've got no bread,' the white boy said. He had halted in surprise at the suddenness of their appearance before him. They must have been hiding behind one of the trees that were planted at intervals along the pavement. 'I don't bring bread from school.'

They did not move. Michael shifted his school case from one hand to the other and took a pace forward. Silently, the African children stood aside. As he passed them, Michael was conscious of the movement of their eyes; when he turned to look back he saw that they were standing still to watch him go. The boy was holding one of the girl's hands in his.

It was this that made the white child pause. He was touched by their dependence on one another, and disturbed by it too, as he had been by the way they had suddenly come before him, and by their watchfulness and silence after they had uttered their customary, begging request. Michael saw again how ragged and dirty they were, and thought of how hungry they must be. Surely he could give them a piece of bread. He was only three blocks from home.

He said, 'I haven't got any bread here. But if you come home with me, I'll see that you get some bread. Do you understand?'

They made no reply; but they obviously understood what he had said. The three children moved down the pavement. Only Michael's shod feet crunched on the sand; the footfalls of the others were silent. They walked a little behind Michael, and to one side of him. Once he asked them if they went to school, and the boy shook his head; when he asked them if they were brother and sister, the boy nodded.

When they reached Michael's house, he went inside and told Dora, the cook-girl, that there were two piccanins in the lane outside, and that he wanted her to cut some bread and jam for them. Dora grumbled that she was not supposed to look after every little beggar in town, and Michael answered her angrily, 'We've got lots of bread. Why shouldn't we give them some?' He was particularly indignant because he felt that Dora, being of the same race as the two outside, should have been even readier than he was to help them. When Dora was about to take the bread out to the back gate, where the children waited, he stopped her. 'It's all right, Dora,' he said in a tone of reproof, 'I'll take it,' and he went out into the sunlight, carrying the plate in his hand.

'*Stukkie brood*,' he called out to them. 'Here's your *stukkie brood*.'

The children stretched their hands out eagerly, and Michael let them take the inch-thick slices from the plate. He was pleased to see that Dora had put a scraping of apricot jam on the bread. Each of them held the bread in both hands, as if afraid of dropping it. The girl's mouth worked a little, but she kept her eyes fixed on the white boy.

'What do you say?' Michael asked.

They replied in high, clear voices, 'Thank you, baas.'

'That's better. Now you can eat.' He wanted to see them eat it; he wanted to share their pleasure in satisfying their strained appetites. But without saying a word to him, they began to back away, side by side. They took a few paces, and then they turned and ran along the lane towards the main road they had walked down earlier. The little girl's dress fluttered behind her, white against her black body. At the corner they halted, looked back once, and then ran on, out of sight.

A few days later, at the same time and in the same place, Michael saw them again, on his way home from school. They were standing in the middle of the pavement, and he saw them from a long way off. They were obviously waiting for him to come. Michael was the first to speak, as he approached them.

'What? Another piece of bread?' he called out from a few yards away.

'Yes, baas,' they answered together. They turned immediately to join him as he walked by. Yet they kept a respectful pace or two behind.

'How did you know I was coming?'

'We know the baas is coming from school.'

'And how do you know that I'm going to give you bread?' There was no reply; not even a smile from the boy, in response to Michael's. They seemed to him, as he glanced casually at them, identical in appearance to a hundred, a thousand, other piccanins, from the peppercorns on top of their heads to their wide, calloused, sand-grey feet.

When they reached the house, Michael told Dora, 'Those *stukkie broods* are waiting outside again. Give them something, and then they can go.'

Dora grumbled once again, but did as she was told. Michael did not go out with the bread himself; he was in a hurry to get back to work on a model car he was making, and was satisfied to see, out of his bedroom window, Dora coming from the back gate a few minutes later with an empty plate in her hand. Soon he had forgotten all about the two children. He did not go out of the house until a couple of hours had passed; by then it was dusk, and he took a torch with him to help him find a piece of wire for his model in the darkness of the lumber-shed. Handling the torch gave Michael a feeling of power and importance, and he stepped into the lane with it, intending to shine it about like a policeman on his beat. Immediately he opened the gate, he saw the two little children standing in the half-light, just a few paces away from him.

'What are you doing here?' Michael exclaimed in surprise. The boy answered, holding his hand up, as if warning Michael to be silent. 'We were waiting to say thank you to the baas.'

'What!' Michael took a step towards them both, and they stood their ground, only shrinking together slightly.

For all the glare and glitter there was in the streets of Lyndhurst by day, it was winter, midwinter; and once the sun had set, the air turned bitterly cold as swiftly as the light disappeared. The cold at night wrung deep notes from the contracting iron roofs of the houses, and froze the fish ponds in all the gardens of the white suburbs. Already Michael could feel its sharp touch on the tips of his ears and fingers. And the two African children stood there barefoot, in a flimsy dress and torn shirt, waiting to thank him for the bread he had had sent out to them.

'You mustn't wait,' Michael said. In the half-darkness he saw the white dress on the girl more clearly than the boy's clothing; and he remembered the nakedness and puniness of her black thighs. He stretched his hand out, with the torch in it. 'Take it,' he said. The torch was in his hand, and there was nothing else that he could give to them. 'It's nice,' he said. 'It's a torch. Look.' He switched it on and saw in its beam of light a pair of startled eyes, darting desperately from side to side. 'You see how nice it is,' Michael said, turning the beam upwards, where it lost itself against the light that lingered in the sky. 'If you don't want it, you can sell it. Go on, take it.'

A hand came up and took the torch from him. Then the two children ran off, in the same direction they had taken on the first afternoon. When they reached the corner all the street lights came on, as if at a single touch, and the children stopped and stared at them, before running again. Michael saw the torch glinting in the boy's hand, and only then did it occur to him that despite their zeal to thank him for the bread they hadn't thanked him for the torch. The size of the gift must have surprised them into silence, Michael decided; and the thought of his own generosity helped to console him for the regret he couldn't help feeling when he saw the torch being carried away from him.

Michael was a lonely child. He had neither brothers nor sisters; both his parents worked during the day, and he had made few friends at school. But he was not unhappy in his loneliness. He was used to it, in the first place; and then, because he was lonely, he was all the better able to indulge himself in his own fantasies. He played for hours, by himself, games of his own invention – games of war, of exploration, of seafaring, of scientific invention, of crime, of espionage, of living in a house beneath or above his real one. It was not long before the two African children, who were now accosting him regularly, appeared in some of his games, for their weakness, poverty, and dependence gave Michael ample scope to display in fantasy his kindness, generosity, courage and decisiveness. Sometimes in his games Michael saved the boy's life, and was thanked for it in broken English. Sometimes he saved the girl's, and then she humbly begged his pardon for having caused him so much trouble. Sometimes he was just too late to save the life of either, though he tried his best, and then there were affecting scenes of farewell.

But in real life, Michael did not play with the children at all: they were too dirty, too ragged, too strange, too persistent. Their persistence eventually drove Dora to tell Michael's mother about them; and his mother did her duty by telling Michael that on no account should he play with the children, nor should he give them anything of value.

'Play with them!' Michael laughed at the idea. And apart from bread and the torch he had given them nothing but a few old toys, a singlet or two, a pair of old canvas shoes. No one could begrudge them those gifts. Michael's mother certainly didn't. What she was anxious to do was simply to prevent her son playing with the piccanins, fearing that he would pick up germs, bad language, and 'Kaffir ways' generally from them. Hearing both from Michael and Dora that he did not play with them, and that he had never even asked them into the backyard, let alone the house, she was satisfied.

They came to Michael about once a week, meeting him as he walked back from school, or simply waiting for him outside the back gate. The spring winds had already blown the cold weather away, almost overnight, and still the children came. Their words of thanks never varied, whatever Michael gave them; but they had revealed, in response to his questions, that the boy's name was Frans and the girl's name was Annie, that they lived in Green Point Location, and that their mother and father were both dead. During all this time Michael had not touched them, except for the fleeting contact of their hands when he passed a gift to them. Yet sometimes Michael wished that they were more demonstrative in their expressions of gratitude to him; he thought that they could, for instance, seize his hand and embrace it; or go down on their knees and weep, just once. As it was, he had to content himself with fantasies of how they spoke of him among their friends, when they returned to the tumbled squalor of Green Point Location; of how incredulous their friends must be to hear their stories about the kind white *kleinbaas* who gave them food and toys and clothing.

One day Michael came out to them carrying a possession he particularly prized – an elaborate pen and pencil set which had been given to him for a recent birthday. He had no intention of giving the outfit to the African children, and he did not think that he would be showing off with it in front of them. He merely wanted to share his pleasure in it with someone who had not already seen it. But as soon as he noticed the way the children were looking at the open box, Michael knew the mistake he had made. 'This isn't for you,' he said abruptly. The children blinked soundlessly, staring from the box to Michael and back to the box again. 'You can just look at it,' Michael said. He held the box tightly in his hand, stretching it forward, the pen and the propelling pencils shining inside the velvet-lined case. The two heads of the children came together over the box; they stared deeply into it.

At last the boy lifted his head. 'It's beautiful,' he breathed out. As he spoke, his hand slowly came up towards the box.

'No,' Michael said, and snatched the box away.

'Baas?'

'No.' Michael retreated a little from the beseeching eyes and uplifted hand.

'Please, baas, for me?'

And his sister said, 'For me also, baas.'

'No, you can't have this.' Michael attempted to laugh, as if at the absurdity of the idea. He was annoyed with himself for having shown them the box, and at the same time shocked at them for having asked for it. It was the first time they had asked for anything but bread.

'Please, baas. It's nice.' The boy's voice trailed away on the last word, in longing; then his sister repeated the word, like an echo, her own voice trailing away too. 'Ni-ice.'

'No! I won't give it to you! I won't give you anything if you ask for this. Do you hear?'

Their eyes dropped, their hands came together, they lowered their heads. Being sure now that they would not again ask for the box, Michael relented. He said, 'I'm going in now, and I'll tell Dora to bring you some bread.'

But Dora came to him in his room a few minutes later. 'The little Kaffirs are gone.' She was holding the plate of bread in her hand. Dora hated the two children, and Michael thought there was some kind of triumph in her voice and manner as she made the announcement.

He went outside to see if she was telling the truth. The lane was empty. He went to the street, and looked up and down its length, but there was no sign of them there either. They were gone. He had driven them away. Michael expected to feel guilty; but to his own intense surprise he felt nothing of the kind. He was relieved that they were gone, and that was all.

When they reappeared a few days later, Michael felt scorn towards them for coming back after what had happened on the last occasion. He felt they were in his power. 'So you've come back?' he greeted them. 'You like your *stukkies brood*, hey? You're hungry, so today you'll wait, you won't run away.'

'Yes, baas,' they said, in their low voices.

Michael brought the bread out to them; when they reached for it he jokingly pulled the plate back and laughed at their surprise. Then only did he give them the bread.

'Thank you, baas.'

'Thank you, baas.'

They ate the bread in Michael's presence; watching them, he felt a little more kindly disposed towards them. 'All right, you can come another day, and there'll be some more bread for you.'

'Thank you, baas.'

'Thank you, baas.'

They came back sooner than Michael had expected them to. He gave them their bread and told them to go. They went off, but again did not wait for the usual five or six days to pass, before approaching him once more. Only two days had passed, yet here they were with their eternal request – '*Stukkie brood,* baas?'

Michael said, 'Why do you get hungry so quickly now?' But he gave them their bread.

When they appeared in his games and fantasies, Michael no longer rescued them, healed them, casually presented them with kingdoms and motorcars. Now he ordered them about, sent them away on disastrous missions, picked them out to be shot for cowardice in the face of the enemy. And because something similar to these fantasies was easier to enact in the real world than his earlier fantasies, Michael soon was ordering them about unreasonably in fact. He deliberately left them waiting; he sent them away and told them to come back on days when he knew he would be in town; he told them there was no bread in the house. When he did give them anything, it was bread only now; never old toys or articles of clothing.

So, as the weeks passed, Michael's scorn gave way to impatience and irritation, irritation to anger. What angered him most was that the two piccanins seemed too stupid to realize what he now felt about them, and instead of coming less frequently, continued to appear more often than ever before. Soon they were coming almost every day, though Michael shouted at them and teased them, left them waiting for hours, and made them do tricks and sing songs for their bread. They did everything he told them to do; but they ignored his instructions as to which days they should come. Invariably, they would be waiting for him, in the shade of one of the trees that grew alongside the main road from school, or standing at the gate behind the house with sand scuffed up about their bare toes. They were as silent as before; but more persistent, inexorably persistent. Michael took to walking home by different routes, but they were not to be so easily discouraged. They simply waited at the back gate, and whether he went into the house by the front or the back gate he could not avoid seeing their upright, unmoving figures.

Finally, he told them to go and never come back at all. Often he had been tempted to do this, but some shame or pride had always prevented him from doing it; he had always weakened previously, and named a date, a week or two weeks ahead, when they could come again. But now he shouted at them, 'It's finished! No more bread – nothing! Go on, *voetsak!* If you come back I'll tell the garden boy to chase you away.'

From then on they came every day. They no longer waited right at the back gate, but squatted in the sand across the lane.

Michael was aware of their eyes following him when he went by, but they did not approach him. They did not even get up from the ground when he passed. A few times he shouted at them to go, and stamped his foot, but he shrank from hitting them. He did not want to touch them. Once he sent out Jan, the garden boy, to drive them away; but Jan, who had hitherto always shared Dora's views on the children, came back muttering angrily and incomprehensibly to himself; when Michael peeped into the lane he saw that they were still there. Michael tried to ignore them, to pretend he did not see them. He hated them now; even more, he began to dread them.

But he did not know how much he hated and feared the two children until he fell ill with a cold, and lay feverish in bed for a few days. During those days the two children were constantly in his dreams, or in his half-dreams, for even as he dreamed he knew he was turning in his bed; he was conscious of the sun shining outside by day, and at night of the passage light that had been left on inside the house. In these dreams he struck and struck again at the children with weapons he found in his hands; he fled in fear from them down lanes so thick with sand his feet could barely move through it; he committed lewd, cruel acts upon the bare-thighed girl, and her brother shrieked to tell the empty street what he was doing. Michael struck out at him with a piece of heavy cast-iron guttering. Its edge dug sharply into his hands as the blow fell, and when he lifted the weapon he saw the horror he had made of the side of the boy's head, and how the one remaining eyeball still stared unwinkingly at him.

Michael thought he was awake, and suddenly calm. The fever seemed to have left him. It was as though he had slept deeply, for days, after that last dream of violence; yet his impression was that he had woken directly from it. The bedclothes felt heavy on him, and he threw them off. The house was quite silent. He got out of bed and went to look at the clock in the kitchen: it was early afternoon. Dora and Jan were resting in their rooms across the yard, as they always did after lunch. Outside, the light of the sun was unremitting, a single golden glare. He walked back to his bedroom; there, he put on his dressing gown and slippers, feeling the coolness inside his slippers on his bare feet. He went through the kitchen again and on to the stoep, and then across the yard. The sun seemed to seize the back of his neck as firmly as a hand grasping, and its light was so bright he was aware of it only as a darkness beyond the little stretch of ground he looked down upon. He opened the back gate. Inevitably, as he had known they would be, the two were waiting.

He did not want to go beyond the gate in his pyjamas and dressing gown, so, shielding his eyes from the glare with one hand, he beckoned them to him with the other. Together, in silence, they rose and crossed the lane. It seemed to take them a long time to come to him, but at last they stood in front of him, with their hands interlinked. Michael stared into their dark faces, and they stared into his.

'What are you waiting for?' he asked.

'For you.' First the boy answered; then the girl repeated, 'For you.'

Michael looked from the one to the other, and he remembered what he had been doing to them in his dreams. Their eyes were fathomlessly black to look into. Staring forward, Michael understood what he should have understood long before: that they came to him not in hope or appeal or even in reproach, but in hatred. What he felt towards them, they felt towards him; what he had done to them in his dreams, they did to him in theirs.

The sun, their staring eyes, his own fear came together in a sound that seemed to hang in the air of the lane – a cry, the sound of someone weeping. Then Michael knew that he was the one who was crying. He felt the heat of the tears in his eyes, their moisture running down his cheeks. With the same fixity of decision that had been his in his dreams of violence and torture, Michael knew what he must do. He beckoned them forward, closer. They came. He stretched out his hands, he felt under his fingers the springy hair he had looked at so often before from the distance between himself and them; he felt the smooth skin of their faces; their frail, rounded shoulders, their hands. Their hands were in his, and he led them inside the gate.

He led them into the house, through the kitchen, down the passage, into his room, where they had never been before. They looked about at the pictures on the walls, the toys on top of the low cupboard, the twisted white sheets and tumbled blankets on the bed. They stood on both sides of him, and for the first time since he had met them, their lips parted into slow, grave smiles. Michael knew that what he had to give them was not toys or clothes or bread, but something more difficult. Yet it was not difficult at all, for there was nothing else he could give them. He took the girl's face in his hands and pressed his lips to hers. He was aware of the darkness of her skin, and of the smell of it, and of the faint movement of her lips, a single pulse that beat momentarily against his own. Then it was gone. He kissed the boy, too, and let them go. They came together, and grasped each other by the hand, staring at him.

'What do you want now?' he asked.

A last anxiety flickered in Michael and left him, as the boy slowly shook his head. He began to step back, pulling his sister with him; when he was through the door he turned his back on Michael and they walked away down the passage. Michael watched them go. At the door of the kitchen, on their way out of the house, they paused, turned once more, and lifted their hands, the girl copying the boy, in a silent, tentative gesture of farewell.

Michael did not follow them. He heard the back gate swing open and then bang when it closed. He went wearily back to his bed, and as he fell upon it, his relief and gratitude that the bed should be there to receive him changed suddenly into grief at the knowledge that he was already lying upon it – that he had never left it.

His cold grew worse, turned into bronchitis, kept him in bed for several weeks. But his dreams were no longer of violence; they were calm, spacious, empty of people. As empty as the lane was, when he was at last allowed out of the house, and made his way there immediately, to see if the children were waiting for him.

He never saw them again, though he looked for them in the streets and lanes of the town. He saw a hundred, a thousand, like them; but not the two he hoped to find.

FRESH FIELDS

When I was a student there was one living South African writer whom I, like most of my friends with literary inclinations or ambitions, greatly admired. That writer was Frederick Traill, poet, essayist, and novelist. To us it seemed that Traill, almost alone in the twentieth century, had shown that it was possible for a man to make poetry out of the forlorn, undramatic landscapes of our country; out of its ragged *dorps*; out of its brash little cities that pushed their buildings towards a sky too high above them; out of its multitudes of people who shared with one another no prides and no hopes. Because Traill had done it, we felt that with luck, with devotion, we might manage to do the same. Like Traill, we might be able to give a voice to what had previously been dumb, dignity to what previously had been without association or depth; in our less elevated moods, we could hope simply that like Traill we would be able to have our books published in London, and have them discussed in the literary reviews.

Traill was for us, therefore, not only a poet, he was a portent or a promise. It was taken for granted among us that Traill should live in England, whence all our books came; his exile, indeed, was part of the exhortatory significance of his career. In England, Traill had remained aloof from the political and artistic furores of his time. He had issued no polemics; he had not voiced his opinions of Britain's foreign policies; he had lived in obscurity throughout the war. The little that we knew of him in South Africa was that he lived in the country, well away from London, that he had always shunned publicity, and that he was known to few people.

All of this, I found out when I first came to England a few years after the war, was true. Everybody had heard of him; nobody knew where he lived; many people thought he was dead, for it was a long time since he had published his last volume of verse. For me the revelation of that first visit to England can be described by saying that in England I saw, wherever I looked, the word made flesh – made brick, too; made colour; made light; made trunk and leaf. But in the midst of this sudden solidification or enfleshment of almost everything I had ever read, Traill remained no more than a name to me. All around me was the country that other writers had described and celebrated; the one man who had uttered the words for my own distant country remained unknown. Whatever gossip I could pick up about him, I treasured eagerly; but there was very little of it. I heard that he was married; that he was childless; that his wife was ailing. And that was about all. Eventually, when I met a director of the firm which had published Traill's books – Parkman was the man's name, Arnold Parkman – I blurted out to him the admiration I felt for Traill, and my sense of frustration that there seemed no chance of meeting him. The publisher replied, 'You should write to him. I'm sure he'll be pleased to hear from you.' He must have seen that I was taken aback by the simplicity of the suggestion, because he added, 'Frederick's really a very friendly man, you know. I wish he wrote more, that's all.'

'So do I,' I said.

But I made no promise to write to Traill. Like many people of my generation (I suspect) I wished to lead some kind of 'literary life' without in any way appearing to do so. The thought of writing, as an aspirant author, to a great name – and

Traill's name was a great one to me – made me feel embarrassed, pushful, and, worst of all, unfashionable. That kind of thing, I felt, might have been all very well twenty or thirty years before; but in post-war, comfort-clutching, cigarette-grabbing, shabby, soiled Britain – no, it just wouldn't do. All the same, when the publisher told me that Traill lived in South Devon, and gave me the name of the village in which he lived, I made a careful note of it. I felt I had a proprietary interest in South Devon; my girlfriend's parents lived there, and I had visited them, and had travelled about a little in the area.

I didn't remember seeing the name of the village, Colne, on any map or signboard; but when I next visited my future in-laws, I took out a large-scale map and found the village on it without any difficulty. And one fine day (the day was really fine: in mid-summer, cloudless and hot) I set out on a cross-country bus trip to Colne. The trip promised to be a long one, involving two or three changes, and I did not know what I would do when I got there; I did not even know the name of the house in which Traill lived. But I set out on the trip as though it was something I had always intended to do, and without any doubt that I should succeed in seeing him.

Colne was pleasant without being picturesque. It had a stubby little church with a tower hidden behind trees, it had a village store and a whitewashed pub with a bench and table in front of it, it had a police station, a village hall and a war memorial. The road did not run straight through the village, but turned, spread itself between the pub and the store, and then swung upwards again, towards Dartmoor. For miles the road had been climbing, and from Come one could look back and see fields and woodlands taking turns at sweeping up or down or over the curves of hills, or lying in sunken valleys. Above them, on the far side of Colne, was the bald, high brow of the moor, its nakedness made more emphatic by the rich, close signs of cultivation everywhere else. Below Colne, the land had been measured and measured again, parcelled into little lots by hedges which met at corners, ran at angles from one another, lost themselves in the woodlands, emerged at angles beyond. Every view offered its own ranges of green – so many of them, from the palest yellow-green of the stubble where the first fields had been cut, to the darkness of the hedges, which you would have thought to be black, had they not been green also.

Most of the houses in Colne seemed to advertise Devonshire Cream Teas, but I went to the pub where I was offered a plate of biscuits with some cheese. I took the food and a lager, and went outside to eat my meal in the sun. The little open space in front of the pub was almost at the edge of the village, not its centre, and I looked out directly on a hedge, the road, a field, an open barn. There were few people about. I saw the village store being closed for the lunch hour; some workmen who had been bending over a tractor in the barn nearby went into the public bar; a moustached old man with a military bearing and a hard red skin went into the saloon bar. Several carloads of tourists passed along the main road on their way to the moor; several other cars came from the other direction, from the moor, with bunches of heather stuck into their radiator grilles. Three packed coaches went up in a convoy: I had heard the complaint of their engines, in the quiet of the afternoon, from miles away.

Then I saw Frederick Traill walking towards me. Though he had rarely been photographed, I knew it was him immediately. He was tall, he was bent, bald, and old. I felt a pang to see how old he was; the photographs, my own image of him, had prepared me to meet a younger man. He walked by me, with a glance down at the table, through his small steel-rimmed glasses. I was sure that I was betraying some kind of confusion; I was embarrassed by the crumbs on the table. But he walked on without a second glance, and I turned to see him go into the pub, bending his head at the door. His tweed jacket was peaked over the back of his neck; it hung loosely, wide over his hips.

I finished my food in a hurry; I did not want to be caught with it still in my hands when he came out. But I need not have worried, or hurried. The minutes passed; the workmen came out and went back to their tractor; a car carrying two men and two women stopped a few yards from me, and they all went noisily into the bar. I could have followed them, but I sat where I was; I felt that I would rather approach Traill where no curious or affable barman could overhear us, no stranger could stare. As I sat there I rehearsed how I was going to introduce myself to him; what I was going to say to him. Vainly, foolishly, I even permitted myself the fantasy that he might have heard of me, might have read something I had written, though I had so far published only a couple of stories in the most obscure and ill-printed of little magazines.

In fact, when I approached him as he came out of the pub, he shook his head almost as soon as I opened my mouth. 'Mr Traill?' I had said, and he stood there, shaking his head, looking at me and over me at the same time, his glasses low on his small nose.

'You aren't Frederick Traill?' I felt foolish, and small – literally small, because he was much taller than I, and had the advantage of the step as well.

Still he shook his head. But he said, 'Yes, I am Frederick Traill.'

I was relieved to hear him speak, and not only because he had acknowledged his identity. He kept his mouth half-closed as he spoke, but his accent was unmistakable: it was my own. 'I thought you must be,' I said. 'I recognized you from your photographs.'

He looked suspiciously at me; then moved forward, as if to come down the step. I took a pace back. 'I hoped I might see you,' I said. 'I heard from Arnold Parkman that you lived in

Colne. I'm staying near High Coombe for a few weeks. I'm from South Africa originally.'

I caught a glance from his small, pale-blue eyes. 'You are? What part of South Africa?'

'Lyndhurst.'

For the first time he smiled faintly. 'I know Lyndhurst. I used to visit an uncle of mine there, when I was a boy.'

'You wrote *Open Mine* about it.'

'Yes, I did,' he said, without much apparent interest in what he was saying; without surprise that I should have known the poem. He stepped down and began walking away; I hung behind, at a loss. I might have let him go, without another word, if I hadn't thought to myself, *That man there is Frederick Traill*. I saw his bald head, and beyond it the Devon countryside; and I felt that if I let him go the encounter would seem no more than a childish dream of my own.

How I was to wish later that I had let him go! But I did not. I called out, 'Mr Traill.'

He stopped and turned to me. 'Yes.'

'I wanted to talk to you,' I said. 'Your work meant so much to me, when I was in South Africa. And – and to lots of people I knew. I'd be so glad if I could – if you would let me –'

'I don't give interviews,' he said bluntly.

The oddity of the remark did not strike me at the time; how many people could there have been who had made the pilgrimage to Colne in order to interview him for the press? 'I don't belong to any newspaper,' I replied.

'No?'

'No, it's just that I've read your work.'

He seemed to consider for a moment what I had said, and then asked hesitatingly, 'What did you want to ask me about?'

'Everything.'

Again he smiled faintly, as if from a distance. 'Well, as long as you don't expect me to answer everything ...' The gesture of his shoulders was an invitation to me to join him, which I eagerly did. Together, we walked up through the village; then we turned from the main road and went up a stony little lane. There were a couple of small houses on the lane, but we passed these, and came to a wooden gate, set at the right angle between a brick wall on one side and a stone wall on the other. The stone wall ran on with the lane, until trees hid it from sight. 'This is the back entrance to the house,' Traill explained, as he led me through the gate, and closed it behind us. 'The lane goes right round to the front.' Then he said, 'My vegetable garden; I spend a lot of time on it.' The vegetable garden was big and obviously kept up with great care. The house itself was an old rambling double-storey cottage with a slate roof and walls half-clad with slate. The house leaned, it bulged, it opened out unexpectedly at doors and little windows; it straightened itself at a chimney that ran all the way down one wall. We walked around the house, past a walled flower garden; in front of the house there was a meadow, as green and sunken as any pond, with a gravelled drive running to one side of it. The entrance to the drive was hidden behind a bank of trees. Beyond those trees, at a distance of many miles, the single pale curve of a hill filled the horizon.

It was a lovely, ripe, worked-over place. We sat down in deckchairs on a little lawn in front of the house, and talked casually, for a little while, about the weather and the view. But eventually the conversation turned to Traill's work. I told him of the admiration I felt for it; I told him something of what I and my friends had felt his career to be for us; I said how sorry I was that he had not written anything for so long. While I talked I kept looking at him, taking in, for memory's sake, his long, slack figure, with his legs crossed at the ankles and his hands clasped behind his head; his bespectacled, small-featured face, with its clusters of wrinkles at the sides of his mouth and eyes. His head was almost entirely bald, and his scalp was faintly freckled. I could see that he was pleased by what I was saying, but I felt that he was saddened by it too, and eventually I fell silent, though there was much which I hadn't yet said to him and though I was disappointed that I had not drawn him out to speak more.

But he said nothing about his work; instead he asked me about mine. He asked me what I had done, where I had published; he questioned me about themes and settings. He had read nothing of my work, but his questions were all kindly, and he spoke to me as I had hardly dared to hope he would: as a professional speaking to an apprentice to the same trade or craft. His voice was deep; his manner of speech was lazy; still he spoke through a half-closed mouth. I was all the more surprised, therefore, when, without changing his position or opening his mouth wider, yet speaking with great vehemence, he said suddenly, 'Go home!'

For a moment I thought he was simply dismissing me, and I got up, confused and taken aback. Again he said, 'Go home!' and added a moment later, with one hand waving me back into my chair. 'Don't do what I did! Go home!'

I sat down again, and stared at him. 'Can't you understand what I mean?' he said. 'You'll do nothing if you stay here. It's your only chance, I tell you. Go home. Get out of this place.'

He leaned forward and said bitterly, 'How many years is it since I've published anything! And that's why I tell you to go back to South Africa. I know, I know,' he said, waving off an interruption with one hand, though I had not spoken, 'I know you'll tell me that South Africa's provincial, and dull – except for the politics, and who wants that kind of excitement? – and there's nobody to talk to. And here there's everything – books, and people, and everything you've ever read about. Elm trees,' he said sardonically, and pointed to the trees at the bottom of the meadow – 'and meadows,' he added, 'and villages like Colne. It's wonderful, you can't imagine anything better. You can't imagine ever tearing yourself away from it. But can't you see that as you live in it, year after year, all the time your own country is getting further and further away from you? And then what do you do?' He slumped back in his chair and put his hands behind his head again. 'I can tell you,' he said. 'You sit here, looking at the elm trees and the meadow. You work in the garden; you go for a drink at lunchtime; you go to the market-town once a week, and sit in the cinema there. They've got three, you know, in Mardle, three cinemas! And you try to work; and there's nothing there for you to work on, because you've left it all behind.'

We were both silent, though I could see that he had not yet finished what he had to say. 'I tell you,' he went on presently, 'when I came here I had my store with me, and I began unpacking it, and the more I unpacked the more there seemed to be. I felt free and happy, ready to work for a lifetime. All around me was this – all this – just what I had hankered for, out there in the veld. Until one day I found that there was no more work for me to do, the store was finished. And then what was I to do? Where was I? What did I have left? Nothing – nothing that's really my own. So now I'm dumb. Done for.'

This time he had finished, and still there was nothing I could say. At last, not so much because I was curious and wished to draw him out, but simply because I felt sorry for him, I asked, 'Why didn't you go home? You could have, all these years.'

He looked at me oddly. Then he said, 'My wife isn't well. She hasn't been well for many years. I suppose you could call her bedridden, though it's a word she hates to hear.'

'I am sorry.'

He said nothing to this; shortly afterwards I got up from my chair; I had to be going back to the village, to catch my bus.

'You must be off?' Traill asked.

'Yes, I'm afraid so. It really has been a privilege meeting you, Mr Traill. And I do appreciate the way you've given your time to me.'

'Oh – time! I've got lots of time.'

He saw me off as far as the back gate; right at the end, as we said goodbye and shook hands, he seemed reluctant to let me go. 'All this you understand,' he said, 'is my wife's.' He did not gesture, but I knew him to be referring to the house and the grounds. He stood with his eyes half-closed, and the sunlight glinted off the top of his head. 'She loves this place. So do I really. It was quite impossible for me to leave. How could I?' Then he grasped my hand again, and said firmly, 'Go home, while you can. Don't make the mistake I made. Go home!'

He turned and went through the gate; I stood for a moment in the shadowed lane, with the sunlight streaming above me and falling in bright patches on the grass of the bank on the other side. There was no sound but that of his footsteps, beyond the stone wall. I did not like to think of what he was going back to; of what he lived with. Yet the place was beautiful.

The place was beautiful, England was beautiful: rich, various, ancient, crowded, elaborate. But I was much dispirited, as I rode away from Colne in the bus that evening. The warnings and the advice Traill had given me echoed all the fears I had felt about England, even before I had arrived. Yet his life, and the work it had produced, we had conceived to be our models! Give up England, or give up writing, Traill had seemed to say to me; and I wanted to do neither.

I was much surprised and flattered when I received a letter from Frederick Traill a few weeks later. It had been addressed to me at one of the magazines which I had mentioned to Traill as having published a story of mine. In the letter Traill asked me to send on to him, if I would, something of my work, published or unpublished, as he would really be most interested to see it. The day on which I received the letter I made up a parcel of carbon copies of stories and other pieces, most of which had been going from magazine to magazine for months, and posted the parcel to him, with a letter in which I thanked him for the interest he was showing in my work, and again for his kindness to me when we had met.

I began waiting for a reply almost immediately. One week passed, a second, a third. Two months after I had sent the manuscripts away I was still waiting for a reply. Four months later, when I thought about it at all, my impatience had given way to a sense of injury which I tried to convince myself was unwarranted. Six months later I was astonished to read a long narrative poem by Traill which was unmistakably a reworking of one of the unpublished stories I had sent him.

Traill's poem was published in one of the leading literary monthlies. Delighted to see Traill's name on the cover, I had bought a copy of the magazine at a tube station. I read the poem sitting on one of the benches on the platform. The train for which I had been waiting came in and went out, and still I sat there – hotly, shamefully embarrassed, as though I had been the one who had committed the offence. I had no doubt that the offence was gross; but I did not in the least know what I could do about it. How could I write to him, the man whom I had so much admired and had wanted to emulate, accusing him of having stolen my plot, my character, my setting? There was no doubt that he had done so, none at all; there could be no question here of 'unconscious reminiscence'. As I sat on that station bench I cursed myself for my curiosity in going to see Traill; I damned myself forever wanting to have anything to do with writers or writing. Within the general flush of shame I felt resentment and anger, too. The crook! The phoney! With his cottage in the country, and his bald head, and his sick wife, and his advice. His advice! I went home and drafted twenty letters to Traill, but I tore them all up. Shame was stronger than anger. I just couldn't say to him what he had done, let alone tell him what I felt about it.

Not only could I not write to Traill; I could not tell anyone else about it either. The sense of shame I felt held me back; and so too did my feeling that no one would believe me. It enraged me to think that Traill had relied on the strength of his position as against mine, and on the very shamefulness of what he had done, to secure my silence. I couldn't smile at what had happened (after all, it had happened to *me!*) nor, though I tried, could I find much comfort in the lofty thought that it was better to be cribbed from than to crib.

When in the 'Forthcoming Features' panel in the same magazine I saw shortly afterwards an announcement of another long poem by Frederick Traill, I went back to my pile of manuscripts and chose one among them as the most likely for Traill to have stolen from this time; I was not wrong. The poem appeared – a long poem in dialogue. Again, it had my characters, my setting, even a scrap or two of my dialogue. I felt strangely proud of having made the correct guess, when I read the poem; then I realized that it hadn't been a guess at all. I had chosen correctly because I knew Traill's work so intimately.

Mockingly, winkingly, the idea suddenly presented itself to me of writing a story with the deliberate intention of suiting it to Traill's purposes, and of sending it on to him, challenging him to make the same use of it as he had made of the others. The idea came as if it were no more than a joke; but that night, all night, I was working on the joke. The next evening I had finished the story. Like the others, it was set in South Africa; like the others, it was based on a reminiscence of my boyhood. I typed it out and before I could get cold feet I put it in an envelope and posted it off to Traill, together with a note saying that I was pleased to see that my stories had stimulated him into writing once again, and I hoped he would find the story I was sending him equally profitable. It was a sly little note, really, an innuendo, like the submission to him of the story itself, but I didn't feel ashamed of it. To tell the truth, now that I had approached Traill, even in this way, I felt a lessening of shame about the whole series of events; for the first time began to think of them as comical, looked at in a certain aspect.

Then I prepared to wait for Traill's response, which I fully expected to read, in due course, in the pages of one of the literary magazines. What I did not expect was that I should answer a ring on the door one afternoon, shortly after I had come back from the school at which I was then teaching, and find Traill waiting shyly for me on the porch. He was wearing a fawn raincoat and a hat with its brim turned down at the front and the back; he looked ill-at-ease and more rustic, in Swiss Cottage, then I had remembered him as being in Devon. 'I hoped I'd find you in,' he said awkwardly. 'How are you?'

I stared at him. In my imagination he had become a monster of hypocrisy and unscrupulousness; but he stood before me simply as a rather slow and soft-spoken old man, with a small, tired, bespectacled face. 'Won't you come in?' I asked; and then, while he hesitated, I remembered what my room looked like. 'Actually,' I said, 'I was just on my way down to have a cup of tea somewhere. Won't you join me?'

'With pleasure.'

We went to a tearoom which has since disappeared; it is now a bamboo-decorated coffee bar. But then it was still a sombre, Edwardian, mahogany-coloured affair. The panelled walls and the massive chairs and tables were agleam with polish; the waitresses wore long black multi-buttoned dresses and little green caps on their heads; an open fire burned in a grate. The food, inevitably, was execrable. Traill was hungry, as it turned out, and had to eat a meat pie which was a little paler outside, and a little darker inside, than the sauce in which it lay. I just had tea. While he ate, Traill told me that he very rarely came up to London; it was difficult to leave his wife as they had to get a woman to live in the house while he was away; in any case he did not much care for London. But he had had to come up to attend to various business matters, and he had thought that it would be a good opportunity to look me up.

Was he going to make his confession now? As I waited, I was wondering how I was going to respond to it? Coldly? Angrily? Or pityingly? But Traill gave me no opportunity to adopt any predetermined attitude. He said in a firm, guiltless voice, 'Those stories of yours, they're pretty ghostly, derivative stuff, aren't they? The last one you sent me is by no means the worst, in that way. And you do know,' he went on, 'who they're derived from, don't you?'

His blue eyes were severe in expression, and they stared directly at me. 'It gave me a strange feeling, at first, to meet my own ghosts like that,' he said. 'It was very disturbing; I didn't like it. When I read the stories I felt … how can I describe it to you? … that was where I'd been, yes; there was where I had come from. But none of it was clear, none of it was right, those ghosts had never really lived. Then the more I read the clearer it became to me what the ghosts were trying to say. I understood them. I knew them,' he said, 'even if you didn't.'

'So you took them –' I interrupted.

'Yes,' he admitted calmly. 'And surely you can see that I made a better job of them than you did. My poems are better poems than your stories are stories, if you see what I mean.'

'But even if that's true –!'

'You mean, I still had no right to take your ideas? I thought that's what you'd say. And I sympathize with you, believe me. I'd sympathize even more if you hadn't told me what you did about my work, and what it meant to you. And if I hadn't been able to see it for myself, in the work. Your ideas? Your ideas?' he repeated with scorn; and then, as if collecting himself, 'All the same, I'm most grateful to you. Those manuscripts of yours have stimulated me, in all sorts of ways, they've set me going again. I'm tremendously grateful.'

He fell silent abruptly, leaving me struggling for breath, for relief, for release. When I finally brought out my reply it surprised me almost as much as it did Traill. 'Then you can have the lot,' I said. 'And you're welcome to them. I don't want any of them. I don't want to be like you. I don't want to go home.' Suddenly I discarded a burden I had been carrying for too long, and all sorts of scruples, hesitations and anxieties fell away with it. 'I'll take my chance right here, where I am. It's my only hope. If I don't strike out now, I'm sunk. And if I am to be sunk,' I said, 'I'd rather it happened now, than when I'm at your age. You can have what you've already got, and you can have all the stuff that's still in my room. It's all yours, if you want it. Take it, take the lot.'

'I will,' Traill said simply, after a long silence.

So we parted amicably enough, outside the house in which I boarded, Traill with his arms full of the files I had thrust enthusiastically upon him. 'Good luck,' I said; I had difficulty in restraining myself from clapping him on the back. There went my youth, I thought, looking at the bundle in Traill's arms; but I felt younger and more hopeful than I had for many months, than I had since coming to England.

I still feel that I did the right thing. The only trouble is that Traill has just published a new and very successful volume of poems; whereas I still live on hope, just on hope.

THE EXAMPLE OF LIPI LIPPMANN

In Lyndhurst, if a Gentile spoke enviously to a Jew about how rich the Jews of Lyndhurst were, how clever they were, how well they did in business, the reply was often made – 'Well, it's not really true about all the Jews. Just look at Lipi Lippmann!' No one, not even the biggest anti-Semite in the world could say that Lipi Lippmann was rich or clever or did well in business.

Lipi Lippmann once said that the Jews of Lyndhurst should pay him to remain poor, his poverty was so useful in arguments. But the joke was received in silence; it was felt to be in bad taste. The Jews of Lyndhurst were ready to use Lipi Lippmann's poverty to propitiate an envious Gentile, but they were ashamed of him nevertheless; ashamed of his old Ford lorry, laden with fruit and vegetables, going from door to door; ashamed that Lipi was the only white man who bickered among the coloured and Indian hawkers at dawn in the market place. Every other Jew in town was a licensed wholesaler or a licensed hotel-keeper, a licensed dentist or a licensed doctor; but Lipi Lippmann had remained nothing but a licensed hawker. And his only son, Nathan, was nothing but a licensed radio operator in the South African Airways, who still did not earn enough to support his ageing father. What an incongruous job Nathan's seemed to be, anyway, for a son of Lipi Lippmann! 'How's the airman?' people sometimes asked Lipi patronizingly, when they saw him; and Lipi looked up at the sky, wrinkling his brow, and said, 'He's fine, still up in the air.' In fact Nathan had been on the ground staff for a long time, but Lipi did not know this, for he and Nathan wrote to each other so seldom. Lipi himself had never flown in an aeroplane; he never listened to the radio either.

Lipi was a small man, with the head of a large one: his cheekbones were strong and prominent, his nose was bony and arched, his eyes were set wide apart. He was a widower, and lived by himself in a tiny single-storied house in one of the oldest suburbs of Lyndhurst. Around Lipi's house were houses as small and as shabby as his own, with the same high stoeps in front, and the same iron roofs above. In the backyards behind the houses there lived troops of raucous African servants who, with their dirty bare feet and torn clothes, were as different from the trim, white-overalled servants in the wealthier suburbs as the employers in the one district were from those in the other. All Lipi's neighbours in the street were Afrikaner railwaymen or mineworkers; and their children sometimes shouted '*Koelie-Jood*' after him – *Koelie* being an insulting term for an Indian, and thus being a disdainful way of referring to Lipi's trade. But the mothers of these children always waited for Lipi to return home at the end of the afternoon, when they bought from him at cut prices the softened carrots and moulting cabbages he had been unable to sell elsewhere. Then the children also came round, and asked Lipi if he had any *ertjies* for them. Often enough Lipi would produce a handful of pea pods which were no longer green, but grey and pale brown or white, and distribute them among the clamouring children. When they had dispersed, he would pack the empty crates neatly together in the back of the van, tie them down with rope, and go into his house.

Nobody followed him inside it. Once inside, he took off his hat, collar and tie (he always wore rather stiff detachable collars, even in the fiercest heat) and washed himself in the small, smelly bathroom. His 'girl' – a withered Basuto woman whose grandchildren played about in the backyard – served him his supper. Soup, meat and vegetables, and stewed fruit, followed one another in unvarying succession, while Lipi slowly read the paper from front to back. After supper he sat on his stoep, with the light burning above him, listening to the street noises and the shunting of trains in the distance. He never sat up late. Saturday was his busiest day, so he went to synagogue only on the high festivals; but he always went to the evening meetings of the local Zionist society. At these meetings he sat in the front row, listening intently and nodding his large head, almost like a man at prayer, to every word that was said.

That nod was Lipi's characteristic gesture; it looked like a gesture of acquiescence, of acceptance, yet it never appeared to bring to an end the debate he seemed to be having with himself. He nodded at Zionist meetings, he nodded when he drove his lorry, when he bargained with the housewives, when he sat alone on his stoep. He nodded in the same way when he came home from work one day and found that while he had been away and the girl had been paying her regular afternoon visit to a friend in the backyard of a nearby house, someone had broken into his house and robbed him of everything that could be put into a trunk and carried away. Almost all his clothes were gone, including his best *shul*-going suit; so was the money box in which he kept the few pounds he earned one day and laid out for stock the next day. The thief, or thieves, had also taken the single bottle of whisky Lipi kept hidden in his wardrobe; an old gold fob-watch and chain he had bought on the occasion of his marriage, and which he had not worn for years; two silver napkin rings, with his own and his wife's initials engraved upon them; a couple of tablecloths. Someone, it was clear, had been unable to believe that Lipi was in fact as poor as he had appeared to be; someone must have had the fantasy that Lipi was a miser, and had been hoarding money

96

and valuables over the years. Whoever it was – a black man or a white one – was no doubt disillusioned now; and he had left the marks of what looked like rage in the splintered drawers thrown upon the floor, the razor-rents in the armchair in the front room and the mattress in the bedroom, the wanton destruction of the basin in the bathroom.

Because the basin was smashed, Lipi went into the kitchen and washed himself carefully at the sink, and then, in his shirt sleeves, came into the front room of the house. All day it had been hot; now, with the sun hanging low in the west, the heat seemed to have a settled, brooding quality, quite different in its intensity from the morning's direct glare, or the throb of noon. The windows of the room were wide open, but no breeze came in through them; it was as warm indoors as it was outside. Lipi stood in the middle of the room, staring at the drawers of the sideboard upside down on the floor, and the hideous lumps of blue and white stuffing protruding from the ripped armchair. A strange, cracked sound came from his breast; this was followed by a sigh, as if something broken inside him sought to knit itself together again. He hunched his shoulders higher and went to the window. His shoulders shook, and again he uttered that abrupt sound, which was again followed by the faint complaining wheeze.

Lipi was laughing. When his girl came back she found him standing at the window, looking across the stoep and garden into the bit of street beyond. Seeing the wreckage in the room and the blood on Lipi's knuckles, she thought he had been in a fight with the intruders. Lipi could not explain to her how he had laughed and bitten at his own knuckles, laughed and bitten at himself, like a madman, with the smashed room behind him.

It was the girl who went running to the neighbours with the news, and the neighbours who telephoned the police. The police found Lipi standing alone in the room. While one man in the police squad went around looking for fingerprints, the other, perturbed by the fixity of Lipi's expression, and the sudden jerky nods of his head, tried to get him to sit down. But Lipi would not move; he did not seem to know what the man wanted of him. Readily enough, however, when the policeman asked him to make a statement, he began to detail what had been taken from him. There was his best suit, and the other clothes; his gold watch and the bottle of whisky; there was his money box.

'Money box?' the policeman interrupted. 'What kind of money box? How much was in it? Where did you keep it?'

'How much was in it?' Lipi repeated. He laughed loudly, looking beyond the policeman. 'A fortune, what do you think? All my money. The work of a lifetime was in the money box. Isn't that enough? Enough – enough – for what? What do I want? I want to go to *Eretz Yisroel* before I die. That's how much money there was in the money box.'

'Mr Lippmann –'

'Yes,' Lipi cried out, 'put it down in your book, why not, put it down that there was money to go to *Eretz Yisroel* in the money box, put it down. What difference does it make now?' Lipi laughed and shouted, he gnawed at his fists, he cried out that before he died he wanted to go to the Holy Land, and now he knew he never would be able to. He was a poor man, he had always been poor, but he had had one ambition, one hope; now he saw what nonsense it had always been. 'I look around and see my whole life is rubbish, here it is in this room.' When the policeman told him that he should get in touch with his insurance company, Lipi laughed for the last time. 'Where am I insured, who insures me? It is lost, everything is lost. Put it down.' Lipi began kicking at the furniture, tearing at the few strands of black and grey hair that usually lay flat on his scalp. Eventually, a doctor was called and he administered a sedative; Lipi fell asleep in the bedroom, on the torn mattress, with the wardrobe doors still hanging open and various articles the thieves had not bothered to take scattered about the floor. By that time a small curious crowd of people had gathered on the pavement outside, and the news of Lipi's loss had spread all over the neighbourhood. The amount of loss was exaggerated as the story went from one servant or housewife to the next, though no single exaggeration was greater than the one that the policeman, at Lipi's bidding, had written into his book.

The next morning the story was in the local paper. Lipi was described as 'a well-known city fruiterer and greengrocer'; his loss was estimated at 'several hundred pounds, which Mr Lippmann had been saving to fulfil his lifelong ambition of visiting the Holy Land'. The police, the report added, were continuing their enquiries.

A few days later another report appeared, in which it was stated that several leading members of the Lyndhurst Jewish community were offering a reward for information leading to the arrest of the thief or thieves; the report stated also that it had been decided that, should the money not be recovered, a fund would be established to make good Mr Lippmann's loss, and thus enable him to fulfil his lifelong ambition of visiting the Holy Land.

For Lipi had become a hero, even something of a martyr in Lyndhurst, and especially so to the members of the Lyndhurst Jewish community. If they felt any embarrassment or shame in connection with him now, it was only because they had been ashamed of him and embarrassed by him in the past. His poverty now appeared to them noble; his ambition to visit Israel exemplary; his attempts to realize that ambition inspiring; his disappointment pitiable. There was none among the well-to-do Jews of Lyndhurst who did not feel himself humbled by Lipi's humility, shamed by his self-sacrifice. When Lipi went to *shul* he was now greeted with great friendliness, even with deference; in the streets Jews and Gentiles alike stopped his lorry to express their sympathy with him and to assure him that from now on they would buy all their fruit and vegetables from him. The police continued their investigations, without success. Three months after the burglary had taken place, the paper published a photograph showing Lipi being presented with a return air ticket to Israel and a cheque large enough to cover his expenses during the visit. The presentation was made by half a dozen leading members of the Jewish community, among them an ex-Mayor of Lyndhurst, the local rabbi, and the chairman of the Zionist society. Many Gentiles, including some of Lipi's neighbours, it was said, had contributed to the fund.

Lipi dreamed that he was in Palestine. It was a dream he very often had, and the landscape was familiar to him, though it was unlike any he had ever seen. In front of him, pale ploughed fields stretched away to a group of white houses, with red-tiled roofs, in the distance; behind the houses were hills, vaguely outlined. Nothing grew from the fields, yet they were not barren; there was no sun in the sky, but the scene was evenly filled with light; no one stirred about the houses, yet Lipi knew that there were people living in them. As he had done a hundred times before, Lipi began walking towards the houses.

As always, Lipi awoke before he reached the houses. Immediately he was fully awake, in the darkness, confronting once again, with the poignance of the dream still upon him, the enormity of the lie he had told, and its consequences. Lipi had not anticipated anything of what had happened since he had told the policeman, in a frenzy of rage and self-hatred, that the thieves had stolen from him savings he had never had. Lipi could not even remember telling the lie to the policeman; if it had not been for the report in the newspaper the next morning he would never have believed that he had in fact done so. All Lipi could remember of that afternoon when he had come back to find his house in disorder, was a stunned sense of humiliation and anger, which had not at all been directed against the strangers who had come into the house, fingered and thrown about his meagre possessions, and taken those few they had thought it worth their effort to carry away. Lipi's rage had been directed against himself; against his own poverty and powerlessness; against the lifetime he had spent toiling in the sun, for so little reward, for a house that ten minutes could despoil, for possessions that ten pounds could buy.

These emotions, as he lay in his bed at night, with his departure for Israel only a few days off, Lipi could remember. But what had taken place subsequently was all an absurdity, a confusion of noise, of darkness and light. His own frenzy, and the faces of the policemen, the reports in the newspaper and the friendliness of strangers, the rumours of the collection that was being made for him and the tense, jovial little ceremony when he had been handed his tickets and money – all these were less substantial than a dream, far less substantial than the dream he had just had of Israel. But the tickets and the money were real, and had been given to him; they were waiting for him now at the bank. (How many jokes had been made at the ceremony about the money being safe from burglars in the bank; how many about Lipi being able to teach his son to fly when he came back from the trip.) What a lifetime of work had failed to bring him, a single lie had made possible; and Lipi lay in his bed and marvelled at the world, and especially, of all the world, at the city of Lyndhurst. With a satisfaction that was sweeter than any he had felt since he had been a young man lying beside his wife, Lipi knew that at last, at last, he would be able to settle the problem that had for so long been a dear, familiar, secret riddle to him: he would be able to see if Israel really looked as it did to him in his dreams.

But later that same night, Lipi woke again. His own beating heart had shaken him out of sleep; his body was filled with a dread that his mind was still ignorant of. Baffled by the warm, thick darkness around him, hardly knowing who or where he was, Lipi again remembered, as when he had woken earlier, the journey he was about to make. Was he afraid of the burglars? Did he fear that the police might find them, or that they might come forward themselves, and expose his fraud? But that was an anxiety that had visited him before, and that had never had the power to make him lose his own sense of himself. It was another fear that possessed him now, and it was as impenetrable and insistent as the darkness around him. He could not believe that the landscape of his dreams would accept him, if he came to it as a liar and a fraud. It would reject him – he did not know how – it would thrust him from itself, it would disgorge him as unclean, a tainted thing.

In the morning Lipi rose and went to see the ex-Mayor, who had formally handed to him his travel tickets and money, on behalf of the Lyndhurst Jewish community. The ex-Mayor was a builders' merchant who had inherited his business; he was twenty years younger than Lipi and twice Lipi's size; his manner was authoritative and his complexion rubicund; he wore spectacles with heavy black rims, though his eyesight was excellent without them. He had not only been Mayor of Lyndhurst for a time; he had also been the captain of the local golf club and the president of the local Red Cross Society; he was still chairman of the Chamber of Commerce and a member of the City Council; and at public meetings, and even when he was alone with his wife, he was in the habit of putting forward his own career as an illustration of the cordiality of what he called 'inter-faith relations' in Lyndhurst. He received Lipi with the benevolence of a man who knows he has done well by his visitor; but his benevolence had altogether disappeared by the time Lipi had finished his confession. However, the ex-Mayor was a man of decision; and he said nothing to Lipi of his rage at the deception Lipi had practised upon the people of

Lyndhurst, or of his own personal indignation at having been shown up as a sentimental fool, or even of his anxieties about the possible effects of Lipi's confession on 'inter-faith relations' in Lyndhurst. Instead, he told Lipi, 'Look, I want you to leave for Johannesburg at once, and wait for your plane there. You can go on the train tonight. And I don't want you to say a word of this to anyone else, do you hear? Not a word. As far as I'm concerned, this conversation never took place. I haven't heard you, and no one else ever will. Now go, go on, go on, I'll send my car around to pick you up tonight. Do you understand? Just go!' Only at the very end did the ex-Mayor add, with sudden ferocity, 'And I wish you'd never come back!'

Bewildered, Lipi allowed himself to be hustled out of the office; he found himself on the placid, sunlit pavement, his hat in his hand. Around him the people of Lyndhurst went about their business, and Lipi joined them, though he had no business to attend to. In his ears there was a voice that shrieked that everyone, everything in the world was tainted; that he had nothing to fear. All day he wandered about the town; he was seen standing outside the shops in the commercial district and walking down the middle of streets in residential areas far from his own; he was even seen in the African locations around the town, where people stared in amazement at the spectacle of a white man, alone and on foot, making his way between the mud and iron huts laid down in rows upon the veld. At nightfall Lipi found himself in the railway shunting yards; and there, too late, he was glimpsed by a horrified engine driver, in front of whose slowly-moving locomotive Lipi fell. What the engine driver most vividly remembered, what he always mentioned when he subsequently told his tale to others, was how Lipi had brought his hands to his ears, at the very moment of his fall.

A verdict of accidental death was returned at the inquest. The coroner added that the death was all the more tragic in coming so very shortly before the deceased could realize his dream of making a pilgrimage to the Holy Land. Lipi's funeral was enormous; and it was noticed that the ex-Mayor of the town was among those who seemed most affected by grief at the graveside.

AN APPRENTICESHIP

It was only for three or four years that David Palling and I were close friends; but when I look back now it sometimes seems as though we shared our entire boyhoods. Season runs into season in the memory; and in all of them I see David's spare, loose figure, his bright red hair, his freckled face with its tiny nose and pale blue eyes; I hear his high-pitched voice, with its plaintive note when he spoke and its raucous note when he sang. He was a year or two younger than I was, but was the same height, and this seemed to wipe out the difference in our ages. Our elder brothers were friends, too; but their friendship was not nearly as close as ours. Being so many years older than David and I, they could not compete as openly and strenuously with one another as we could; they could not cry in front of each other as we were still able to; they tired more quickly of the games of backyard cricket that gave us so much pleasure; they could not laugh as hysterically as we did over puns, scraps of gibberish, the clothing of dandy Africans we passed in the streets, our own grimaces and postures.

Three or four years: how many enthusiasms, in those years? The breeding and racing of homing pigeons was a constant care, a constant, shared source of interest. But there were many others. Fruit stealing was a recurring enthusiasm, every summer, when we – whose parents regularly brought home from the market place crates of grapes, apricots, peaches, plums, and figs; whose backyards were filled with unpruned trees that dropped their small, sweet fruit into a vinous litter at the foot of each trunk – would go out at night to denude the trees of all the suburban houses around ours. Through sandy, dusky lanes, where groups of chattering African servants gathered, we made our way, until we came to a lane that was clear; then we scrambled over brick or iron fences and into the rustling darkness of the trees; when any back door opened, or a light was switched on, or a voice was raised in challenge, we fled wildly, with pounding hearts, down the lanes, across the tarred, lit streets, into the stretches of unbuilt-upon veld that still lay between each group of houses. The bosoms of our shirts would be full of fruit; if the fruit was soft, its juice would trickle down our chests and under our belts, as we ran; if it was hard and inedible we would, when we were safe, throw it at each other, or at street lamps, or give it to the bands of tattered piccanins who also roamed the streets and lanes of the town.

By daylight, during school holidays and over the weekends, we hunted lizards in the veld, mice in the outbuildings in our backyards; we organized elaborate foot and bicycle races; we built wire slides, and slid down them, hanging on for dear life to the piece of iron piping through which the wire was threaded; regularly we stole onions, potatoes, fat, and a frying pan from the kitchens of our houses, and went into the veld to fry potato chips over fires of grass and sticks. Our chips never came out of the pan crisp and brown; we always produced a coagulated, hot mass of stuff, black on the outside and white inside, which was sometimes so nauseating that we turned it over entirely to the piccanins who invariably gathered around us. No matter how isolated was the spot where we chose to do our cooking, these piccanins would appear; their eyes large and black, their shins frail, and their hands so toughened that they could scoop up the chips almost straight from the fire. We took their presence almost as much for granted as we did the rocks, grass, and thorn trees of the veld around us, and the gleam of iron roofs in the distance. On Saturday afternoons we went to the matinée at one of the town's three bioscopes, and lit cigarettes when the lights went out; we talked incessantly of girls, but did little about them, except to ride our bicycles round and round the house of this or the other girl whom we had chosen especially to admire; sometimes one of us would join the family of the other for a formal outing – a picnic by the river, a day trip to a farm, a visit to one of the open mines in the town.

I had a fantasy about the members of the Palling family; I believed them to be 'typical'. I suppose the main reason why they appeared to me so typical was simply the fact that they were Gentiles and we were Jewish; it was from this difference that all other differences seemed to spring, more or less directly. It was not just that they celebrated Christmas and Easter, while we celebrated Passover and *Yom Kippur*. My parents spoke with a foreign accent; the Palling parents did not. Mr Palling was in employment as the chartered secretary of the local branch of a building society; my father managed his own business. The Palling parents called each other 'Mother' and 'Father'; mine did not. Mr Palling went every Sunday morning, in a white shirt, white flannel trousers, and a blazer, to play bowls at the local club; my father did not. The Pallings' house was always clean and orderly; ours was not. My parents discussed politics endlessly – local politics, Zionist politics, the war in Europe; the Palling parents never did. Our house was full of books and newspapers, and we were constantly going to the town library; the Pallings' house was altogether bare of reading matter. I and my brothers did well at school; the Palling boys did not. We argued with our parents; the Palling boys did not.

I would not have chosen to live without books or to do badly at school, or to be afraid of my father; but still, I deeply envied the Pallings for what I thought of as their typicality, their apparent resemblance to all the families in books, films, and newspaper advertisements. And I envied them because they seemed so much safer, so much more secure, than ourselves. The Palling boys did not have to read in the newspapers about the massacre of their fellow-Jews in Europe; they did not have to protest against anti-Jewish remarks made by boorish schoolmasters or uglier things said in the playground by schoolboys; they did not have to bear a special burden of guilt and sympathy towards the blacks; they did not have to flinch inwardly when their parents mispronounced an English word.

How simple it was, it seemed to me, to have Mr and Mrs Palling for one's parents – or to be Mr and Mrs Palling! Mr Palling was on first-name terms with everyone on his street and all the teachers at school; his brow was untroubled, his chin was always beautifully shaven; polygonal, rimless glasses rested firmly on his little round nose; his expression was entirely innocent, even obtuse, except for the puckered, prim set of his mouth. (If it hadn't been for David's red hair he would have been the image of his father, everyone said.) Mrs Palling's face was more refined than her husband's: her nose and lips were thinner, her brow was wider, her cheeks were drawn in a little, always, as if in reflection. She was tall for a woman, as tall as her husband. She too seemed to be on first-name terms with all the housewives in the neighbouring houses, and drank tea and smoked cigarettes with them in the mornings; in the afternoons she usually rested on one of the beds in the boys' bedroom, and smoked or dozed or just lay there looking at the ceiling. Both she and her husband belonged not only to the bowls club, but to numerous other organizations: the Sons of England (though they had both been born in South Africa); the Methodist Social Guild (though neither of them were great churchgoers); the Rotarians and the Rotary Anns. They did things which it was quite impossible for me to imagine my parents ever doing: they went dancing, they played cards, they held each other around the waist and called each other darling, they came home making jokes about how they had had too much to drink at Joe's or Betty's or Bill's or Bob's. They were typical, typical in every respect, I was sure; and I coveted the peace and assurance which I was convinced their typicality must give them.

But my envy turned into something else when David and I were playing one day in the garage of the Pallings' house, and we overturned a box which contained in it, tied with red and blue ribbons, bundles of passionate letters that Mr Palling had written twenty years before to the girl he was later to marry. I read only three or four of the letters before David, who had been busy reading from another bundle, snatched them violently, shamefacedly, out of my hand, and threw them back into the box, together with the letters he had been reading. What he had read (and whether or not he ever went back to the box) I do not know; but those letters I had seen seemed to me altogether incredible, bizarre, even insane. In the letters Mr Palling raved, he talked of salvation and damnation and despair, of the moon, the stars, her beauty, his unworthiness; he grovelled, he abased himself, he pleaded; he boasted wildly of 'others'; he threatened to commit suicide. Mr Palling! To Mrs Palling! Was it possible? I could not imagine them any different from what they were as I knew them; and to my shocked, incredulous imagination it seemed that if he could have written to her like that, then any emotion was possible for anyone, anywhere. Was it typical to write to a woman of her breasts and arms, of prostrating yourself beneath the soles of her feet; typical to swear to her that if she did not yield you would leave her for others who would; typical to speak of that night, her voice, our love, our single heart? And was it typical, too, to conceal and contain these passions within an outward show of respectability, of total conventionality? Then there was no one

109

in the world who was safe; then everyone lived amid his own dangers.

But I did not realize what the reading of the letters had done to me until ten or twenty minutes later. I went into the house with David, and at my first sight of his mother – who had received those letters, who must have written others like them – my mouth went quite dry and the air seemed to escape from my breast in a single shudder. I was in love with her. It was the last and most passionate enthusiasm I felt during my friendship with David; it was the one that he knew nothing about.

Like most of the pains one endures, the dumb, hopeless lust of puberty and adolescence is quickly forgotten, once it is over. Only in dreams do we sometimes recall it, in its intensity, shame and ignorance; only in dreams are we ever so determinedly driven to an end that remains totally mysterious to us, even while we are driven towards it. I loved Mrs Palling and I did not know what the word meant and could not say it to myself, let alone to anyone else; I could not do anything about the love I felt, except to watch Mrs Palling, and to make as many occasions as I could for watching her. I could only urge David that we should play in his yard rather than my own; that we should play indoors rather than in the yard; that we should go into his room, where in the afternoons I knew his mother lay, resting.

The room was always warm, summer and winter, for its windows got the afternoon sun. Yellow curtains were drawn across the windows, and the light that came through them was pale gold in colour, and evenly diffused over white walls, the black dressing table, and the patchwork counterpanes on the beds. Mrs Palling lay on the bed furthest from the window, that of David's brother; she was always fully-clothed, except for her shoes, which lay where she had kicked them off on the floor. On the chair to the side of the bed there was an ashtray, a packet of cigarettes, and her lighter. One arm lay alongside her body, the other was usually lifted from the elbow; and the smoke from her cigarette, blue at the tip, grey and gold as it thinned and dispersed, rose slowly towards the ceiling. The dress she wore showed the outlines of her legs. In the room there was a warmth and dryness that my senses strained towards, hungered for, as I stood at the door, afraid to enter, unable to go. Dryness is the only word I have for what it was about her that made her seem so unendurably desirable to me. I was afraid I might fall or faint if I moved, if I spoke.

She spoke – sometimes drowsily, sometimes alertly, always in a friendly manner; she asked what we wanted or where we were going to play. At first I was filled with chagrin that she should have spoken to me in exactly the same way as she spoke to all David's other friends; later, even her indifference became a part of her attraction for me. I longed for a word or a gesture from her to explain the mysteries which she suggested to me; which I knew she had enacted; which I was sure, at times, must fill her imagination as obsessively as they did my own. But if I caught so much as a curious glance from her pale eyes I was filled with confusion and embarrassment: such a glance was enough to drive me back, away from the room.

It was only for those dazed moments in the bedroom that I now valued David's friendship; for no others. All the pursuits we had followed together seemed to have become unprofitable and boring; they had meaning only because they led me to or from the woman I loved. I looked down upon David, because he was so ignorant of what I felt; but, oddly enough, I felt no jealousy of Mr Palling. Rather, I felt compassion towards him, because he had suffered what I was now suffering; at the same time, I was grateful to him for having shown me what it was possible to feel towards his wife. It was to him that I owed the revelation of the length of her limbs, and the piercing dryness of her presence in the bedroom. It was to him, too, that I owed my pride at my own understanding when, 'out of the blue' as everyone said, the Pallings' marriage suddenly broke up.

David announced to me one day, in the middle of a school term, that he and his brother were going to an aunt in Cape Town for a few weeks; then he burst into tears. When I reported this to my parents they exchanged an odd, wry, satisfied glance, and told me that there seemed to be some 'trouble' between Mr and Mrs Palling, and that I should not make a nuisance of myself by going to their house. What the trouble was they would not tell me, but I soon found out all the same. Quite unexpectedly, Mr Palling had walked out of the house and had gone to live with an Afrikaans woman in a rundown area on the other side of the town. The scandal was talked about for weeks, and we eventually learned almost all its details. Apparently, Mr Palling had been seeing the other woman for months, some said for years. In her distress Mrs Palling had sent the boys away to a sister of hers in Cape Town; but she continued to live alone in the house. She was begging her husband to come back; she tried to see him, she phoned him, she wrote him letters, but he remained obdurate, he swore he was never coming back.

I felt myself to be the only one in the neighbourhood who was not shocked or surprised at the development; I had long known, ever since I had read those letters in the garage, that such things could happen, that anything could happen, to anyone. But I was also sure that there was no one in the neighbourhood who could have been more deeply excited than myself about the event. Every morning on my way to school, when the sun still skulked behind trees and rooftops, I went out of my way to pass the Pallings' house; in the afternoons, on my way back from school, when the sun stood high and its own heat sprang back at it from every pitched roof and flat road, I came past once again, more slowly. I lingered at the gate, looking into the garden I had once been able to cross, at the windows of rooms I had once entered; when I reached the corner of the street I stopped and looked back, hoping that Mrs Palling would come out. The thought of her alone in the house, in the bedroom, for me to speak to (I had not once spoken to her alone; always I had been with David when I had seen her) made me often walk back, if there was no one in the street to observe me, and stand once more at her gate.

One day I simply pushed the gate open. Never, in all my fruit-stealing expeditions with David, not even on the occasion when we had been caught and taken down to the police station by an irate householder, had I felt such fear as I did when I found myself walking up the little gravelled path of the garden. I felt that the sun was watching me; the house was listening to me, the path was ready to roar at me. As I walked I repeated over and over again to myself the question which was to be the pretext for my approach to Mrs Palling: When was David coming back? When was David coming back? I gained the shade of the stoep, and rang the doorbell. Already, I was exhausted.

I heard the muted trill of the bell, and a little later the sound of footsteps in the hall; I saw a vague shape in the glass in the upper half of the door. But I could not step back. The door opened. Barely six inches away from me stood Mr Palling. He was dressed in an athletic vest and a pair of trousers; his feet were bare.

I was so surprised that I could not speak, but simply stared forward at him. Somehow, the fact that on a weekday afternoon he should have been at home, instead of at work in his office, seemed to be as shocking as anything else in the situation. For a moment I don't think he recognized who I was; then, brusquely, he asked me what I wanted.

The shock of his appearance had driven my prepared question out of my head. Instead, I asked blankly after the woman I had come to see. 'Where's Mrs Palling?'

'She's gone. She's not coming back. Why do you want to know?' His expression was peevish; it seemed to me almost menacing. Before I could answer, I heard a woman's voice – not Mrs Palling's – calling from inside the house, 'Who is it?' Mr Palling answered without turning his head. 'A friend of David's.' Then he added, staring directly at me, smiling without a trace of amiability, 'My wife's admirer.'

The shame I felt seemed to burn down to my toes. They knew! She had known, and had told him! I wanted to cry out that it wasn't true; but another impulse restrained me. I heard myself say, 'You admired her too.'

The blow that fell on my cheek was hard, but it did not hurt. I heard him shouting; vaguely, I ducked another blow, then turned and ran down the gravelled path. At the gate he caught up with me, while I was struggling to open it. He shook me and hit me again; he almost threw me over the gate. But he could not shake out of me my gratitude to her, my exultation that my secret had been no secret at all to her, those past afternoons. His violence and rage could only prove that what I had begun to learn from her was indeed worth knowing, was worth living a lifetime to know.

TRIAL AND ERROR

He was a tall thin man with fair hair, a long nose, and a chin with a deep cleft in it. Her face was round and childlike, framed in straight brown hair cut in a fringe across her brow. She was thin too; but her bust was full. The very first time he had seen her he had noticed the way she walked, slightly stooped, as if her own deep bosom were a burden to her.

They were both South Africans; they had been among the first to join the great trek of young, white, educated, liberal-minded, English-speaking people out of what was obviously a doomed country. It was so easy, so sensible, to leave behind the sunlight, squalor and confusion of South Africa to come to England, where everybody spoke English, where there were so many other liberal-minded people, and where there were so many opportunities for him to do the work he wanted to do. He had taken a good Honours degree in economics in South Africa and had subsequently done some research work there; on the strength of this he was given, in England, a job in the extramural department of a provincial university. They had no money, but it was easier to be poor in England than it had been in South Africa. In England there was a tradition, after all, of high thinking and bleak living; their own poverty could appear to them almost glamorous. How many of the novels and biographies they had read had told of writers, thinkers, artists, living as they did: on the outskirts of a little Midlands village, in a stone cottage with windows askew in the walls, a smoky grate in the living room, and a small garden at the back, where, to their surprise, daffodils and primroses came up in the spring, out of the black, sodden earth.

So it was not just that they ran away from South Africa; they ran towards something, too: towards a way of life that was settled and orderly, to the company of like-minded people, to the academic distinction he hoped one day to win. For though Arnold Bothwell liked to think of himself as a political radical, he was far from being a revolutionary of any kind; he held much the same views as most of his colleagues about the cold war, race prejudice, capital punishment and the dangers of the mass media. It was only in a country like South Africa that he could ever have been regarded as a dangerous subversive, a suitable subject for enquiries by the detectives of the Special Branch. He was conscientious about his work, both in its public aspect, which involved the organization of rather dreary, stultifying evening classes in three or four towns within some miles of the village, and in preparation for his doctorate. He was given to understand that if he succeeded in gaining a good degree he might expect an internal appointment, and in due course he did indeed get a good degree and an internal appointment.

But that took many years; in the meantime he and Jennifer continued to live in the village. They had no family in England. Often, at first, they were lonely; and they never succeeded in making friends with any of the villagers. The village itself was an ugly straggle of a place, several streets of brick and black slate in raw, straight lines. All around were green fields, and on them were scattered a few farmhouses with clumps of trees; the sea was not far, but one did not feel its presence. A large church stood off from the village, set among the fields, and Arnold and Jennifer frequently walked to it on weekdays, especially after the baby came, when they would let him play in the grassy churchyard, among the gravestones.

In later years Arnold was to think of that time as the happiest in his life; though at the time he was hardly conscious of all he was afterwards to recollect with so much poignance. Or, rather, he did not imagine that his opportunity fully to enjoy these things would be so fleeting. Everything he and Jennifer did together was a discovery: their housekeeping, their walks to the churchyard, their trips to the seaside, their visits to the pub, where he and Jennifer would sit hand in hand listening to the people around them, their excursions by bus to the great industrial town, an hour's ride away, where the university was. They were in a foreign country; and yet they were at home. It was a discovery to them simply that England should have been so open and warm in summer; so cold and dark in winter. On winter mornings the touch of the bedclothes which they had not warmed with their limbs was so cold that they would press closer yet to one another, while the yellow mornings of fog, the grey mornings of rain, irresolutely lightened against the bedroom window. In summer, at midnight the sky was still radiant, and when he or Jennifer got up for a drink of water or to go to the lavatory, the warmth of the air seemed to tail languidly over their naked bodies.

And there was his work. The classes in dusty schoolrooms and institutional halls may often have been dreary; but he gained confidence in his ability to conduct them, and the more self-confident he became the more he found in them to enjoy. He attended seminars at the university; at home he read and made notes, or listened to Jennifer reading aloud her essays to him. She had not graduated from the South African university where they had met; instead, she had given up her course, very shortly after meeting Arnold, and had then worked in an office while they were saving money to come to England. But now she had started working again for a degree – not in economics, for that, they had gravely agreed, might involve them in competition with one another, but in sociology. At first she was conscientious in her studies and he in helping her. But he could not hide from himself the fact that her essays were never really any good; and this dismayed him deeply. They had always taken it for granted that their marriage was one between intellectual and moral equals. Even to think of it being anything else would have seemed to them dishonest, shameful, reactionary; a kind of treason against the ideals they were sure they both shared; a blow at his pride as much as at hers.

So he found many soothing reasons for the lack of merit in her work. She had not yet settled down in England; she was more an intuitive type of person than an intellectual; sociology was not, perhaps, the field to which she was best suited; the examination requirements were really very narrow; her housework was a continual distraction. Jennifer listened complacently when he put forward these excuses on her behalf; however, if he offered any direct criticism of her work she took it badly. She complained that he was trying to score points off her; and this complaint quickly led to others. She complained that he lacked ambition or he would have got a better job; that the cottage was poky; that she was lonely; that she was bored; that Arnold didn't love her.

'Sweetheart, I do love you, you know that.'

'Then why do you say such horrible things about my work?'

'Because I'm trying to help you!'

'You're not. You're trying to discourage me, I don't know why.'

'Jennifer, how can you say things like that? It's ridiculous. I'm just being objective.'

'Oh! Oh!' Her round cheeks stood out in surprise. 'So when you're *objective* then you can see that I'm stupid, and can't understand the books I read, and can't write two sentences together without making a mistake. Is that what you're saying?'

'Ach, it's impossible to explain things to you.'

'You see? You see? All you do is insult me. You must think you're the only real intellect left in the world. The only man in the world, too, I suppose. What do you want me to do? Worship you?' She laughed derisively, in a way he hated. 'Worship your great brain? Go down on my knees and thank you for condescending to marry me? Is that what you want?'

She almost invariably got the better of their arguments: she was so much more unscrupulous and single-minded about them than he was. And Arnold was frightened by the rage she could rouse in him; a rage which sometimes led him to shout and swear at her, and at other times, which were even worse, left him simply watching her. In silence, with a kind of perverted pride in his own clear-sightedness, he watched how inattentive she was when he read *his* papers to her; how easily he was able to predict her judgement of situations, her responses to the stories he told her; how absorbed she could become in radio quizzes and competitions on the back of cornflake packets; how quickly and coyly she rose to the bait of a compliment, with a mock-modest widening of her eyes and a simper around her mouth; how unshaken her confidence in her own intellectual abilities appeared to be. Because he was thoroughly nettled he stopped offering excuses on her behalf; but he also stopped offering criticisms of her work. Who cared if Jennifer took this wretched degree or not? What was it worth if it drove them apart from one another?

Both of them knew, however, that what they had revealed in these rows did not begin or end with the question of her academic talents. When she fell pregnant they were relieved, though nervous. They postponed the plan for her to take a degree until, as they said, 'this baby's out of the way'. Now there was no longer any reason for her to read her essays to him; occasions which they had both secretly come to dread, for they had led so often to tears and reproaches on her side, anger and watchfulness on his. Now he could get on with his job with a clear conscience, knowing that Jennifer had something of her own to keep her busy. He thought of the baby, so far as he thought of it at all, as Jennifer's affair; he couldn't believe that its arrival would much affect him. So the greatest of his discoveries, in those years, was the discovery of his own passion as a father.

'Why don't people *write* about it more?' he used to demand of Jennifer. No one had ever warned him of the pleasure he would get from handling the baby's smooth limbs, of touching his hair, of smelling him after his bath, of just watching him eating his food, of listening to his random sighs and chuckles, of recognizing in his eyes, with their mysterious bluish irises and extraordinarily unsullied whites, the recognitions that the baby was himself making. No one had ever warned him of the tenderness he would feel at seeing the baby's shoes or trousers; of the absorption he would fall into watching the tiny, precise beauties of his face. Nor had he been told that the chores of paternity would be made easily bearable by love; so that the cleaning of a napkin was a job he grumbled at and yet could find satisfaction in, and that when he woke to the baby's cry at unearthly hours of the morning he was rewarded by the clasp in his arms of a living bundle that clung to his shoulders, and snuggled against his breast with minute, comfort-seeking movements of the loins, and thrust against him round absurd knees whose weakness made him feel weak too. 'Why don't people write about it?' he complained, and yet he was proud that what he was feeling had come as a surprise to him; that it had sprung entirely from within himself, instead of having been tainted by words in books and magazines, laid down for him in patterns set by others. In comparison with what he felt as a father it seemed to him that so much else in his marriage and work was mere imitation, a mere groping towards states of mind and feeling he wished to have because he had read or been told they were desirable.

Jennifer, too, was tender to the baby, but in a more amused, less anxious way than he. The baby, Timothy, loved her more; Arnold saw that early. He did not begrudge her the baby's love. It was only fair, he felt obscurely, as if the weight of that love could redress a balance between himself and Jennifer that had somehow gone awry.

By the time Timothy was two years old, Jennifer could no longer complain of being lonely. Slowly, Arnold had succeeded in making friends among the people he met on his visits to the university, the Fabians whose society he had joined in one of the nearby towns, the social workers and schoolmasters whom he met in the course of his lecturing. For Jennifer's sake, Arnold was quick to invite people to visit them at their cottage, and almost every weekend they had visitors or went visiting others. Jennifer had lost the wistful, rather resentful shyness she had had in her manner when Arnold had first met her, and which for him had always been associated with her stooped, endearing walk; she was now almost bold when she met strangers. She was looking handsomer than ever before. Her arms and legs were fuller; at the same time her face had become a little drawn, and her brown eyes showed up the better as a result. She knew that people looked at her when she walked down a street or came into a room. Her teeth were bad, so she smiled seldom, and when she did it was 'inscrutably', with her lips closed.

She had never gone back to her books, and Arnold had never urged her to do so, though there had been times when he had felt a malicious impulse to put her to that test again. So he felt curiously guilty when Jennifer turned on him, as she eventually did, and accused him of deliberately thwarting her ambitions, of having no wish to see her achieve anything independently of him, of denying her opportunities to fulfil herself. 'You just want me to be a housewife,' she raged. 'You don't think I'm capable of anything else. Cleaning Timmy's napkins and cooking your food: that's your programme for me for the rest of my life. Well, it isn't enough. I want something else. I want something more.'

'But what do you want to do? Do you want to start your course again? I've never said that you shouldn't.'

'You've been so encouraging about it, haven't you? All this time you've been pressing me to do it, haven't you?'

'Jennifer, you can start tomorrow, if that's what you want.'

Jennifer turned away. 'No, I don't want to do that,' she said. 'Anyway, I'd probably fail the exams.'

The confession did not seem to have cost her much; but it hurt him. 'Sweetheart, you could do it easily. I'll help you.'

'Mister Magnanimous!' she jeered.

That was the way their 'discussions' now began to go; and they soon became more violent than any they had had before Timothy's birth. No matter how calmly they tried to talk of their plans for the future, they ended up with raised voices, averted faces, and a feeling of stupid, unbridgeable distance between them. These quarrels took place most frequently on Sunday evenings, when the visitors they had had for the weekend had gone, and the two of them were left once again to confront each other and the beginning of yet another week.

It was in the course of one such Sunday evening that Jennifer suddenly announced, while she was washing the dishes, that she wanted to go to London.

He stood at the kitchen door. 'What do you mean: you want to go to London?'

'I want a holiday. I want to get away from this place. I want to look around and feel myself my own boss for a little while.

Can't you understand? You don't have to look at me like that. People do it all the time.'

'And Timothy?'

'He can stay here with you. I'll go during the vacation. You'll be able to manage.'

In the years of their marriage they'd hardly been separated from each other for more than a day, and the idea seemed monstrous to Arnold. Monstrous; and yet suddenly harmless. How simple it would be if a holiday was really what Jennifer needed! A change would surely do her good. And it was true that people did this sort of thing all the time. 'Do you think you could do it?' he asked, still surprised at the simplicity and enormity of the idea.

'Of course.'

'But where would you stay?'

'With the Rowans,' she said, naming a couple they knew from the university, who had recently settled in London. 'I'll write and ask them if they could put me up. I'm sure Peter and Anne won't mind.'

'So you've got it all worked out.'

'Yes,' Jennifer said defiantly.

Her defiance won him over; not because he feared it, but because he thought it so childlike. 'All right, go ahead and write to the Rowans. If they'll have you, it can be done, I'm sure.'

Jennifer spoke tenderly to him. 'You mustn't spoil Timothy while I'm away.'

'Oh, I will,' he promised her, smiling. 'I'll spoil him like mad.'

And he did. They saw Jennifer off at the railway station, Timothy's hand clasped in his own, and then they returned to the cottage. For a fortnight they lived off his favourite delicacies, most of them out of tins. The first few days the child would sometimes stop in his play, raise his round, fair face, and ask, 'Mama coming?' and Arnold would reply, 'Mama's coming soon.' Later Timothy seemed to forget his mummy, except when they visited places that were for him particularly associated with her, like the grocery shop in the village or the chemist. Arnold played elaborate games with Timothy's Dinky toys and went through his picture books at all hours; he took him on visits to friends and on excursions to fire stations, railway stations, a small airport outside one of the towns, and the seaside; wherever they went he bought Timothy sweets and toys. Timothy was on the whole a good boy, able easily to amuse himself, and often Arnold simply sat in the living room or out in the garden reading and watching Timothy play his own obscure games with sticks and cardboard boxes and the little wooden men from his bus set. A woman came in every morning to help with the housework, and she looked after Timothy while she was in the house; this regular break helped to prevent Arnold from getting stale at the task. In all, though he was frequently impatient with Timothy, and though they had a few awful stand-up rows, with Timothy shrieking like a red demented creature and Arnold unable to contain his own anger and flinging the child down in his cot and leaving him there to yell, the time passed more quickly and easily than Arnold had expected it to.

The day before Jennifer was due back, there was a letter from her.

> Dear Arnold, I love you and I love Timmy, and that is why it's so difficult for me to write this. I am not coming home. I didn't tell you, but Anne wasn't here when I came. I should have left straight away, but I didn't, and now something has happened that neither Peter nor I ever expected. Please try and understand. Kiss Timothy for me. I can't help myself, my darling, believe me. Jennifer.

The letter had come with the afternoon's post. For how long he stood staring at it in his hand Arnold did not know. More than anything else he felt incredulity, and with that incredulity, a kind of shame for Jennifer for making such a fool of herself. But she was a fool, a fool, a fool – what else could she be, why should he deny it? The clichés in the letter filled him with a disgust that was almost like a satisfaction: look at them, look how she writes, he wanted to say – but to whom could he say it? Only to her; and she was gone. He looked about the house; every object in it seemed strange to him, because none of them knew what had happened. His eye fell on the telephone, and he ran to it, to put through a call to the Rowans' flat.

He did not know their number, so Trunks told him to call Directory Enquiries. When Directory Enquiries, after an interminable delay, gave him the number, Trunks told him that all the lines to London were engaged, and that they would call him back. For fifteen minutes he waited in the living room, with Timothy playing around his feet. Arnold could not bear to look at the child. Then Trunks phoned to say that there was no reply from the given number.

'Try again!' Arnold shouted.

The voice at the other end was indifferent. 'We will, sir.'

But Timothy knew something was amiss. With a sense of panic Arnold watched the alarm gather in the child's face. 'Timothy – sweetie boy –!' he said, and took hold of him just before he burst into tears. Arnold uttered endearments and curses, not knowing what he was saying, and caressed the child's shoulder blades under the palm of his hand.

Still there was no reply from the Rowans' number. Jennifer and her lover must have run away from the flat, for that evening at least, fearing that he would phone. Arnold knew he should be finding out what time the next train left for London, and packing his clothes and Timothy's; instead, he waited, gave Timothy some supper and finally put him to bed. He would go to London in the morning. He was afraid to go that night. He could not face the thought of Timothy and himself, in search of a mother and a wife, wandering around the huge, dark, crowded city, which he had visited briefly on only two occasions previously, and where he had no friends. Acquaintances he did have there – people he had met since coming to England, and some South Africans who had settled there – but no one to whom he could turn for succour, from whom he could demand shelter. He was afraid even of the train ride to London, at nightfall, past dusky fields, innumerable small stations, towns with lights in rows and rooftops pitching and falling like waves. And London beyond them all, still to be confronted.

When Timothy was asleep, Arnold left the cottage, with all its lights burning, and went up the main street of the village. But he turned out of it, afraid that he might be seen, and walked down a side street that soon became nothing but a path. He did not know where he was going. In the half light trees and outhouses and the posts of fences looked shaggy, unfamiliar, unlike their daylight selves. Random phrases and images jostled for a place in his mind and slipped out of it. He imagined himself saying to his colleagues, 'My wife has left me,' and hoped he would say it gravely, without a nervous or apologetic smile. He remembered some notes he had made earlier in the day, then reproached himself for being so unfeeling as to think of work at a moment like this. When he thought of Jennifer embracing another man, her hair dark on some pillow, her body supine and exposed on some bed, he felt neither anger nor jealousy; merely nausea. He shouted out, 'Bitch!' and a moment later said tenderly, 'Jenny.' He clenched his fists and went through a pantomime of a fight, striking out in the air, grunting and gasping for breath. Then he thought that when Jennifer returned he would never have to pity her or feel guilty towards her again, and the idea at first relieved him, then made him feel like a crook, a pimp, a maker of bargains. He looked over his shoulder to see if anyone were watching him, and imagined himself calmly returning the greeting of a passer-by, who would never guess what lay behind the exchange of commonplaces between them. But, though he strained his eyes into the gloom, he could see no one in front of him or behind him.

He was at the entrance to the church. He stood at the gate and looked across the churchyard; he could see only the dark shapes of some trees, and the bigger shape of the church itself. Why had he come here? He lifted his eyes to the overcast, lightless sky. There was no one to whom he could pray. He was altogether alone with his problem, with his life. It appalled him to think of the lightheartedness with which he and Jennifer had left the country of their birth and come to a foreign land, where they had no family and few friends. As if they wouldn't have been lonely enough anyway, with nothing to guide them except for a few ideas that they had taught themselves out of books and conversations! It seemed to Arnold that he was more ignorant than the most ignorant savage, for all the books he had prided himself on having read, all the views he held, all the lectures he had given. He did not know what his marriage had meant, where they had erred in it, what he should do or feel now that it was breaking up. He would die one day, and he did not know how he would be buried. If Timothy were to die, he would not know what instructions to give, to dispose of the little corpse.

He turned and ran, fearing that he might find Timothy dead when he returned home. There might have been a fire in the cottage; or a leak of gas; or a sexual maniac might have broken into it while he was away. He ran faster, and the breath came out of his body in groans; he stumbled and almost fell, but ran on as blindly as before. Soon he was back in the high street. Now there were people to see him run, but he did not notice how they looked over the net curtains in their living rooms, or paused in their conversations on doorsteps, and watched him go by. Only when he was a few yards from the cottage did he slacken his pace abruptly. The lights still burned brightly; the house seemed quiet. Surely, Timothy was all right. Then he saw a figure pass across the window of the front room, and in what seemed one leap he had burst through the front door.

Jennifer looked up, startled at his noisy entry; startled, too, by the expression on his face, the drops of sweat on his forehead, his gasps for breath. But he was the first to speak; he said incredulously, 'You! You're back?'

'It looks like it, doesn't it?' A moment later she asked, 'You got my letter?'

He nodded. He stood in the doorway of the living room, unable to come forward. She sat on the couch, looking up at him, her hands resting on her lap.

She said, 'I'm sorry. I was hoping I'd get here before it arrived.'

'Well you didn't.' In an odd, complaining tone, he said, 'I might have gone to London. And then what would have happened?'

'We would have missed each other,' Jennifer answered wryly, looking away, as if irritated by the absurdity of the complaint.

They were both silent. Jennifer rose and came to him, and took him by the hand. They stood holding hands, a pace apart from one another.

'I'm sorry, Arnold. It was all a terrible mistake. I don't know how it happened; I don't even know what really happened. I must have been mad.'

'And now?'

'I'm sane again.'

He released his hand from hers, and stepped past her into the room; then he turned to look at her. He saw her slight, stooped figure, her deep bosom, her arms hanging at her sides. Her face was lowered, hidden from him, under her fringe of dark hair. He remembered saying to himself that when she came back he would never again have to feel guilt or pity towards her. He did not know if that were true. All he knew, as he stared at her, was that his fear of being left alone was stronger than anything else he felt; stronger than his pride; stronger even than his hatred of her.

With an effort he lifted his hands and put them on her shoulders.

'Jennifer, don't do it again, don't do it ever again.'

'I won't,' she promised.

She drew a little closer to him. Slowly his head sank forward, he buried his face in her neck. They stood together, quite still, as though their trouble would pass over, if only they did not move.

THE PRETENDERS

Jeremiah Mawgan was an American whose father had taken part in the Californian gold rush of '49; Mawgan himself, as a very young man, had mined unsuccessfully for silver on the Comstock lode in Nevada. Like thousands of others of all nationalities, Mawgan had set out for South Africa immediately the news of the first diamond rush had reached him, and had joined the crowds of diggers who were turning over those mounds of earth that can still be seen, like the barrows of prehistoric men, stretching for miles in the now-deserted veld to the west of Lyndhurst.

At that time the territory on which the diamonds had been found belonged to no one, or to everyone. The Boers in the Transvaal Republic claimed it; the Boers in the Orange Free State claimed it; the chieftains of three or four nomad, cattle-grazing, half-caste tribes claimed it; only the Liberal Government in Great Britain refused to claim it, on the grounds that the diggings would soon peter out and that Britain already owned enough useless desert in Southern Africa. And then Jeremiah Mawgan, who had had no luck as a digger, claimed the territory, too – on behalf of the State of Diamondia, of which he declared himself to be the first President.

Mawgan's political success was considerable, at first. The diggers had no wish to pay taxes and claims-rent to either of the two Boer Republics; still less did they wish to come under the rule of any of the half-caste chieftains. So they cheered when Mawgan and a group of his friends threw a Boer magistrate into the Plat River, set fire to a *kraal* belonging to the Batlapin tribe, and then solemnly raised the flag of Diamondia (a silver diamond in a blue field) in one of the largest of the digger encampments. Mawgan appointed cabinet ministers and policemen; he sent stern but friendly messages of greeting to Queen Victoria, to the presidents of the Boer Republics, and to the Kaiser; he made speeches and issued proclamations.

His 'administration' did not last long, and was squalid while it lasted. His 'police' were a crowd of bullies who extorted protection money ('taxes') from the diggers; Mawgan himself sold arms to the tribal chieftains, for use against the Boers, from whom at the same time he tried to coax bribes ('fiscal appropriations') for keeping the tribesmen down. Altogether, he indulged himself to the top of a variety of bents. He wore medals of his own devising, a grey top hat, and green-tinted spectacles; in his hand he carried a long leather *sjambok* which he used on his half-caste servants and on diggers who opposed him. He dressed his male servants in a kind of livery, and, it was rumoured, took them into his bed. He drank heavily, and tried to forbid others from drinking at all. He issued 'Mawgan-money' and declared it to be the only valid currency in the territory he governed. The diggers soon repented of the enthusiasm with which they had acclaimed him.

When diamonds were discovered many miles to the east, on the tract of ground which was later to become the city of Lyndhurst, Mawgan at first tried to extend his authority, such as it was, over the new diggings too. But by that time, there were simply too many diggers for Mawgan's bands to be able to terrorize them all; by that time, too, the imperial government had at last woken up to the importance of the diamond fields, and was prompt to lay claim to them, in the face of strenuous protests from the Boers, the tribal chiefs, and Jeremiah

Mawgan. Immediately the British proclamation had been issued, a group of diggers set out, with a drum of tar and a sack of feathers, towards Mawgan's 'White House' – a whitewashed iron shack on the bank of the Plat River. But they found when they got there that Mawgan had already fled. He was never heard of again. The most popular supposition was that he had been murdered, either by his own 'police' or by a group of tribesmen, and stories were widely circulated about the 'Mawgan Diamonds', which he was believed to have stolen in the days of his power, and for which it was said he had been murdered. But other stories were that Mawgan settled down, under another name, and became a shopkeeper in the Eastern Transvaal; that he became a digger on the Witwatersrand gold fields; and that he simply went back to California.

More than eighty years after the Republic of Diamondia had come to its end, there were few people in Lyndhurst or anywhere else in South Africa who had ever heard of Jeremiah Mawgan – until the announcement was made that the Pan-Anglo Film Company was to come to Lyndhurst to make a motion picture about Jeremiah Mawgan and the early days on the diamond fields. The people of Lyndhurst were understandably excited by the news; but a tremor of excitement seemed to run through the entire country when it was announced that the star of the company would be none other than Bland Giffard, the American movie star.

'Bland Giffard Seasons', at which Bland Giffard would make personal appearances, were promptly arranged for cinemas in Johannesburg and Cape Town; official bodies in these cities, and in others, offered him mayoral banquets, public processions through their streets, and the opportunity to open fetes, golf tournaments, motor rallies and agricultural and industrial exhibitions. Chain stores sold flags with 'Welcome Bland Giffard' printed on them; and a group of newspapers ran a competition for the members of the 'Bland Giffard Fan Clubs' which had suddenly sprung into existence among teenage girls all over the country. Every competitor had to write an essay on 'Why I think Bland Giffard Is The Greatest', and the prize offered to the winner was 'An Evening With Bland Giffard'.

In Lyndhurst we did not begrudge the other cities what they could get of Bland Giffard. We could afford to be generous, for we were to enjoy his presence for a month or more, no one was quite sure how long. In addition, we were to be the hosts to the other, lesser-known stars who would be accompanying Bland Giffard, and to the director and assistant director, cameramen and assistant cameramen, continuity and make-up and wardrobe girls, public relations men, scriptwriters and assistant scriptwriters – none of whose names were at first known, but whose professions all sounded glamorous enough to us. Long before the company arrived, the local newspaper had published photographs and profiles of the more important of the company's members, together with details of the hotel space booked for them, the excursions to sites of interest which had been organized for them, and the civic, sporting and cultural events at which they would be present. On the day on which it was announced that several hundred 'extras' would be hired in Lyndhurst itself for the shooting of the film, a crowd gathered outside one of the local cinemas, and dispersed only after the harassed manager of the cinema had given an assurance that a recruiting office would be set up in due course, and had also distributed among the crowd copies of a large photograph of Bland Giffard himself.

That gathering outside the cinema should have been taken as a warning of the effect which the arrival of Bland Giffard and the Pan-Anglo Film Company would have on Lyndhurst. But no one could have foreseen the effect these arrivals would have on young Benny de Jager, and the extraordinary old man who became known as 'the claimant'. After Benny de Jager had brought the company's visit to its terrible and unexpected climax many people did feel, however, that their own excitement may have contributed something to the disaster. So they tried to blame the newspapers for what had 'come over' them; they blamed the well-known immorality of film people, and the political situation (which they said had everybody's nerves on edge); the English-speaking blamed the Afrikaans-speaking and the Afrikaans-speaking blamed the English-speaking; both groups of whites quite reasonlessly blamed the Coloureds and Africans (who, having been thoroughly excluded from the pleasures of the visit, were thus made responsible for its pains); some people blamed the drought. But it wasn't the weather or the political situation or even the newspapers that made so many of the white people of Lyndhurst queue up to become extras; that sent them out into the streets again and again to cheer when Bland Giffard passed through; that made them fill the bars and lounges of the hotels where members of the company were staying, and go excitedly to public functions at which members of the company would be present, or to drive out repeatedly to the ford on the Plat River where the actual shooting of the film took place; that made every woman with social ambitions compete furiously for the privilege of inviting members of the company to her house for cocktail parties. During the visit of the company, parties were given more frequently than ever before in Lyndhurst, and people drank more heavily at them, and laughed more loudly, and quarrelled more fiercely, and boasted more extravagantly, and flirted more outrageously with each other than they had been known to before. Marriages broke up while the Pan-Anglo Film Company was in Lyndhurst; other marriages were suddenly announced; many virginities were quietly surrendered. Model children shouted at their parents and took the next train to Cape Town or Johannesburg. And that was not the worst, as we all know. Not by any means. Between them, Benny de Jager and the crazed old 'claimant' saw to that.

On the morning the recruiting office for extras finally opened, a few weeks before Bland Giffard's arrival in town, young Benny de Jager appeared outside the office, dressed up in black jeans, high black boots, and a black shirt with white leather fringes over the breast pockets and at the hips. Round his waist he wore a belt studded with little circles of brass, like the tops of drawing pins; and on his head a large black hat with a broad, turned-back brim. His guitar was slung across his back.

Some of us had known about the guitar. Benny de Jager had played on it as a member of a local dance band; he had sung to it in solo numbers. But the black cowboy suit in which he strutted and swaggered alongside the queue of would-be extras, was a complete surprise. Condescendingly he greeted his friends, ignored the jeers of strangers, and uttered aloud, to no one in particular, his opinion of the people in the queue. 'Creeps,' he said. 'So you're going to be extras? Big deal! Big, big deal!'

'And you? What are you going to be? The Lone Ranger?' Benny de Jager shrugged. 'Don't know,' he said. 'I don't know what they'll offer me.'

There it was. Benny de Jager was convinced that he was going to be a film star. He had never revealed this ambition or intention, before; but he spoke now without any doubt whatever. He was a slight, good-looking boy, with clear blue eyes, neatly-parted brown hair, and an ingenuous expression; the son of a local auctioneer. His skin had a childlike freshness and smoothness; one might almost have expected it to smell faintly of soap. He worked in his father's business by day, and played in the band a couple of nights a week; he went frequently to the cinema. It was said later that he had amassed over the years a huge collection of film magazine and annuals, which he had kept in his room and never shown to anyone; and that he had also taken a home correspondence course in dramatic art. But we did not know this at the time. I doubt if it would have made any difference to the people in the queue even if they had known.

Embarrassed because they were his friends, his friends were the first to tell him to piss off. Despite de Jager's certitude, no one believed that he would ever become a film star: a fact which is a little surprising, considering how credulous the people of Lyndhurst were to show themselves in the following weeks. But their scepticism here shows their essential modesty; they knew their own place in the world even if de Jager didn't. The kindly disposed felt pity toward him, mingled with amusement; others were angry and scornful, as if he had insulted them. They were given many opportunities to show their feelings, for though he had not signed on to become an extra, de Jager could not keep away from anyone or anything even remotely connected with the making of the film. Nor would he take off his cowboy suit.

In those weeks, while we were awaiting Bland Giffard's arrival, the town was slowly filling with members of the company; most of them Englishmen and women, for Pan-Anglo was a British firm with whom Bland Giffard had gone into a partnership for the making of this one film. They arrived singly or in groups; the small Scots technicians, who spoke in incomprehensible accents and got drunk in bars all over town; the elegant, suede-shod public relations men who spoke in BBC accents and got drunk in a few bars they had picked out for reasons known only to themselves; the middle-aged women, variously employed, who were all alike in having black, pointed eyelashes that stood out in individual spikes from their eyelids; the well-known character actors whose faces you were sure you had seen before, but couldn't remember where; the pretty little English starlet who was to play opposite Bland

Giffard, and whose big opportunity for stardom this film was; finally, the director himself.

De Jager wooed them all indiscriminately. He offered to appear before the director and his assistants at auditions; he had cards printed inviting members of the company to a series of informal entertainments in his home. In hotel lounges and even in the street he volunteered to sing to them, or simply tried to tell them of his ambitions. None of them responded to his invitations. Most of them learned to move away rapidly when they saw him coming. The managers of some hotels forbade him to enter their premises. One evening a group of technicians made him sing to them for an hour, told him that he was immensely talented and that they would certainly bring him to the attention of the director, and then hid his guitar in a rubbish bin in the alleyway behind the hotel. De Jager found it only after a frantic search, while the technicians roared with laughter at obscene suggestions as to where he should look for it.

Benny de Jager's blue eyes showed anger and bafflement, under his neat dark brows; but he did not complain. They mocked him, he said, because they were envious. It was the fate of all heroes, of all artists, of all true aspirants to fame, of all who had the power to impose themselves on the consciousness of the world. He was not to be discouraged. And eventually he decided, in silence and isolation, that there was only one man among those who were coming to Lyndhurst who would not feel envious of him. It stood to reason, de Jager thought, that one artist would be able to pick out another; that one great man would recognize the potentiality of greatness in another. In his imagination, fed on too many films, Benny de Jager anticipated the glance Bland Giffard would cast upon him, and how in that glance indifference would yield suddenly to hope and surprise; he heard Bland Giffard say to the people around him, 'Who is that man? I want to speak to him'; he felt Bland Giffard's hand within his own, and Bland Giffard's arm across his shoulder. De Jager imagined himself dancing for Bland Giffard, singing for him, enacting brief scenes in front of him; he saw the two of them returning to Bland Giffard's hotel, where they would relax over a drink and Giffard would tell stories of his own early days, while the crowd gathered outside and chanted, 'We want Bland!' and 'We want Benny!' Then Bland Giffard and Benny de Jager would come out on the balcony together, and wave to their fans.

The script of the film bore little relation to anything that was known about the life of Jeremiah Mawgan. Nothing in the film, it was clear, was intended to give offence to anyone – the Boers did not appear in it, except for a few lovable farmers, nor the native tribesmen, nor even the English authorities until the very end. In fact, it was the villain in the picture who was a man rather like the real Jeremiah Mawgan. The hero, the Jeremiah Mawgan of the movie, was a man like no one in the world – a roving lover of justice, a digger indifferent to wealth, a ferocious but gentle fighter, a passionate but honourable lover. The villain tried to bribe him, then to threaten him, then to seduce him with one of his many women; the terrorized diggers refused to listen to him. His tent was burned down, his claim was flooded, his animals were poisoned, his gear was wrecked. But he fought on, single-handed, and the woman who had tried to seduce him fell in love with him, the diggers slowly came round to supporting him, and eventually he was able to drive the villain and his cut-throats out of the district. Jeremiah Mawgan was then elected president of the Republic of Diamondia by an overwhelming vote; he established a hospital, instituted a court to arbitrate on disputes between diggers, and formally opened a presidential ball in the open air. But when the British arrived and begged him on behalf of the Queen to stay and carry on with his good work, he refused. 'Not even for me?' whimpered the woman who loved him, and Mawgan wistfully but resolutely replied, 'Not even for you. It's time I moved on. I'm a roving man.' The last sequence of the film showed how even hardened diggers wept to see Mawgan go; and how, as he rode away from the camp, his figure seemed to grow larger and mistier to the spectators, as if he were a spirit rather than a man; a vision that they themselves had evoked. 'He'll be coming back,' one digger in the crowd said. 'Whenever we need him, I guess he'll be around. Or a man like him.'

Shooting from this script began in earnest a week or two before Bland Giffard's arrival in Lyndhurst, on a location on the banks of the Plat River, about fifteen miles west of the town, in the direction of the original diggings. Sequences were shot and shot again, in what appeared to be haphazard order. The extras plunged into the river and helped to haul tented wagons across it; they rocked diligently at their 'cradles' and combed through the pebbles on the sieves which the cradles carried; they scattered into the veld when the villain and his henchmen passed by, and gathered in muttering, gesticulating groups among their tents after he had left. Much of the time they did nothing at all, while sequences involving only the professional actors were put in front of the cameras, or the director and his assistants conferred with the cameraman and his assistants. Then the extras sat in the shade of the thorn trees and ate their sandwiches, or queued up outside the mobile canteen for tea, or strolled to the perimeter of the location to talk to friends and relations who had driven out from Lyndhurst and who stood peering curiously at the activities going on inside the wire.

Benny de Jager was invariably among these visitors and picnickers from Lyndhurst. His clothes no longer looked so odd, now that many of the extras were wearing garments somewhat similar to his, and several times de Jager simply slipped through the wire, like some of the other visitors, and wandered unnoticed about the encampment, looking at everything, talking to no one, except occasionally to himself.

De Jager was waiting for Bland Giffard; everyone was waiting for Bland Giffard. Bland Giffard did not let us down. He came riding into town from the airport in a huge pale blue convertible, with its hood down; he sat in the back seat of the car, smiling across the width of his face and waving with one hand to the groups on the street corners. At the hotel the police had to clear a way for him through the pushing, cheering throng, and he sauntered slowly between the ranks of policemen, shaking this or that outstretched hand, and saying over and over again, 'Hi!' and 'Glad to see you all!' At the entrance to the hotel he turned to face the crowd and said a few words in his professionally resonant, thrillingly American voice. 'A great moment for me ... so many friends here in Lyndhurst ... anxious to meet you all ... to work with you ... history ... wonderful town ... thanks again ... great ... I'll be seeing you.'

He looked grotesque, like no one else the people in the crowd had ever seen before, and they cheered with satisfaction. So this was Bland Giffard! – who had so often triumphed over villainous district attorneys, corrupt sheriffs, smooth-talking Communist spies, and entire bands of sallow cityfied gangsters. He was very tall; his hair was thick and dyed bright yellow; his shoulders were broad, his jacket was short, his trousers were narrow. Everyone had seen his face enlarged a hundredfold; gigantic close-ups had dwelt upon the droop of those eyelids; advertisements had stretched that smile across the width of entire hoardings. Yet the face of the man in the hotel entrance was bigger than anyone had expected it to be. Under his yellow hair there were regular, unbroken expanses of brow and nose and chin; the very skin of his face seemed to stand off further from the bones than the skin of an ordinary man, so that his face seemed not only abnormally wide and long, but abnormally deep too. His eyes were the size of those marbles the children of Lyndhurst used to call 'ghoens'; his yellow sideburns, which had been grown long for the part of Jeremiah Mawgan, were almost pelt-like; each tooth appeared to be the size of a thumbnail. He looked neither young nor old; neither handsome nor ugly; neither weak nor strong. He looked like a man wearing a mask; yet if you were to tear it off, you felt there would be the same cushioned mask underneath; and beneath that the same mask again, of the same size as the first.

The crowd changed, but did not disperse, throughout the afternoon; as time passed the stories about Bland Giffard's appearance grew wilder, both in praise and denigration. People said that he was wearing a wig, and lipstick and rouge; that his teeth were false, his shoulders were padded, his heels were built-up; that he looked like a drunkard, a drug addict, an old man; in spite of his widely-publicized marriages and divorces, they said that he looked like a homosexual; they said that there was something about his eyes that made you shiver. But others said that he was younger and much more handsome than in his pictures; that he was so modest and sincere he had been moved to tears by the reception that Lyndhurst had given him; that even if you hadn't known who he was, and had passed him in the street, you would have known him to be a great man; that already he could speak Afrikaans; that he had pressed lucky silver dollars into the hands of those who had been able to touch him. A curious thing was that some people repeated, with equal sincerity, both the praise and the abuse.

Everyone agreed, anyway, that he was not a man who wasted his time. He paid courtesy calls on the mayor and the offices of the Lyndhurst General Mining and Exploration Company (on whose ground the film was being shot), he visited the local cinemas, he conferred for a day or two with his colleagues. Twice Benny de Jager, who had written and

141

telegraphed several times to Giffard and had repeatedly tried to phone him since his arrival, thrust himself in front of the actor when he emerged from the hotel, struck a chord on his guitar, and broke into a song; each time Bland Giffard smiled in what everybody said was the kindest way, and told de Jager, 'Not now, youngster, I'm a busy man.' De Jager was hustled away on both occasions by the people around; the second time Bland Giffard called out after them, 'Don't break his guitar,' before striding on to the waiting convertible.

Then Giffard went out to the location. Preoccupied though he was, on his arrival there he took the trouble to walk among the extras, asking individuals how they enjoyed working on the film, and laughing heartily at their more or less enthusiastic replies. Having thus roused the extras to a pitch of excitement they had not felt before, Giffard disappeared, to change and to be made up for the particular sequence which was to be shot that morning.

After the usual shouting through loudspeakers, and the shuffling confusion of the extras; after the director had several times thrown up his hands in despair and people around him had buzzed and sworn at each other and contradicted each other's orders, the extras and actors were at last marshalled into position. A man shamming dead lay in the middle of them, with a woman kneeling at his side, and Bland Giffard appeared, dressed in a beautifully tailored pair of high boots and a beige frock coat. His eyes glittered from the chemicals that had been dropped into them, and his skin was unnaturally smooth and suffused with a strange roseate hue. Slowly he made his way through the throng, and stood aghast over the man whom the villains were supposed to have murdered minutes before.

'That's fine,' the director cried. 'Now let's go, and keep going.'

Again Bland Giffard made his way through the throng, and stood aghast over the murdered man. And with many interruptions, and retakes, and consultations, and more cursing, the scene proceeded. But no sooner had Bland Giffard come to the end of his first great speech appealing to the diggers to stand together, than there came a quavering cry from behind the throng of extras. 'It wasn't like that,' the voice cried out. 'Not like *that*.' Then it uttered a single jeer of amusement or scorn.

The director yelled, 'Cut!' before yelling, even more loudly, 'Who the hell is that?' Bland Giffard was frowning; the men around the director were poised to eject the offender who was slowly making his way through the arc of extras, towards the open space in front of the cameras.

He emerged at last in front of Bland Giffard. 'That's not the way to do it,' he said. 'You don't know your own job!' Again, he uttered a shrill jeer.

The stranger's appearance was so remarkable that for a moment no one spoke or moved. He was a tiny, shrivelled, tattered old man, bent far forward at the hips and supported by a stick he clasped in both hands; his breast was almost parallel with the ground, and he had to strain his head upwards to lift his gaze to the people in front of him. His face was so deeply wrinkled as to be almost featureless; instead of features it seemed to have folds, merely, all of the same dull brown colour. But his tiny eyes were bright. He was wearing a hat, a khaki shirt without buttons, and a pair of soiled khaki trousers; on his feet were a pair of broken canvas *takkies*. No one there had ever seen him before.

He raised one brown, shrivelled, paw-like hand from his stick and pointed it at Bland Giffard. 'You've just got no idea,' he said, his head shaking slowly from side to side. 'You don't know who you're supposed to be.'

143

He was dotty, an old mad man. Everyone relaxed, even Bland Giffard. 'Who let him in?' the director demanded. 'Get him out of here.'

With a glance at the people around him, Bland Giffard asked, 'No idea about what, old-timer?'

The patronizing tone in which the question was asked seemed to infuriate the old man. Disconnected words and squeaks came out of his throat. Then, clearly, he said, 'My name – using my name! Who do you think you are?'

Loudly, raising his voice above the hubbub made by the people who were pressing forward to hear what was happening, Bland Giffard asked, 'What is your name, old-timer?'

'Jeremiah Mawgan!' the old man shrieked. 'What do you think it is?'

Before they laughed, the crowd recoiled, in a movement of superstitious horror and astonishment. Then they laughed immoderately, hilariously, pushing against one another and collapsing on the ground, and repeating over and over again, 'Jeremiah Mawgan, Jeremiah Mawgan.' Even the director – a plump, irritable, heavily freckled man, who had never before been known even to smile – stretched his short legs in front of him and shouted with laughter. The old man himself stood with a vague smile on his face, obviously delighted with the reception that had been given to his announcement.

But there was one man in the crowd who did not laugh. Benny de Jager had stolen among the extras in order to get as close as possible to Bland Giffard, and had stood among them throughout the shooting of the scene. Now, before his staring blue eyes, he saw another scene enacted; the one he had so vividly imagined for himself so many times. But it wasn't Benny de Jager that Bland Giffard looked at with astonishment and curiosity; it wasn't about him that Bland Giffard said, 'Wait, let's listen to the man; let's hear what he's got to say for himself.' Nor was it Benny de Jager's hand that Bland Giffard clasped warmly a few minutes later, or his shoulders that felt the weight of Bland Giffard's arm, as Giffard turned and faced the whole group and said, 'Well – it's a good story, and I think we should give a cheer to the man who told it.' When the applause died down, Giffard said, 'I'm not going to let you go, old-timer; I want to hear more of your stories.' He bowed deeply, and added with a smile, 'Mr Mawgan, sir, may we now proceed with our work?' Then he led the old man aside and sat him down on a canvas chair. Applause broke out again, even the old man clapped, as Giffard returned to his place in front of his cameras; everyone had been affected by the courtesy and good humour he had displayed. Giffard acknowledged the applause with a raised hand.

'All right, all right, back to work. Where were we?' the director cried.

When shooting for the day was over, Giffard sat down with the old man, and the public relations men gathered around them. With the frankness and geniality that the film magazines always referred to in their descriptions of his character, Giffard questioned the old man about his past, and about his present way of life. Soon a cavalcade of cars, with Bland Giffard in the leading car, was speeding along the main road towards the dorp of Klaarwater, a few miles further west along the Plat River. For it was there that the old man lived; there, he claimed, that he had the proofs that he was indeed Jeremiah Mawgan.

Iron roofs; low whitewashed walls; a few tiny shop windows filled with fruit, bread, celluloid toys and bolts of cloth; the steeple of the Dutch Reformed Church; the rocks and reeds of the Plat River below – one could take in Klaarwater at a glance, even though it was spread for a great distance over the veld. Dusty double tracks ran circuitously between isolated clusters of dwellings, and were lost to sight among rocks or thorn bushes. Here and there a faded noticeboard attached to the roof or verandah post of one or another shack gave evidence of Klaarwater's past: *J. Kruger: Licensed Diamond Buyer or M. Levine: Licensed Diamond Buyer*, the notices said; but the shacks were inhabited by families of poor whites or coloureds who stared anxiously at the lurching cars as they approached, and curiously only after they had passed by.

It was to a group of shacks like the others that the old man directed the car. But he did not live in one of the shacks; he lived in what was in effect an outhouse to the shack nearest to it: a windowless, ceilingless structure which was made entirely out of corrugated iron and a few struts of wood. Air and light came in through the door. On a wooden fruit crate next to the bed there was a tin mug, plate, teapot, and candleholder with a misshapen stub of a candle thrust inside it. The bed itself consisted merely of a set of springs raised off the earth floor by piles of bricks at each of its four corners. There were a few thin blankets on the bed, a picture calendar hanging from one of the beams holding up the roof, and several neat piles of newspaper on the floor. Otherwise the room was entirely bare. It smelled heavily of cheap tobacco.

Excitedly, the old man led the way into his shack, and as many as possible of the people who had come in the cars crowded in after him. Bland Giffard was the first among them. The old man went straight to his bed, and with trembling hands began to search under the blankets. When he found what he was looking for he uttered a little cry, and rested for a moment, without moving, his hands still thrust forward. Then he pulled out a bundle of papers and waved them in the air. 'Here!' he cried with delight. 'I knew I had them.' Several people grabbed at the papers, but he would not yield them, he clutched them to his breast. Then he shouted at Giffard, 'You're the man. You must look at them.' He passed them over to the actor, who took them eagerly in his hand.

By this time the excitement in the hut was intense; it was even more intense outside, where the crowd of people from the film company had been swollen by people of all ages, sizes and colours from the houses nearby. None of the villagers knew what was happening; most of them thought that the old man was being arrested by an astonishingly large force of plain-clothes policemen. But the film people were touched once again with the superstitious horror and astonishment they had felt when the old man had first announced his name to them.

Bland Giffard could not read the papers in the dimness of the shack. So everyone who had gone inside it tumbled out once again. Giffard and the old man came out together, and stood side by side in the doorway, with the light of the declining sun directly in their faces. The sunlight was yellow; the irregular shadow of the crowd was black: the veld seemed to hold no other colours. Everyone fell silent; only then did Giffard lower his head and begin going through the papers.

Into the silence, the old man shouted, 'It's all there – see – all about me – all about Jeremiah Mawgan!'

But Giffard slowly shook his head, and without a word passed the papers over to the man standing next to him, who glanced briefly at them, grimaced wryly, and handed them on again to yet another member of the company. So they passed from hand to hand, and everyone who looked at them smiled or shrugged or tapped his forehead with a meaningful finger. The 'papers' were nothing: they consisted merely of cuttings of all the reports which had appeared in the local newspaper about the film which the company was to make. They were all there, the big stories and the little ones, the photographs of Bland Giffard and the starlet, the expurgated life of Jeremiah Mawgan which the newspaper had run on successive mornings one week, the interviews and the civic speeches of welcome to the members of the company, even the description in the

'Camera Club Corner' of the cameras the company was using. But there was nothing else.

'I told you I had the papers,' the old man crowed. 'You can read all about me there. They're writing about me every day. It tells you everything there. You read it in the papers, just like I said.' The crowd moved, hesitated, wavered; people began returning to their cars, some of them looking back pityingly at the old man, who was following his papers as they went about from hand to hand. 'Look after them,' he cried proudly. 'They're my proofs.'

The villagers, still confused about what was going on, were in the meantime offering all the information they had about the old man to anyone who would listen. They called him *'Oubaas Twak'*; they did not know him by any other name. He had been living there for a long time, no one knew how long; but longer than the people in the shacks around his own. The Government had once tried to move him, but he'd come back. He was a nice old man, they said, he never made trouble for anybody, not even when the children teased him because he talked to himself. Everyone used to give him a little money sometimes, and pipe tobacco. No, he had no money of his own. Rent? The owner of the shack nearest to the old man's laughed at the idea of himself as a landlord. Sometimes the old man would get meat from the shops in the village, and tea. How much did an old skinny man like that need to keep him going?

Someone asked, with great hesitation, was he white? The old man's immediate neighbours were insulted at the suggestion that he might be anything else. Weren't they white, they demanded, in voices that insisted upon an affirmative answer more strongly than their appearance actually warranted. Did anyone think they'd have a *Hotnot* living next door to them? The half-castes lived there, they said, with voices that trailed lengthily over the word, as a way of indicating how great was the distance between themselves and the nearest coloured shacks, a hundred yards away.

And that seemed to be all that was known about him. The information – such as it was – was passed back to Bland Giffard and the group standing around him. The papers were back in the possession of the old man, and he was going through them, forgetful momentarily of the crowd, to make sure that none was missing. 'Give the old bugger a pound, and let's go,' a public relations man suggested amiably, but an assistant to the director disapproved of the idea. 'You do that and you'll have the whole village asking for a handout. He's had an exciting day, and a nice ride home, it's enough for him.'

Bland Giffard looked up. 'Is that what you think?' he asked, with less than his usual affability. 'You know a lot, don't you?' Then he approached the old man. 'Will you be my guest while the company is here in Lyndhurst? It'll be a privilege for us to entertain you.'

The assistant to the director looked chastened, the public relations man shook his head gloomily, but everyone else was greatly pleased with Giffard's gesture. It would have been cruel, they said, simply to drive away, leaving the deluded old creature standing alone outside his dreadful shack. And the old man's reply delighted them, in its absurdity and grandeur. 'It's only fitting,' he said. 'You're using my name. I'm entitled to be paid for it.'

'That's right,' Giffard replied, with an inclination of his golden head. 'That's the truth.'

The gravity of his face and voice as he said these words, observers reported later, was wonderful to see. What an actor he was!

So, that evening, Benny de Jager saw the last of his imaginings simultaneously fulfilled and yet brutally denied. The news of what had happened on the location and in Klaarwater had gone rapidly round the town, and a crowd almost as large as that which had first welcomed Bland Giffard to Lyndhurst had gathered outside his hotel. Driven back by the police, the people filled the pavement on the other side of the street, and spread down the block. They began chanting in unison, 'We want Bland! We want Bland!' and others cried out, amid much laughter, 'We want Mawgan! We want Mawgan!' Finally, they were rewarded. Bland Giffard came out on to the balcony of his room; when the crowd saw that he was accompanied by the old man, a huge roar of pleasure and amusement went up. Bland Giffard waved a practised hand to the crowd; the old man waved his stick and did a little jig; he shook Bland Giffard by the shoulder; in the half-light his mouth could be seen opening and closing as he faced the crowd and gesticulated. But not a word of what he was saying could be heard; the laughter and cheers of the mob down below were too loud. Then, gently but firmly, Giffard led the old man back inside the hotel, and a groan of good-humoured disappointment filled the street.

All around him de Jager heard people speaking about Bland Giffard with a devotion they could hardly have expressed more strongly if he had done for each of them individually what he had done for the old man. 'But it's all a lot of nonsense,' de Jager protested a few times to the strangers around him. 'It's all lies. He *can't* be Jeremiah Mawgan.' But no one listened to him. 'Who cares?' people shouted. 'Hell, it's wonderful – taking up the old man like that, and treating him so well – it's just wonderful, man, say what you like.'

At about one in the morning, when the last most obstinate sightseer had left, and only a coloured porter and a white policeman dozed in the hotel foyer, Benny de Jager took up a position in the middle of the street, struck a few chords on his guitar and broke into a song he had only just composed, 'Diamond Town Blues'. A few lights came on in the hotel bedrooms. The policeman emerged from the foyer and told de

Jager to move on. But the young man refused to obey. 'You don't know how important it is,' he told the policeman. 'This is my last chance – his last chance –' he mumbled, then suddenly raised his voice and sang, 'I been waiting for a long time, but I ain't waiting any more. Wanta leave this town 'cos my heart's so sore.' The policeman pushed him; de Jager put down his guitar and pushed the policeman. For a few seconds they faced one another, under the blue lamps, the sound of their breathing loud in the empty street. Then the policeman drew his truncheon. 'Help!' de Jager yelled. 'Bland, it's your chance – help me!' The policeman struck him on the shoulder, lightly, and de Jager burst into tears. Emboldened by this sign of weakness, the policeman hit him again, on the head, and though the force of the blow, and the sound of it, were muffled by de Jager's hard tall hat, he sank immediately to his knees and collapsed in the gutter. The policeman stood over him, baton in hand.

A moment later, the street resounded to the noise of a few hollow handclaps. The policeman, turned and saw Bland Giffard standing alone on his first-floor balcony. 'Good!' Bland Giffard shouted. He was unsteady on his feet; he grabbed at the balcony railing and leaned far over it. 'Do it again! Smash him up! Smash them all!'

He was overheard by a few incredulous hotel guests and members of staff, whom the noise had wakened; and by Benny de Jager, too, who stirred on the asphalt, rose to his feet, shook his fist at Giffard, and staggered wordlessly away down the street, his guitar still clutched in his hand.

People were to suggest, many weeks later, that the blow from the policeman's baton must have injured de Jager's brains; others said that whatever the blow might have done to his feelings, it had made no difference to his brains, which must always have been soft. What is certain, anyway, is that after that

151

last escapade outside Bland Giffard's hotel, de Jager appeared more sane and more calm, to those who knew him, than he had for a long time. He took off his cowboy suit and wore once again the flannels and sports jacket of any other Lyndhurst youth. He no longer went out to watch the filming on the Plat River location; instead, he returned to work in his father's showrooms. When people teased him by asking what had happened to his great plan of becoming a film star, he smiled remotely and did not reply.

The only surprising thing he did, during this period, was to strike up an acquaintance with the old man whom Giffard had brought into town. This was easy enough to do, for the old man wandered all over Lyndhurst, introducing himself as Jeremiah Mawgan, and complaining bitterly to anyone who would listen to him about the travesty of his life which, he claimed, they were filming a few miles away. 'It wasn't like that,' he kept on complaining. 'That's not how I remember it.' The old man had fulfilled the prediction of the gloomy public relations man; he had made such a nuisance of himself whenever he visited the location – buttonholing the director, interrupting the takes, giving instructions to the extras – that he was now forbidden to go there. However, even that public relations man would admit that the response of the local and overseas press to Bland Giffard's 'discovery' of the old man had been remarkably good. The company's official press releases had carefully refrained from suggesting that the old man was in fact Jeremiah Mawgan; but the story of the encounter between the actor and 'the claimant' (as the old man was always referred to) had nevertheless made exciting and heartwarming copy, of a kind that was most valuable to the Pan-Anglo venture as a whole, and of course entirely creditable to Bland Giffard himself.

Many people in Lyndhurst did not doubt that the claimant was Jeremiah Mawgan. Their sense of historical chronology was weak; and the old man was clearly very old. But even these people soon became impatient with his complaints. Who cared what the old man remembered, they asked each other. Did he suppose a whole film could be changed to suit him? Besides, they added, it was just a film; just a story. It didn't have to be true in every detail, did it?

Benny de Jager, however, never appeared to be bored by the claimant's stories. They sat together, the old man and the young one, in corners of hotel lounges, the old man talking, gesticulating and occasionally screeching with rage or amusement; de Jager remaining calm and impassive, but listening intently and at intervals rapidly nodding his head. Or they walked about the pavements together, the old man haphazard in his movements, but still voluble; de Jager upright, precise, and quick to nod with gratification every time the old man broke out uncontrollably with some phrase like, 'All lies!' or 'Do it properly, that's what I say, or don't do it at all!'

What most enraged him about the film was that it seemed to him so namby-pamby, so sissy. 'Do you think that's how I did it – like that?' he would cry, so loudly that he could be heard halfway across a street or hotel lounge. 'Christ! When I wanted a thing I took it! I made them give it to me. I didn't say please, we must help each other, we must love each other. I said to myself, "Take what you want! Show them who you are!" And that's what I did, do you hear me, that's how I became rich and famous. And now they try to turn me into a Boy Scout. Do I look like a Boy Scout? It's all lies, they're telling, all lies.'

'Liars, all liars,' de Jager sometimes repeated passionately, staring straight at the old man, with narrowed eyes. Spasms of silent laughter shook him; they were so intense that even the old man noticed them and looked back at him suspiciously. But de Jager met the scrutiny with a face innocent and impassive once more and the old man would go on talking of the respect that used to be paid him and the luxuries he used to enjoy in the days of his power, or would catalogue again all complaints

153

against the company. Neither of them ever spoke directly of Bland Giffard, until the very end.

In the meantime the making of the film proceeded more or less according to schedule, and without any further interruptions or intrusions, though in Lyndhurst the parties and the competition for invitations to parties, the gatherings on street corners and the drives out to the Plat River, the private scandals and the public gossip about them, all went on. There was so much to do and talk about throughout the company's stay that the incidents involving Benny de Jager and the old man became 'ancient history', as people said, and were almost forgotten. Bland Giffard seduced none of the local women; he was sufficiently attentive to the little starlet to give the gossip writers something to write about, but no more; when he drank (and the rumour went around, after the incident with Benny de Jager, that he got drunk regularly), he did it in his room at night, where there was nobody to see him. He frequently flew away to attend the functions which had been arranged for him in other centres; on one occasion to spend that evening with a Durban girl whose photograph and prize-winning essay were printed in the papers. Every time he returned, he said that he was really so glad to be back, for Lyndhurst felt like another home to him.

At last – too soon for some, too late for others – the work was almost done; and members of the company began to slip away in ones and twos and larger groups. On Bland Giffard's last night in Lyndhurst, the directors of the Lyndhurst General Mining and Exploration Company gave an open-air party for the star himself, the remaining senior members of the film company, and many leading citizens of the town. The party took place in the grounds of a house that had once been the 'lodge' for visiting Legemco directors, and was now a museum. The grounds were extensive and as formal as any in Lyndhurst: there were gravel paths, lawns, flower beds, trellises supporting plumbago and golden-shower bushes, a fish pond, a broad paved terrace in front of the house, where a temporary bar had been set up. Under the bright electric lights in the mild late-summer air, the party looked elegant and animated; but it was in fact more subdued than any other which had taken place during the last few weeks. Only a few of the film people were at all boisterous, and the Lyndhurst people did not try to join that group, as though they were overcome by shyness now that the visitors were about to depart. Bland Giffard made conversation with the two resident Legemco directors and their ladies; then he moved among the guests, exchanging a few words here and there, nodding, smiling. Lyndhurst had been 'wonderful' to him, he said, again and again. In his tie he wore the diamond tiepin which had been presented to him by the Lyndhurst Chamber of Commerce.

Benny de Jager and the old man joined the party simply by walking up the dark, hedge-lined driveway that led to the garden. None of the coloured and African drivers waiting near the entrance dared challenge their right to do so. De Jager saw the lights and the moving figures at the end of the driveway, the white coats of the waiters and the bare arms of the women; he heard the sound of laughter and conversation. Then he saw Bland Giffard's tall figure, and the gleam of his hair. Roughly, he prodded the old man, and pointed in Giffard's direction. The old man halted abruptly, but de Jager pushed him once more, towards the illuminated, stage-like area in front of them. The old man did not pause again; he hurried forward and de Jager followed.

So they emerged into the light, the old man a pace or two ahead of the young one, who was dressed once again in his cowboy suit and wore his tall hat. Half-concealed in his hand, he carried a small shining revolver. Now the old man looked neither to the right nor left, but stumbled on hastily. There were exclamations and some laughter from the guests who saw the strange couple; a few people thought that de Jager, in that

155

costume of his, must be connected with the film company, and some vague idea of charades moved in their minds. The gleaming object in his hand they took to be a glass, like the object in everyone else's hand. Yet an unease at the appearance of the two men spread through the guests; and it was in response to this that Bland Giffard turned, and saw the pair approaching him. Conversation suddenly died away.

The old man almost ran the last few paces towards Giffard, and fell on his knees in front of him. 'I'm not Jeremiah Mawgan,' he gabbled.

'Louder!' commanded the young man, who stood back, his hands flat against his thighs.

'I'm not Jeremiah Mawgan,' the old man screamed. 'My name's Patterson! Do you hear me? Just Patterson!'

Giffard looked up. 'What's going on? Who are you?' he asked de Jager. The old man lunged sideways. De Jager raised the revolver and fired.

Still, many people took it for a joke; something to do with westerns, the kind of joke film people would play. But a scream went up when Bland Giffard pitched forward and fell. De Jager stood alone, the gun still clutched in his hand. He opened his mouth, but no words came out. Then the old man yelled, 'Look at him! There's a real man!'

De Jager stooped suddenly – some say in horror at what he had done. Others, however, insist that he was bowing to the crowd.

As we know, Bland Giffard was not fatally injured by that shot. His life was never in danger. But the assault did put an end to his career as an actor. The bullet, which was of a very small calibre, entered his throat and damaged the laryngeal nerves, before it came to rest within the muscle of the neck. Bland Giffard cannot now speak above a whisper. So he no longer appears in films: instead, he ranches in San Luis Obispo County, California, and he also owns a share in a motel on

Highway 101, near his ranch. He has a reputation among those who have dealings with him, for being morose, withdrawn, and a heavy drinker; but all this, they say, is understandable enough.

The old man is back in Klaarwater. In court he insisted that his name was Jeremiah Mawgan; that he had denied it only in an attempt to appease the cursing, pistol-waving young man who had roused him from his hotel, and, babbling of past incidents, raving of 'the showdown', of 'letting the world see', had then driven him with threats and blows towards the party. However, all the court officials referred to the old man as 'Patterson'; in his summing-up the judge spoke at length of the 'unfortunate consequences to which these senile fantasies have helped to lead'. He was acquitted of being an accomplice in the crime.

In giving evidence on his own behalf, de Jager said of himself only what has been related here. When he passed sentence the judge recommended that the prisoner be transferred as soon as possible to the experimental psychiatric prison which has recently been opened near Bloemfontein.

Perhaps the most surprising aspect of the whole affair, however, was the intense sympathy for de Jager which was expressed all over Lyndhurst while the trial was proceeding. One might have thought, listening to the people who spoke about the trial, that they had always dreaded and hated the power Bland Giffard had had over them, and that in attacking him the young man had acted for them all. They spoke pityingly of his frustrated ambitions; admiringly of his 'courage' and 'sincerity'. Several young girls wrote letters to him containing proposals of marriage. Several young men appeared in the streets of Lyndhurst wearing black cowboy suits with white fringes, and no one laughed at them. Everyone is looking forward eagerly to the serialization of Benny de Jager's autobiography, which will be appearing soon in an illustrated national weekly.

ANOTHER DAY

I was lying in the shade of a peach tree that grew to the side of the lawn. Behind me sprawled our house, with its broad red stoep, its white pillars and white wooden shutters. Overhead, above the thin, tapering leaves of the peach tree, was the clear sky. It was a Sunday morning: one of the vacant, interminable, never-changing Sunday mornings of childhood. My parents were out of the house, but I could hear the African servants talking idly to one another in the backyard. The air was warm; a contrasting coolness rose from the grass underneath me; in my nostrils was the faint, bitter, almond-like scent of peach leaves. Every sensation I was conscious of seemed to contribute to the wide, full stillness of the day; each was part of its calm. I held a book in my hands, but I wasn't reading it.

I was roused by a strange rumbling noise coming from the road. The noise grew louder; within the rumble I could hear the squeak of metal, the crunch of sand or gravel against the tar of the road. Drawn by curiosity, I went to the fence and looked outside.

I was shocked to see what had broken into the morning's suburban silence. The noise I had heard was that of a funeral procession. But what a funeral procession! What a cortège of mourners! What a hearse! On a flat, wooden two-wheeled barrow of the kind used to carry vegetables and coops of chickens in the market square, a metal frame had been erected, from which there hung a canopy of a few black strips of cloth. Beneath this wretched canopy, naked on the planks of the barrow, rested a small coffin. As the wheels turned, metal rims grating on the tar, the barrow shook at every joint; and the coffin on it shook too.

The coffin was a child's. It was a plain wooden box without handles or ornament of any kind. At its corners, roughly sawn, the heads of a few nails shone brightly. The child in the coffin must have been even younger than I was at the time: the box wasn't more than three feet long. Next to it, on the planks, there lay a spade.

The barrow was level with me; then it had gone by. None of the three people following it had noticed me. The man pushing the barrow was a young, strongly built African dressed in a pair of shorts and striped cotton shirt. His head was bare, and so were his feet. The calf muscles of each leg bunched as he took his strides off the balls of his feet, leaning forward slightly against the barrow. His head was lowered, and from his mouth there came a wordless, tuneless chant. Behind him walked two African women, long dresses trailing around their ankles, and fringed shawls about their shoulders and over their heads. They both clutched their shawls together with their hands in front of their mouths, so that their faces were veiled, hidden.

No one else was in the street; no one else seemed to be standing in any of the gardens to watch the procession go by. I went to the gate and began to follow them.

Groaning and rumbling, the barrow went down the road. We covered the distance of one block, a second, a third. Here and there someone working in his garden paused for a moment to stare, or an African walking up the road stopped, shook his head, and went on. No one seemed to associate me with the group. I followed under a compulsion I did not understand but could not disobey, unable to take my eyes off the powerful legs of the man pushing the barrow, the bowed heads of the women, and the light, shaking box that contained the corpse of a child younger than myself.

We passed a police station and some small shops. The road descended into a subway and passed under the railway lines. Beyond the railway the road was no longer tarred; the area was an outright slum, inhabited by poor whites and Cape coloureds, bordered by acres upon acres of the mine dumps which lay all around the outskirts of our town. The dumps were enclosed within a fierce barbed-wire fence, twelve feet high. The group with the barrow turned and followed a dusty, pitted road that ran parallel to the railway lines. Soon there were no houses around us at all. On one side were the railway lines, on the other the barbed wire and the mine dumps.

I thought I knew where we were going. About a mile farther down the road there was an African 'location', thrust down on a flat stretch of ground, where the mining company's wire curved away from the railway. However, when the group came to a fork in the road, only the two women went straight on to the location; the man pushed the barrow some way down the road to the left before halting and throwing himself down in the shade of a little camel-thorn tree that grew to the side of the road. He left the barrow with the coffin on it standing in the sun. The women were soon lost to sight in the confusion of rust-coloured, dust-coloured shacks that stretched away indistinguishably across the bare, level earth. In the strong sunlight the location looked vast but insubstantial.

Hesitantly, hearing the sound of my own footsteps on the road and watching my own shadow in front of me, I approached the man. Only when I was within a few feet of him did I look up. He had drawn himself up at my approach; he was sitting with his knees raised in front of his chest and his arms behind him, propping up his body. He smiled cheerfully at me. His teeth were white, his skin smooth, his face broad.

Over each eye there was a protuberance of bone which might have given his face an angry, lowering aspect if his expression had not been so amused. His eyes seemed to peep slyly at me under his heavy brows.

'What are you looking for?' he asked me, in Afrikaans. His voice was deep, and had an idle, teasing note to it.

I could not answer him. Yet it seemed that he knew what I wanted, and was ready to tell me all he could. He turned his head away from me and looked at the coffin, wrinkling his brow against the brightness of the sunlight beyond the shadow in which he lay.

'The little boy in there – he had a sickness in his chest. They fetch his *ouma*, the grandmother, now. Then we go to the graveyard.'

He held up a single dust-stained finger. 'I do all the work for a pound. Just one pound, and I make the coffin, and I take it where they want me to, and I dig the hole also.'

He fell silent, still regarding me from under his brows, half-threatening, half-quizzical. Then he said: 'You want to look inside? Come!' And he rose swiftly on the word.

I turned and ran. Behind me I heard the man laughing; then a scurry of footsteps in the sand. He was coming after me. Sickeningly, the earth seemed to turn across all its width, like a great, flat, pallid wheel; I could not keep my balance on it. I fell, and looked up. His smiling face was over me.

'Don't run away,' he said. His hands grasped me gently. I was sure he would never let me go. Death itself stood over me, determined to punish my curiosity by satisfying it utterly. What had happened to that other child was going to happen to me. I was going to learn all that he had learned.

I don't remember the man letting go of me, or hearing his footsteps retreating. All I knew when I opened my eyes was that the man's face was no longer between me and the sky. I did not look where he had gone. I got to my feet and took a few paces, but felt too weak and unsteady to go on. There was a ditch to the side of the road, and I crept into it. How long I lay there, with my head on my arms and my eyes closed, I do not know. When at last I stood up, I found that the man and his barrow were gone. I also found, without surprise, that having come so far I felt I must go on.

I could see the wheel tracks that the barrow had left in the sand and I began to follow them. A car passed me, with a swirl of dust at its tyres, and I saw the people in it looking at me curiously. I went on walking. To the left, the barbed-wire fence ran straight, the dumps of earth lying empty behind it. On the right, almost as bare of vegetation as the dumps, was a stretch of veld where a few piccanins were playing with a ball. The spaces around them made their figures look tiny. Then I saw the location's cemetery.

It looked much like the veld where the piccanins were playing, only its surface was more irregular, broken by innumerable little mounds of earth. There was no fence around it. From hundreds of the mounds there gleamed little points of light: reflections from the jam tins which were used to hold the flowers brought by mourners. There were only a few formal tombstones to be seen; there were more wooden crosses, some of them tilted at angles; there were many strips of corrugated iron thrust upright into the ground, with names painted on them. Some of the graves had their borders carefully marked out by small boulders laid in rows on the ground. But most of them were quite without adornment, identification, or demarcation of any kind. It was impossible to tell where each ended or began. There was not a tree, not even a bush, anywhere. Among all the low mounds and humps of earth, the people I was looking for stood out distinctly. There were three women, and the man working with a spade.

The women stood aside from the man, next to the barrow with the coffin on it. They did not seem to be weeping; merely watching and waiting. When the hole was a few feet deep – the rim of it came to the man's waist when he stood in it – he clambered out, wiped his brow, and simply picked up the coffin and carried it in his arms to the grave, holding it in front of his chest. The women cried out briefly, then were silent. The man slid the coffin, end foremost, into the grave and climbed in after it to lay it flat. A moment later he had climbed out again and had set about shovelling the earth inside the hole, working very fast.

The women waited until he had done. Then they turned and began walking towards the location, taking a short cut across the veld. The man, alone once more, pushed the empty barrow to the road, where I was standing. The going was difficult for him, among the graves, and it took him some time to draw near.

Eventually he reached the road. He blew out his breath noisily and smiled. In his deep, mocking voice he said, 'Another time.' He pointed a finger at me and shook it. 'Another day.'

I began walking home, ahead of him. All the way home I heard the rumble of the barrow behind me. At the gate of the house I stood and watched the man go past; I knew he was conscious of me, but he did not look in my direction. He did not need to. His head was lowered, from his lips came that tuneless, wordless chant I had heard before. The muscles of his legs quivered with every long stride he took.

SONIA

Behind the holiday resort were mountains – high, bare, and rock-littered, with much black soil showing through green grass; in front of it the yellow beach and the sea. The resort itself was a sprawl of peeling stucco hotels and boarding houses. Sea sand drifted up through cracks in the pavements. Little lawns and salt-stunted palm trees grew on traffic islands in the main road. A long walk, called the promenade, was raised above the beach on concrete pillars; in the middle of the promenade was a concert hall and a collection of milk bars, hot-dog stalls and amusement arcades. From the resort, trains ran frequently to Cape Town, twenty miles away; other holiday places were scattered farther down the line, at a distance of two or three miles from one another, until you came to the naval base at Simonstown.

The five of us, all schoolboys on holiday, without our parents, had the run of the place – or so we felt. We swam in the sea, we lay for hours on the beach, we ate hot dogs at odd times of day, we tried our luck in the amusement arcades, we sent Fatty Krawitz (because he was the oldest of us) into a bottle store from which he came out with three bottles of cheap Cape wine which we planted ostentatiously on the table of our room. We took the train or hitch-hiked to Cape Town, where we went to cinemas and department stores and loafed about the docks until we were driven away by uniformed officials; we explored the Cape coloured and Malay quarters of the town; we went to watch cricket at Newlands. We were easily beguiled and as easily distracted. After the small, drab mining town on the edge of the Karroo in which we all lived, everything around us was more of a novelty, more of an adventure, than we could ever bring ourselves to admit to each other. The number of people in the streets and on the beaches was a source of excitement; the sound of the sea at night would not let us rest; the persistence of the pure, thin twilight surprised us every evening, rousing obscure longings, secret melancholies, imprecise lusts.

Incessantly we looked out for girls. We schemed to get introductions to them in the sea, on the promenade, in the amusement arcades. But Sonia Ritstein we ignored, though we saw her every day and though she was not so much less good-looking than many of the girls we were eager to walk up and down with on the promenade or tried to coax into the darkness beneath it.

We ignored Sonia for no better reason than that she was the daughter of the widowed Mrs Ritstein, who ran the boarding house we were living in and whom we regarded as a figure of fun. Mrs Ritstein was a woman with a large bosom that had very little breath inside it; she conducted her business in frantic, gasping spasms of activity, when she rushed up and down the stairs, complaining about her guests to her guests, and repeatedly asking God why she went on year after year. When these spasms were over she sat torpid on the porch ('for a breath of air') or joined the guests at cards in the lounge.

Sonia was the youngest of Mrs Ritstein's children, and the only one still at home. She was a tall, slow-moving, rather heavily built girl; she had a long neck and large brown eyes, with sluggish eyelids above them; she wore her red-brown hair piled on top of her head in a loose coil. When people greeted her she flushed slightly, and moved her head back, as if there were some obstruction in her throat which she had to clear before she could answer. Her mouth was broad and somehow without definite outline; it simply seemed to lose itself in her freckled cheeks.

She took no part in running the establishment. Whenever one saw her she was carrying a book in her hand, usually with a finger thrust between its pages to mark her place. One would come across her reading in all kinds of odd corners – in one of the tiny linen rooms, for example, or even, between meals, in the deserted dining room. When she was disturbed she would look up, surprised and guilty, stretching her long neck, and would put the book down on her lap. There was something almost abject in her gaze and manner at these times, as if she wished to escape not merely from the intruder, but also from the embarrassment of being reminded of her own bulky body and inert posture. She seemed to have no friends, either among the holidaymakers or the residents of the town, and when she went to change her books at the little local library, or took her towel and costume to the beach, she did so on her own. Mrs Ritstein complained to anyone who would listen, even to us, what 'a dreamer' Sonia was, how she 'always had her nose in a book', how she 'never lifted a finger to help'. We listened to these complaints without much sympathy.

Secretly, however, I had taken notice of the titles of the books Sonia carried about, and had been much impressed by them. At different times I saw her reading *The Mill on the Floss*, the short stories of Hemingway, an anthology of Elizabethan songs and sonnets, and Tennyson's *Idylls of the King*.

Poor, condemned Sonia! Before the holiday was over we were to learn what shapes her books had given to the pressures that were struggling for release and explanation within her. Just a few months later she was dead, of a tumour on the brain.

> *Haply I think on thee, and then my state,*
> *Like to the lark at break of day arising*
> *From sullen earth, sings hymns at heaven's gate.*

These words, neatly printed in ink on a piece of paper, lay on Fatty Krawitz's bread plate when we came in for lunch one afternoon.

Fatty Krawitz suspected that one of us was playing a practical joke on him. But we were all as puzzled as he was by the message, and looked around the dining room, wondering who had written it out. We didn't doubt, at first, that someone was making fun at him. Not that there was anything especially wrong with Fatty Krawitz; his nickname, which dated from his childhood, did him an injustice. He was merely plump now: a tall, round-faced, round-featured youth, very neat, almost finicky, about his appearance – particularly about his hair, which was always combed precisely away from his solemn yet untroubled brow. He was waiting for his matriculation results to be telegraphed to him by his parents in Lyndhurst. If they were what he expected them to be, he intended going to the university to take a degree in commerce, before joining his father's firm of chartered accountants. He had it all worked out, in his careful way. Fatty was the oldest of us and the most responsible, the least mischievous; we usually heeded the warnings which he uttered with an almost imperceptible stammer, when he thought we had gone far enough. He was by far the strongest swimmer of us all, I remember, and that too added to his prestige among us.

Fatty stared again at the paper, when he had finished staring around the room. 'It's poetry,' he said.

We jeered in mock admiration. 'What a brain! Fatty says it's poetry! How long did it take you to work that out, Fatty?'

'It's Shakespeare,' I said.

'How do you know it's Shakespeare?' Fatty demanded suspiciously. 'Did you write it? You trying to be funny or something?'

'I didn't write it. I just know it's Shakespeare.'

One by one we again denied responsibility for the paper. He could see, we said, that it wasn't in the hand of any of us. So Fatty called over one of the waitresses and asked her if she had seen anyone put it on his plate. She had not. Aggrieved, Fatty looked around the room once more. Sonia was not at her place that day; perhaps if she had been sitting there in her usual heavy, detached way, I wouldn't have thought of her. As it was, I said suddenly, 'It's Sonia!'

'Are you crazy?'

'It must be. Who else in this place goes around reading poetry?'

Fatty was not convinced. When we went up to our room, after the meal, there were two more papers there, one on his bed and the other on the table. The one on the table had his name on it, so that no mistake could be made about the person for whom it was written. On the first paper the scribe asked if she should compare Fatty to a summer's day; he was more lovely and more temperate. On the second she begged him to be true to her, for the world which seemed to lie before them like a land of dreams had really neither joy nor love, nor light, nor certitude, nor peace, nor help for pain.

'What the hell's going on?' Fatty demanded. 'What's it all about?'

But the others now agreed with me that Sonia must be responsible, and we urged Fatty to go and challenge her about it. Whether she had written the messages or not, we were sure we would get a laugh out of Fatty's approach to her.

We were wrong. Fatty allowed himself to be persuaded, and went off to confront Sonia, with the papers in his hand. He was away longer than we had anticipated. When he came back he seemed shaken, positively afraid, and lay on his bed staring up in silence at the ceiling. He ignored our questions, our jokes, our lewd suggestions about what had passed between them.

Eventually we fell silent. When we went down to the beach a little later, Fatty did not come with us.

After Sonia's death Fatty became convinced that she had had what he called (in a hushed tone of voice) a 'premonition', which had made her grab fiercely at what she was determined her life should offer her before it came to its end. For myself, I confess that on hearing she had died I felt an emotion almost akin to relief, a sense that something bizarre and puzzling had been explained. So *that*, I could say to myself, was why she had carried on as she had. It wasn't that I shared Fatty's belief that there was something supernatural or inexplicable about Sonia's premonition. Knowing how she had died, it seemed quite possible to me that her nerves and the cells of her brain had already, when she made her approach to Fatty, begun to undergo clandestine changes which she translated into the fervours of her feelings toward him; that the extravagance and absurdity of her behaviour were the effects of physiological lapses and proliferations which were even then taking place secretly, irreversibly, within her.

For at the age of sixteen I had seen no one of the age of sixteen behave as she did. Her passion for Fatty was announced in poetry, and poetry accompanied it throughout; but this didn't exclude a direct expression of a physical hunger or need that all of us, in spite of our brave talk together in our room and our much less brave fumblings under the piers of the promenade, found incredible, almost shocking. I think that had Sonia been simply 'poetic' in her feelings about Fatty we might have known how to react; had she been just physically forward with him we also would have had no difficulty in finding words to describe her. But that she should have been both at the same time –!

Fatty could not resist her. He couldn't resist the image of himself which Sonia presented to him. He was the man of whom all her poets had spoken. He was beautiful, he was kind, he was passionate, he was gentle, dignified and brave. She admired his swimming, his clothes, the neatness of his hair, the respect his friends had for him. She prophesied all kinds of splendid futures for him – he was to become a great politician, a famous writer, a millionaire, a holy man. When she went to Cape Town for a day with her mother, she sent him a telegram assuring him she did not go in weariness of him, nor in hope the world could show a fitter love for her. When she came back she said how like a winter had her absence been from him, the pleasure of the fleeting year; what freezings she had felt, what dark days seen. And she twined her hands around the back of his neck, looked at him with eyes made bright by pleasure and timidity, kissed him on the lips, pressed her body against his, laughed abruptly, sighed, lowered her head and rested it in the hollow of his shoulder, and broke away to look again at him from the distance of her own extended arms.

We saw this kind of thing frequently, for Sonia now spent as much time as she could in our room; and when she was there she could not keep away from Fatty, or at least from anything that belonged to Fatty. She put her head on his pillow, touched the sleeves of the pyjamas beneath it, played with the laces of the shoes she found under the bed, brushed her hair with his hairbrush and her teeth with his toothbrush. Fatty was embarrassed, of course, by all this, but he was roused, too; there came upon his face at times an expression that none of us had seen before. It was entirely adult – concentrated and yet abstracted, wondering and yet aggressive. But he remained also, throughout, a deeply puzzled boy as well. He was puzzled even by the words Sonia said to him, the lines of poetry she recited to him. He used to consult me about their meaning. ' "Trouble deaf heaven with my bootless cries," ' I remember him repeating slowly to me. 'What does that mean? What kind of cries are those?'

I explained that the word had nothing to do with boots, and Fatty nodded moodily, apparently finding that the removal of this one little source of puzzlement had helped him less than he had hoped.

The rest of the people in the boarding house were, I am sure, unaware that anything was happening to Sonia. When she was on her own her manner remained as shy and graceless as before. Only Fatty – Fatty's presence, or the thought of him when she was talking about him to the rest of us – had the power to set her free, to make her eager and self-confident. Only when she looked at him was the heaviness of her eyelids expressive of emotions or states – languor, luxury, somnolence – we could not really understand or identify but could not help being disturbed by. Only when she was with him did her walk have a fluency and ease which was more like a gathering of physical force than a dissipation of it. Despite our shock and embarrassment I think that by the end of the holiday we were all in love with Sonia, after a fashion, having seen so much of her with Fatty. He was not the only one who found it hard to resist the beauty which their intentness gave to her features when she looked at him, the pathos of her movements of surrender and submission, the strength and queer gaiety of her shamelessness.

But Fatty was the only one who had to decide what to make of, what to do with, the love which he had roused and which in his cautious way he couldn't help reciprocating. Sonia's passion presented him with a large moral problem, about which he consulted us liberally. The problem was whether or not he should 'go all the way' with Sonia. She was ready to go all the way with him; she made no secret of it, and she had a place, her own bedroom, where this could be accomplished. But Fatty hung back, not knowing if he should. Needless to say, we envied him his problem, though we never doubted that it was a real problem. Would it be right for Fatty 'to take advantage' of her, when he didn't feel about her as she felt about him? Would it be fair? Should you want to go all the way with a girl you 'really cared for'? Wouldn't you 'lose your respect' for the girl if you did? The logic of our questions indicated that it would be wrong for Fatty to sleep with Sonia if he loved her, and wrong for him to do so if he didn't. So when, if ever, would it be right? All in all, though we spent much time on them, our deliberations on the subject were not of much help to him.

Sonia had her own simple, certain answers to all these questions; she reproached Fatty, sometimes teasingly, sometimes respectfully, always gently, for his unnecessary doubts and scruples. While he hesitated, the days went by – days so crowded with sunshine and salt water, with unfamiliar sounds and faces, that each seemed interminable and yet was over too soon, over before we had done with it all that it had seemed to promise. The whole holiday lasted less than a month, though it seems much longer, even now, after so many years have passed.

For our last day we had planned a picnic on the mountainside with some girls we had met. Sonia and Fatty were to come with us, and Sonia had for once gone around the boarding house issuing orders, and overcoming her mother's objections to them, for lavish hampers to be packed for us. But, at the last moment, Fatty announced that he and Sonia would not be coming with us, after all. It needed only one look at Fatty's face for us to know why. None of us objected to his decision; more remarkably still, none of us laughed at it. We did not mention either of them all day.

The picnic was successful: we came back late, weary, sun-dazed, with our arms around our girls, dragging our empty haversacks behind us. Sonia and Fatty were in the attic room, lying together on Fatty's bed. Fatty asked us what sort of a day we had had, and we told him. There was no need for us to ask what sort of a day he and Sonia had had. Fatty was slow and solemn with pride; in everything he said he seemed to be condescending from a great distance to the rest of us. Sonia was less altered in manner than he was; she was merely calm and contented. It seemed that her poets had not deceived her, and Fatty had not disappointed her.

Sonia cried heartbrokenly on the station platform when she saw us off. The first letter from her to Fatty came when we had been back in Lyndhurst for only two days. He showed me the verse she had written at the end of it:

> *Therefore the love which us doth bind,*
> *But fate so enviously debars,*
> *Is the conjunction of the mind,*
> *And opposition of the stars.*

They continued to write to one another until her letters abruptly stopped coming. Then Fatty heard both about her illness and her death in a single letter from her mother.

Fatty is today the father of three children; he still works in the firm which he joined, as he had planned, straight after leaving the university. He deserves his nickname once again, though no one ever calls him by it. Thinking of him as he now is, and remembering Sonia's passion for him, I no longer find it so easy to believe, as I once did, that she was already ill when they met. Perhaps that was as much of a delusion as Fatty's belief that she had had a supernatural 'premonition'. The truth may be that she was just a girl with an extraordinary gift for love: a gift which she had only that one chance, during our summer holiday in her mother's boarding house, to exercise.

THROUGH THE WILDERNESS

1

I met Boaz, the Israelite, at a time when I was doing nothing. I was idle, stagnant, dead still.

This was just after my twentieth birthday, when I should have been at my most energetic, restless, and ambitious. Or so I used to tell myself. Instead, I was stuck fast, as if forever, in my home town, Lyndhurst, in South Africa. Not long before I had excitedly made my plans to go to Europe, to go to Israel, to travel as far as I could into the waiting world. But having been compelled to cancel those plans just a few days before I had been due to leave, I remained at home, like someone in a thrall, unable to move, without sufficient energy even to want to do so.

I suppose I'm exaggerating a little when I say that I was doing nothing. There were three things which I did regularly, and which could possibly be called work. At least they were activities of a kind. I went to the hospital every day to visit my father. I took Hebrew lessons three times a week. I went once a week to the farm my father owned, to deliver rations to the 'boys' and to count the sheep.

2

The sheep-counting was something of a farce. Have you ever tried to count a flock of two hundred-odd sheep being driven in a cloud of dust from one *kraal* to another adjacent to it, through a narrow gate? Tried without being practised at it, I mean? I was town born and bred (small town, admittedly; town nevertheless). I had just spent three years at the university in Johannesburg. I was no farm boy, no cattleman, no shepherd.

Driven by two diminutive, barefooted herd boys, who waved large sticks over their heads and yelled fiercely in Tswana and Afrikaans, the sheep milled together, ran in every direction, bleated furiously, and came running in bunches through the gate, where I stood with Piet, the herd boys' father, each of us to one side. We counted them as they ran, their woolly coats quivering, their eyes ablaze with terror, their foolish, triangular mouths open. The dust they raised in the air was green and acrid, made of the dung they had dropped on previous occasions.

Invariably, at the end of each counting there was a discrepancy between the figure I had arrived at and the figure given to me by Piet. Invariably, my figure was somewhat lower than his. Each of us having announced his figure, an embarrassed pause would follow.

A question hung unspoken in that silence: Was Piet stealing the sheep? It was a question I found impossible to answer. If I was right one week in finding the total to be two hundred and twenty-five, say, then surely I was wrong the next week in finding it to be two hundred and forty-five. Or was I? What was there to stop Piet, after a larger than usual depredation, from insinuating ten or twenty of his own sheep into my father's flock when the time came for them to be counted? For he did have a small flock of his own, of which he was a most attentive keeper, about which he bargained and bickered and came to obscure arrangements with Africans on neighbouring farms. I couldn't tell his sheep from any other; they were all the same black-headed Persian type, with dusty off-white bodies; none had been branded or dyed distinctively.

Piet was gentle with me, but unyielding. He would clear his throat, breaking the silence between us; he would gesture soothingly with the hand that clutched the bowl of the small, unlit pipe he almost invariably carried. He was a slight, untalkative, middle-aged man, with a mouth pursed forward in an expression of melancholy, dogged doubt; around his mouth, on both sides, there ran two deep wrinkles, like a pair of elongated parentheses. He looked reflective, sceptical, and somehow urban; his face might have been that of a lawyer, or a petty shopkeeper perhaps, a seller of stationery and stamps. But he was a shepherd, nothing more, and his clothes were almost as ragged as those of his children. His shirt was a mere accumulation of patches; his shoes were so hard, large, and cracked, they might have been made of unseasoned timber. I was pretty sure he put on those shoes only in honour of my visits, and went around barefoot the rest of the time. On his head he wore a brown woollen cap with an implausible pompom.

'Nee, my baas,' he might say. 'Twee honderd drie en dertig.'

Two hundred and thirty-three. He had counted them, and that was his total. I had counted and got two hundred and twenty-seven. So this week the discrepancy was only six. Last week it had been nineteen. The week before it had been fourteen. What was the truth? Would I never know it? What was I going to do now?

I did what I always did: I stared hard at Piet, who met my gaze with a look of dutiful, dignified submission. Pouting, head drooping, pompom hanging forward, he waited for me to pronounce judgement. Sometimes I said we should count the sheep all over again, which we would do amid renewed dust and confusion, with results as unsatisfactory as before. More often I said that we would count them more carefully, more slowly, next time. Then we would leave, while the sheep, still protesting, would be driven out of the *kraal* and down the slope to the grazing lands.

They had more than three thousand acres to graze in, those sheep. Three thousand acres of pale grass, stunted black camel-thorn trees, and innumerable nipple-shaped, knee-high ant heaps of dried earth; the whole area being divided by wire fences into 'camps', with an iron windmill and an iron water tank in each one. You could see every windmill and tank, you could see all three thousand acres, and God knows how many hundreds of thousands of acres beyond – belonging to Pope, to Van Aswegan, to Huyssteen, to Jaap Burger, to the Lyndhurst General Mining and Exploration Company – from the farmhouse where I always parked the car. Behind the farmhouse there was a ridge of *koppies*, and the slight elevation on which the house stood was enough to give a view that stretched all the way I had come. The only irregularity on the horizon were the mine dumps of Lyndhurst, sixteen miles away. From there the white dirt road ran through one farm after another; past the ridge behind the farmhouse it was lost to sight. Out of curiosity I had once followed it beyond the farm, and had found that it arrived eventually at a miserable, shadeless huddle of iron-roofed buildings called Platkop, thirty miles further on.

It was called, for some reason, the Samarian Road. Why Samarian? What had it to do with Samaria? None of the farms along its route was named Samaria, so far as I knew.

Anyway, that was the road, that was the view, from the sagging wire fence that separated the sand of the veld from the sand of the farmhouse 'garden'. The house itself was a low iron-roofed building, whitewashed inside and out, divided into four small rooms. The only item of furniture still in it was a hatstand. A real, elaborate, varnished hatstand, with fierce antlers for hats arching out of a kind of node near the top, and two rings of wood around its lower half, to contain umbrellas. Umbrellas? In that climate? I used to go into the house to see that everything was in order. Each time I found that more whitewash had flaked from the walls and that more and more insects appeared to be occupying the place. Black and yellow striped hornets made their nests plumb against the walls, spiders spun their webs in corners, ants hoarded their food in nests between floorboards. Overhead, between the iron roof and the buckled beaver-board ceiling, I could hear faint scurryings and crepitations – birds, perhaps, or mice, were nesting there.

'Everything' was always 'in order'. The only disorder, the only visible movement in the house, was that of the motes of dust that swarmed and twinkled in columns of sunlight coming in through the windows. The walls sent off a cloud of white dust if I struck them with the palms of my hands, and I often did it, partly for the sake of seeing the dust fly, and partly for the sake of the flat, echoless sound, where no other sound was. Then I would go out. The veld always surprised me, when I came out: the house was so cramped and meagre, the veld so very large. Yet in point of life there didn't seem to be all that much to choose between them:

But, waiting around the car would be Piet and his family, and Kagisho and his family. Kagisho, the other 'boy', Piet's assistant, was many years older then Piet; he was frail and Bushman-like in appearance, with a skin that had a queer reddish or golden tint. Around them sprawled, squatted, and slept their many children. I say slept because that's what the youngest children were doing, slung in fringed shawls on their mothers' backs. I would have thought both women to have passed the childbearing age; but they obviously had not. For that matter, I would have thought Kagisho to be beyond the child-propagating age. But perhaps he had handed his wife over to Piet with the same alacrity he showed when I once heard Piet ask him to hand over the pay I had just given him.

I paid Piet and Kagisho once a month; every week each family was given so much mealie meal, so much sugar, so much tea, so much tobacco. In addition I sometimes off-loaded salt or sulphur or bonemeal for the sheep. Whether or not the sheep ever got these rations I do not know. And there were usually one or two other items that Piet had asked me to get the previous week – a bottle of cough mixture for one of his children, or some kaffircorn malt which he used to brew his own beer. I always brought the children packets of barley sugar, which each came up in turn to receive, in cupped hands. They thanked me formally for these. Once when one of them forgot to do so he was reminded by Piet, who sent the delinquent tumbling with a single, savage blow across the back of the head.

So my 'work' on the farm would be over. I'd tell Piet to expect me at the same time the next week, and get into the car. The women would smile and bob their heads, hands clutching their long skirts; the children would wave; Piet would send *groete* – greetings – to the *oubaas* – my father; Kagisho, who was always both industrious and ineffectual in the off-loading, would give a sudden start as though he too feared a blow from Piet, and hastily send his *groete*, as well, to the *oubaas*. Somewhere along the road I'd pass the sheep on the way to the particular camp they were grazing in, and I'd wave to the solitary boy herding them. And so, home.

There were just two ways of going home: one was very fast, the other very slow. It was purely a matter of mood which way I did the journey; it never made a difference to anyone else. I had no appointments to keep. When I travelled fast, my ambition was to cover the sixteen miles between the farm and the town in fifteen minutes. This was not at all easy to do on an ill-kept, corrugated dirt road, which curved zealously around every clump of thorn bushes, and which was interrupted at least half-a-dozen times by narrow cattle grids. Many of the curves were almost blind, where the thorn bushes grew particularly thickly, and all of them were made trickier by the drifts of sand at their sides. I had some narrow escapes on that road, and so did the oncoming motorists I sometimes found myself confronting in a cloud of dust, to the sound of blaring, astonished horns and skidding tyres.

When I went slowly I'd drive as slowly as I could in top gear, until the car began to stall, then I'd change down into second and do the same; then the same in first. I'd accelerate to seventy miles an hour, switch off the ignition, and see how far the car would go before coming to a halt. I would turn the car round so that it faced the farm again, put it into reverse, and drive backwards for a couple of miles. Many times I simply stopped the car at the side of the road, walked a little way into the veld, and lay down on the sand and tufts of grass, shielding my eyes from the sun and looking straight up into the blue sky until it swam with a multitude of tiny, squirming shapes that were dark and bright at the same time. Or I stared at a particular thorn bush, trying to impress it so firmly on my mind that I would be able to visualize it in every detail an hour later, when I would be back in Lyndhurst. But I found that usually it was something nearby that I hadn't been concentrating on, seeing only out of the corner of my eye, which I would really remember: the knobbly, hard surface of an ant heap, or a particular tuft of grass, or the bland, flat face of a locust, its eyes like tiny beads pasted on, which had jumped on to my trouser leg.

I was seldom disturbed by anything other than insects. A car, or some solitary African on foot or on a bicycle, might pass on the road; I dare say they were curious about the empty car standing on the roadside, but insufficiently so ever to come and look for me. I was on my own, surrounded by a flat, blank vacancy of sky and veld, a world of pale colours and strong light. It was abysmally dull, null, motionless, limitless, meaningless.

Eventually I would drive on to meet the main tarred road, where the view opened out on the town itself: low iron roofs, which always looked black in the strong sunlight; a group of taller buildings in the town centre, also black; some trees, the same; mine dumps of green sand in a rough circle around the entire scatter of the place. I used to skirt the town, going home along a bypass road which had pairs of tram tracks running parallel to it, for some distance, before they branched off into the veld, making for no visible destination at all. Poles, no longer carrying cables, arched over the tracks. God knows when they had been laid down, and with what expectations. The expectations had clearly not been fulfilled, but the tracks and poles still marched bravely and aimlessly across the bare veld, under the wide sky.

3

So much for my 'work' on the farm. As for the Hebrew lessons ...

All the attempts that had been made in my childhood to teach me Hebrew had ended in failure. I had been determined that they should. For all the usual, obvious reasons. I had associated the Hebrew language with being alien, set apart, exposed; implicated in what I was convinced at an early age was a continuing, unendurable history of suffering and impotence; involved with a religion in whose rituals I could find no grace, no power, no meaning, and that had no connection I could discern with the dusty, modern mining town in South Africa in which I was growing up. I can still remember how intensely I hated the very pictures in the books from which we had been taught Hebrew. They were old books, who knew how old, and the pictures in them were ugly, small, cramped, full of thick black lines. The boys who appeared in the pictures were physically puny, dressed in skullcaps, long jackets, and grotesque knickerbockers; they had earlocks hanging from their temples; they were imprisoned in rooms that looked both overfurnished and poverty-stricken; they sat in devout, learning postures, receiving instruction from bearded rabbis or winding their phylacteries around their arms. I cannot describe the claustrophobia, the anguish of embarrassment and distaste, they roused in me. Was I learning Hebrew to become like one of those boys? Was that the prize? I would sooner have died.

So I hadn't learned much more than the script and a handful of words and constructions in all the years I attended, or failed to attend, the classes conducted in the synagogue hall by Mr Saltzmann, the local community's ritual slaughterer, ritual circumciser, and instructor to the youth. I had never learned to understand the prayers that I heard sung, muttered, or sighed in the synagogue. I had never read any of the volumes in Hebrew that filled the bottom row of the big bookcase in our living room: the Bible and commentaries on the Bible, the works of various poets and historians in modern Hebrew. Those books, imposingly bound in imitation leather, and in a peculiarly hairy green cloth, and in multi-coloured marbled boards, were my parents', never mine.

Yet – or hence – here I was, a Zionist now, learning Hebrew once again. And what was more, learning it from the same Mr Saltzmann who had tried so hard to teach it to me in my childhood. Three times a week we sat at the big table in the dining room, surrounded by sideboards with mahogany roses worked all over them, mirrors in heavy frames, a clock in a glass and mahogany case five feet tall, complete with pendulum, which unfortunately did not work. When we looked up from our books we stared into a marble fireplace, and a mantel that incorporated a melancholy lithograph of three sheepdogs in a hut somewhere in Scotland. One could tell that the hut was in Scotland because the largest of the dogs was standing guard over a plaid and a tam-o'-shanter, presumably the property of the shepherd, who was nowhere to be seen. His absence lent a touch of drama to the picture which it otherwise sadly lacked.

Inevitably, in these surroundings, so intimately familiar to me that in recollection they seem to belong to an inner world of dream rather than to any external world of fact, I got to know Mr Saltzmann far better than I ever had as a child. With his bitten nails, his lined brow, his shoulders of unequal height, his unexpectedly strong head of wavy, silver hair, his pallid skin, he looked exactly as he had years before. Then I had thought of him only as a threat and a bore; now I came to know him as an assiduous reader of newspapers, as a rather dissatisfied husband and family man, as a small-scale speculator in real estate, as an enthusiast for certain finer points of Hebrew grammar. We discussed, in a desultory, subdued way, such topics as the meaning of life, the prospects of an afterlife, the future of the State of Israel, and the relation between science and religion. On all these subjects I thought Mr Saltzmann surprisingly cautious, in view of the position he held in the community. He did not seem to know just where he stood. Yet I did not feel it would have been right to accuse him of insincerity when he led the prayers in synagogue, or when he cut the throats of chickens, cattle, and sheep in the ritually prescribed manner. Far from it. In holding fast to his orthodoxy Mr Saltzmann seemed to me as sincere and single-minded about what he was doing as a man washed overboard in the middle of the ocean would be in clutching at a spar. If you were to be so heartless as to ask such a man if he 'believed' in his spar, you would get the same kind of answer that Mr Saltzmann gave to me. What else was there? Why throw it away? Who can be so choosy?

But we didn't spend all our time in conversation; we did pay some attention to our books. The book we used chiefly had been published by the Zionist Organization of America, and was as modern and secular as it possibly could have been. In simple Hebrew it described the adventures of the family Cohen, who sailed one day on a ship to Palestine, and who were so enchanted by everything they saw that they decided to settle there without further ado. On the whole these Cohens were a devoted but charmless family, easily excited into fits of enthusiasm and much given to explaining things to one another. By the end of the book I was up to everything they did and said; I understood their laborious conversations and their few, feeble jokes. In fact, by the time I'd finished the book I was beginning to fancy that already I knew more about the Hebrew language than the poor Cohens ever would; that I had already grasped something of its inner spirit, of its harshness, its archaic severity and compression, its lack of sinuosity, all of which were illustrated for me not just in its sounds and constructions but even in its epigraphy.

Privately, without telling Mr Saltzmann, I took some of the Hebrew books from their place in the bookshelf, and worked through various passages that I found I could cope with. The easiest passages for me to read, all questions of grammar aside, were in the Bible, both because the stories I chose were already familiar to me, and because I could always check my understanding of what I'd read against the English version. One of the first of the tales I went through in this way, reading the Hebrew and English in alternation, was that in which God 'proved' Abraham by asking of him the sacrifice of 'his son, his only son, whom he loved, even Isaac', before accepting the sacrifice of a ram caught in a thicket instead. 'And afterwards they rose up and went together to Beersheba; and Abraham dwelt in Beersheba.'

It was a curious experience to read it all in the original Hebrew for the first time, knowing that in Beersheba, which I had hoped to have visited by that time, there once again dwelt a Hebrew-speaking people who, like myself, were reputed to be descended from the tribe of Abraham and Isaac. How long, and in how many places, everything had been going on: fathers, sons, death, sheep, thorn bushes, the lot.

4

'And Abraham expired and died in a good old age, an old man and full of years; and was gathered unto his people. And Isaac and Ishmael his sons buried him in the cave of Machpelah, in the field of Ephron …'

Well, it hadn't been quite like that. My father hadn't died. Modern medical science, personified by Dr Friedenberg and his colleagues, had seen to that. Nor was he all that old. He had in fact only just retired from work. Three months previously, seeing that none of his sons showed any interest in it, he had sold the cattle-feed plant he had established in the town many years before. Which, as everyone said, was a blessing, in view of what happened to him.

What happened to him, firstly, was that he woke one morning with a stomach ache. This wasn't altogether unusual; he was both choleric and dyspeptic by temperament. He dosed himself liberally with milk of magnesia, wandered about the house in dressing gown and pyjamas, complaining to anyone who would listen to him about how rotten he was feeling, and then went to bed. Before driving into town that morning I went into his bedroom and asked if there was anything I could do for him. He answered with a peremptory 'No!' The curtains were drawn against the rays of the sun, but every corner of the room was irradiated with a faint yellow light that seemed more baffling to the eye than darkness itself. He had some kind of antiquated air-conditioning outfit in his room, a box-like affair the size of a small refrigerator, which rattled and wheezed and produced no cool air at all, so far as I could judge. The noise was distracting; his irritability was embarrassing; his illness was obviously not serious. I left him and went into town. My final exams at the university were a couple of weeks behind me, and my departure for Israel was booked for a few days ahead. I was a busy man, then; or felt myself to be one.

When I came back I found our family doctor in my father's room. There was a smell of disinfectant in the air. When I greeted my father there was no answer; he lay on his back with his head turned aside. I leaned over him and saw something glittering in the tiny hollow of bone next to his eye. His face contracted and he groaned; that bright spot shivered and disappeared. Only then did I realize it had been a tear.

The doctor had been putting his things into his case; he beckoned my mother and me to follow him out of the room. In the passage he said, 'I've given him something to ease the pain. He should settle down.' He added in a puzzled tone, 'It's the intensity of the pain that I don't like. If he isn't much better by tonight he'll have to go into hospital. For observation.'

The pain hadn't eased by evening; it had become far worse. His temperature had risen sharply; his groans rang through the house; he hardly knew where he was. He asked for water, for the doctor, for more blankets, for fewer blankets, for the air conditioner to be turned on, for it to be turned off. Under a grey bristle of beard his face was twisted into a new shape, his eyes shone with a light I had never seen in them before. The previous day he had been a trim, fit, firm-fleshed man just past middle age, no more, vigorous in his movements, pugnacious in his expression, quick in his glances. And even in the morning he had appeared to be, at worst, an unwell, irritable old man indulging himself in a sense of grievance against the unreliability of his own body. But now, within a matter of hours, he had become a tormented stranger, other than himself, other to himself. What one saw in his eyes was not so much pain or fear as a stark incredulous glare of interrogation.

For what seemed minutes on end that glare would be fixed on one point or another in his room; then he would heave up in the bed, his lips uttering sounds, sighs, non-words; he would fall back into brief, uneasy snatches of sleep.

The doctor came again at sunset, and phoned immediately for an ambulance. When it came the patient was wheeled down the garden path on a stretcher, put in the back of the cumbersome vehicle and driven away. Some of our neighbours and the people across the road stood at their gates and watched the spectacle, enjoying to the utmost the solemnity of it all.

Dr Friedenberg was artless, and conscientious. Born and bred in Lyndhurst, trained in Cape Town, he was a stalwart, square-shouldered man, whose ears had suffered much damage as a result of his prowess, during his medical student years, as a rugby lock-forward. When we stood together on the pavement his troubled face loomed many inches above mine in the dying light. He made no pretence at being omniscient. He confessed he was very puzzled. He said he was going to call in the town's one specialist physician immediately, for a consultation. Then they might have to call on the town's one specialist surgeon. Would I and my mother be at the hospital later that evening? I said I would be, and he walked away with his rolling rugby-player's stride to his car. I remember finding the purposefulness of that walk of his absurdly comforting.

My father was operated on early the next morning. At about eleven that night we were called to what proved to be the first of a series of vigils in anticipation of his death. Later he was operated on a second time, and a third; each operation being the result of a crisis, and each in turn producing other crises. There were vigils at midday, at night, in the dead hours of pre-dawn. The hospital was most punctilious in summoning us each time they believed him to be on the point of dying. But there was nothing we could do, once we were there, except sit about interminably in one waiting room or another, or loiter up and down night-empty corridors, looking at the funereal vases of flowers that stood in front of every door.

When we were allowed into his room we witnessed deliriums, bouts of shuddering that looked violent enough to shake his joints apart, prolonged, sunken spells of nausea, when the expression on his unmoving, strangely averted features made one think his flesh had turned in disgust from itself. One night he choked and choked while the nurses spooned from his throat the mucus in which he appeared literally to be drowning. Apparatus of various kinds – stands, tubes, clamps, bottles of blood and saline fluid, oxygen cylinders of great weight in metal cradles – constantly stood or hung about his bed. You might have thought some sort of complicated industrial process was taking place, without which he could not die. A faint smell of suppuration came from his dressings. On his best days, when he wasn't totally unconscious or conscious only of pain and nausea, his hands wandered over the bedclothes, his lips constantly muttered meaningless words. The gaze of his eyes was sightless, turned inward; the interrogation that had been in them was quenched. His nose seemed to grow in length, but everything else about him shrank from day to day, his arms in particular taking on an oddly slight, boyish, negligible appearance. The doctors and the nurses made no secret of their surprise that he was not dead.

He had never been so seriously ill before, and what had happened to him was as shockingly unexpected to us as if he had been the victim of some savage accident. Yet we also had to contend, day after day, then week after week, with the torment of slowness, doubt, and anticipation. During that time I came to think of his death as the true end of his life in a sense that had simply never occurred to me before: death was life's goal, its only certain aim and intention, it was the destination for the sake of which the journey was taken. It was not an unfortunate flaw in nature's arrangements, an institution open to improvement, an arbitrary, unnecessary interruption of life; it was not the last, most deplorable accident we would all have to endure. There was nothing arbitrary or accidental about it. My father's life had been a ceaseless, unknowing, unswerving trek towards these hideous days and hours; they were the summation of his life as well as its undoing. He had moved through time as through a landscape, distracted by a thousand moods, experiences, possessions, achievements, memories, but always, unfalteringly, in one direction only, in this direction. And as with him, so with everyone else who lived, or had ever lived, or ever would. So many deaths already! So many still to die!

Could any discoveries or revelations have been more commonplace? Indeed, no. That was just the point. That was precisely the thought which produced in me a kind of vertigo, associated in my mind with the long, darkly glistening, strictly regular corridors of the hospital. Afterwards, it was the only recollection I had of the stress within my body of shock, pity, or fear.

I had of course cancelled my flight to Israel; I couldn't leave in such circumstances. My departure had been put off indefinitely. I no longer gave it a thought. I could remember how eager I had been to leave home, to travel, to see new places, meet new people, and do new work. But I could no longer remember why I had wanted any of these things, I couldn't find my way back to wanting them.

5

It was then that I met Boaz, the Israelite. I found him on the farm. He came to the car as soon as I arrived one day, and asked if he could speak to me when I had finished what I had come to do.

The first thing you saw when you looked at Boaz was his blind eye. It was swollen, glaucous, without iris or pupil, always open. Its size and fixity were startling, even horrifying. What was more startling still, however, was your realization that while you had been staring at the dead, sightless orb, *he* had been regarding you, unobserved as it were, with his good eye. That one was small, yellow, lively, set under a wrinkled lid.

His head was shaven, his skin was drawn tight against the bones of his face, and lights shone in glints from its darkness. His body was painfully thin, melodramatically so, as if he had willed it to be like that in order to point some obscure yet incontrovertible moral. I wouldn't care to guess his age: he could have been anything between forty and sixty, perhaps more. His clothes were as ragged as those of any other farm African. When he walked it was with odd, stiff, elongated strides; when he stood still, he held himself with an almost soldierly uprightness.

His air of patience was indistinguishable, somehow, from confidence, as he waited near the car, not moving from it, while I went about my business. I had asked him to tell me at once what he wanted; but he had said no, he would rather wait to talk to me, it would be better. He wanted to talk to me alone – 'apart' was the word he used. Puzzled, curious, a little taken aback, I asked Piet, when we were a little distance from the car, who the stranger was; but all Piet would say was that his name was Boaz, that he had arrived on the farm a few days previously, and that he was some kind of preacher. He didn't know any more, Piet insisted, than that.

I'd arrived later than usual that afternoon, and I was more than usually conscientious about the sheep-counting. So by the time we were finished the sun was low in the west, red growing larger; around it were gathering the clouds that invariably appeared in the western corner of the horizon at that hour, after even the most cloudless days. Those clouds, together with the dust that was always in the air, the flat openness of the country, and the strength of the sun, all combined to produce the most spectacular sunsets, day after day: immense, silent, rapid combustions that flared violently into colour and darkened simultaneously. It always seemed suddenly that you became aware that the colours had been consumed and that only the darkness remained; that the day was over, it would soon be full night.

My conversation with Boaz lasted longer than I had expected it to, though the request he actually had to make of me was simple enough. All he wanted, he said, speaking to me in Afrikaans, was my permission to live for a time on the farm, in one of the huts that neither Piet nor Kagisho used. He was an Israelite, Boaz told me. He was a preacher. He travelled about the country on foot, carrying his message to all who would listen. The destination of each of his journeys, he said, became known to him only after he had arrived at it. After each departure he knew that it had been right for him to move on again. Now he was here, having come from Lyndhurst along the Samarian Road; and here, it had been decided, was where he should stay.

An Israelite! Nothing less! Would he tell me who the Israelites were? He did so, at some length. Later I was to look up old newspaper files covering some of the events of which he had spoken. The facts he gave me were accurate enough. About half a century before, under the leadership of a certain Enoch Mgijima, one of the separatist African religious sects had rejected the New Testament as a white man's fiction and 'returned' to the worship of the one God of Israel. Inspired by its prophet the sect grew enormously in numbers and influence among the Africans in the bigger cities, until Mgijima called on his followers to gather at a village called Bulhoek, in order to celebrate the Passover. Several thousand obeyed him, coming together to feast and to pray for the coming of the Messiah. Days passed. Eventually the authorities told the people to move. They refused. One morning detachments of armed police arrived and ordered them to leave immediately. Instead of dispersing, the Israelites tried to attack the police who opened fire at close range. Hundreds were shot down. Those who survived fled or were arrested. Mgijima disappeared. Thereafter the movement went out of sight, was lost to any public record. However, some of the survivors of the Bulhoek massacre continued to meet as they had always done, in tiny, secret conventicles in the larger cities. It was from one of these that Boaz had come.

While he had been telling his story, we had left the car and walked a little way into the veld. Insects whirred out of the tussocks of grass at our feet; a single bird gave a melancholy, repeated whistle; I heard the voices of children from the huts, and in the distance the bleating of the sheep as they went down to graze. A faint evening breeze had sprung up. The blaze in the west was as fierce as it was remote.

His parents, Boaz went on, had been Israelites. They had taken him to their meetings, they had read the Bible to him every morning and evening, they had forbidden him to eat pork. But he had not been interested in their religion. He had wanted to be like all the other children who ran about in the streets and whose parents did not care what they did, or what they believed in, or what they ate. He left home as soon as he could, when he had been fourteen. He had had many jobs, of all kinds, in many places. He did not go home until years and years had passed. Then he heard one day that his father had died, and he decided he should go back, in order to comfort his mother.

During his first night at home he had a dream. He did not see God in his dream, for God could not be seen, but he heard Him.

192

Everything was still and empty in the dream, and out of the stillness God spoke to him as if he were Joshua, saying, 'The book of the law shall not depart out of thy mouth; but thou shalt meditate therein day and night that thou may do all that is written therein. Have I not commanded thee? Be strong and of a good courage; be not afraid neither be thou dismayed: for the Lord thy God is with thee whithersoever thou goest.' He woke, and knew that he had been chosen. He was a chosen man among those chosen people.

'Like I choose this stone,' Boaz said, stooping to pick up a faintly translucent pebble, and holding it out to me on the palm of his hand.

It was a kind that was common enough around Lyndhurst: irregular in shape, smooth to the touch, brown in colour, darkening inward from its shining surface, so that you could see some way into it, rather as with a lump of resin. I knew such stones to be volcanic in origin, like the diamonds that were mined in Lyndhurst. It lay in his hand, its dim light sealed eternally within it.

'Like this stone,' he went on calmly, not at all like a man putting forward a paradox, 'chooses me.'

He brought it closer to his good eye, bending his head over it. 'You think this stone is dead?' he asked me. 'You think it's here for nothing? No, never. It can't move, but it can wait for me, lying here, while all my life I've been coming nearer and nearer to it. You understand? Now I pick it up, and hold it, and look at it. See how it shines! Perhaps it speaks and sings also, only we can't hear it. But God can. Imagine! Imagine!' he repeated fervently, putting the stone to his ear. Then he held it to mine, his clenched hand against my temple.

I could hear only the blurred, small sounds of the evening breeze, nudging at intervals against me, on its journey across the empty country. I did not speak, but Boaz dropped his arm and looked down once more at the stone. With a jerk of his arm he flung it from him. We watched it fly through the air, a fast-moving, diminishing speck that fell out of sight, somewhere beyond the double track that ran down from the farmhouse.

'So it's gone,' I said.

'Gone from us,' he corrected me. 'It's somewhere else now, where it has to be.'

A little later I asked him if he wanted to hold 'meetings' – I couldn't think of any other word to use – while he was on the farm. He was silent. I looked up into his gaunt, disfigured face. He blinded me with his blind eye. Then he said: 'I am holding a meeting now.'

I turned and began walking back to the car, parked forlornly on the rise. He followed me. I couldn't pretend to myself that I had not been moved by his story. I had listened for the song he had said was locked in the stone. I had felt a bond with him in his absurd, wild claim that he, too, was some kind of Jew. Why shouldn't he be? Wasn't it possible that he knew more about the spirit and fervour of the Israelites than I ever would? Yes, just because he was a poor, black, skeleton-thin zealot who had been 'sent' to live in a tumbledown hut on a farm that was nowhere. Just because he was a nut, a religious loony, a dreamer, a hearer of voices, a man you could do nothing with.

But all he had asked from me was permission to stay on the farm. It was easy for me to tell him that he could move into one of the mud-walled, iron-roofed huts that stood in a group some way behind the farmhouse. 'But I don't want any trouble,' I said. 'Not with Piet, not with anyone. Do you understand?'

He held me in the disjunction of his stare or stares before assuring me that there would be no trouble.

6

During the first few weeks that followed, Boaz was as good as his word. When I went out to the farm Piet and Kagisho, who seemed proud to have Boaz living with them, told me that he spent a lot of time praying, and that he preached sometimes to them and to Africans from the neighbouring farms. On these visits Boaz himself invariably made a point of coming to see me, after I had finished with the others. He never asked me for food or money: presumably the others gave him the little he needed.

What he did ask for, however, during our early conversations, was information. Information about the Jews: he wanted to know what I could tell him about the Jewish dietary laws, about the festivals, about the liturgy, about the dispersion of the Jews to all the countries of the world, about Zionism and the State of Israel. Information about myself: he wanted to know who I was, what I was doing with myself, what I had done before he had met me, what I planned to do with my life. Information about current events, which he interpreted in ways I could not follow, according to various texts from the Bible. I answered all his questions as frankly as I could, and he listened carefully. We talked at the car, or in the car, or in the deserted house, or walking about the veld as we had the first time. He was always eager and exalted in his manner; but he was always polite and firm as well. Sometimes when he found himself at a loss for a word his lips would tremble, as if at the strain of containing the force momentarily pent up within him; but there was nothing swooning, babbling, hysterical, or ranting about him, even when he was at his most intense. He was utterly humourless, and utterly direct. He made less of the difference in colour between us – and all the other differences it meant – than any other African I had ever met. That he believed in an omnipresent God and I did not was the only difference between us that mattered at all in his eyes. Or eye, rather.

It was after we had had three or four such conversations that Boaz unexpectedly told me one day that he now knew why he had been 'sent' to the farm. It was his task to convert me to a belief in God. He had been 'chosen' to do so.

195

'Oh no!' I remember exclaiming absurdly, as if he had just broken an item of bad news to me.

'Yes, I will do it with God's help,' he answered. 'You will rejoice when it has been done.'

We were standing where we had stood several times before, on the rise near the car; the sunset was once again blazing away on our right. But in the week that had passed since I had last seen him there had been a brief, fierce, dust-laden blast of wind from the direction where the sun was setting; and it was now much cooler than it had been. Winter was beginning. Boaz had buttoned his threadbare jacket and turned up the lapels. He waited for my response. I could see that he, at any rate, was already rejoicing in what he was to accomplish.

'No,' I said again. 'No, Boaz. You must leave me alone.'

'How can I?' he asked. 'You are not alone. You never have been.'

The next time I went out to the farm Piet said to me, with a curious, sideways, lingering glance quite unlike any I had previously had from him, that Boaz was 'always praying for the baas'.

When we returned from the *kraal* I could see Boaz waiting for me near the car, as he always did. I didn't know whether to avoid him altogether; or to humour him, to pretend that he had succeeded, in the hope that he would leave me alone, leave the farm, thinking his duty done. I could simply tell him to go, to get out, that the permission I'd given him to stay on the farm was withdrawn. Or should I say to him that he would never, never get me to recognize his God, no matter how passionately he prayed for me, or tried to get me to pray with him? That even if there was a God I was by nature deaf to him, blind to him, insensible to his touch on me?

In the end I tried all these ways of dealing with Boaz, as well as another that took me profoundly by surprise, and with which I persisted far longer than I had with any of the others. I tried to believe, as Boaz wanted me to, in a God of life and death, the God my ancestors had believed in through their thousands of years of history; a God who was present in Lyndhurst or on the farm; who cared whether my father recovered from his illness or did not, and who had his reasons for prolonging his life or ending it, as he had with the lives of all other men; a God who would sustain me in my own life, and in the knowledge of whom I would find the purpose and the sense of ultimate value I needed. I tried to pray, I tried to read as much of the Bible as I could in Hebrew and English, I went to the synagogue on Friday evenings and Saturday mornings, I tried to pretend or imagine that I did already believe, in the hope that the genuine belief would follow.

Boaz was not the only one who helped me during this period of trial. Though I did not tell Mr Saltzmann about Boaz, or about what he was trying to do for me, or about what I was trying to do for myself, he must have found my mood or attitude more sympathetic than it had previously been. At any rate, our lessons were soon being neglected more than ever before; and Mr Saltzmann revealed a kind of ironic ardour that he had previously hidden from me. He swayed in his chair, he blew his nose, he made his points in the air with an extended, startled forefinger; he tipped his hat forward with a flick from behind, so that its brim was low over his forehead, and thrust it back to run his fingers through his hair; he spoke of Jerusalem and Babylon and the Vilna Gaon, of Auschwitz, of Isaiah, and the Baal Shem Tov. If Boaz spoke most often of God's power, seeing it figured forth as much in the decisions and acts of every day as in the pageant of nature's cruder effects that was constantly displayed between our bald stretch of earth and the sky above, Mr Saltzmann talked more of God's justice and mercy. He spoke of how unthinkable it was that everything men and women had always had to endure should go unrecorded, unnoticed, unrecompensed, for age after age, empire after empire, life after life; of how inconceivable it was that his, Mr Saltzmann's, demand for justice had no connection with the innermost workings of history, with the intentions of the universe, with the final nature of reality.

In his way Mr Saltzmann, too, was impressive. But I admit his words had less effect on me, when I was in his presence, than those of Boaz: partly because Mr Saltzmann was so much more familiar to me, and so much less fanatical, but mostly because it was Boaz who, after all, had declared my conversion to be his mission. 'Why *me*?' I asked him, more than once, and he invariably answered me, with all passion and sincerity, 'We have been chosen to choose each other. We belong to the people of Israel.' I could not get beyond that conviction, beneath it, over it. 'Is he still praying for me?' I asked Piet once or twice, and he answered me with an air of unsmiling rebuke, 'Always'.

So I went back and forth between Mr Saltzmann in Lyndhurst and Boaz on the farm; often I went out to the farm when I had no business there other than to see Boaz. I made no attempt to bring the two believers together. I felt, almost superstitiously, that I could do so only if I had brought them together within myself; only if through them I had arrived at a comprehension that would make my acquaintance with them both, at that particular time in my life, an illustration of the necessary principles of our shared existence. There were times when I told myself that I was doing no more than studying them as specimens, or that I was practising some kind of hoax on them, or that I was kindly doing them a favour in pretending to be interested in their preposterous beliefs. Yet even when I said such things to myself I remained convinced that if I ever let guilt, embarrassment, or my own ironies inhibit me from what I was doing, I would always regret it, I would always believe that I had let slip an extraordinary chance which would never recur.

Invariably, every day, I still called in at the hospital. To the astonishment of the doctors my father had plainly begun to recover; Dr Friedenberg had finally summoned up the courage to say, 'I think we'll soon be able to say that he's out of danger.' In all, four months were to pass before he emerged from the hospital.

7

Usually when I went to see him he still lay silent on the bed, with an expression on his face that was remote, abstracted, almost aristocratic in its detachment and insubstantiality. However, he was emerging from the utter seclusion of his illness; that seemed clearer to me with every visit I made. One day when he asked me what was happening on the farm, I began to tell him about Boaz. I described how I had found him on the farm, and how he had spoken to me, and what he looked like; I repeated what I had learned from him about the Israelite sect, and about his own life. I tried also to say something about the nature of Boaz's belief in God: how absolute it was, and how direct; how he saw God's purposes plainly written everywhere; how he believed himself to have been chosen by God and yet at liberty to deny his chosen-ness, in a world in which everything was foreknown yet undetermined.

My voice and manner must have shown my father that Boaz had become much more to me than a freak about whom I could tell funny stories. But he made no comment on what I had said. We sat in silence; then he turned over on his side and closed his eyes. I waited for a few minutes before creeping out of the room.

The next time I went to see him I had hardly come into the room before he asked me, with something of his old abruptness of manner, 'Have you been to the farm? Have you told that man to go?'

'What man?'

'The one you told me about. The one who calls himself an Israelite. He must go at once. I don't want him there. I don't want him on my place.'

'Why? What's the matter? What have you got against him, all of a sudden?'

I didn't get a direct reply. After some minutes, however, he began to ramble in a disconnected yet obsessive way about 'that man who calls himself an Israelite'. His voice was so low that I had to strain to hear him; his words were interspersed with the louder sounds of his breathing, or with spells when he merely moved his lips without producing any sounds. The incoherent craziness of what he was saying was made more painful by the physical effort that went into it, and by the earnestness with which he searched my face for a reaction to his words.

That man who called himself an Israelite, he said, was responsible for his illness. He was a usurper, a demon, an evil spirit. He wanted him to die. He came to take what wasn't his. He had to be driven away. At once. Couldn't I have seen it? How could I have let him stay there for so long? What had I thought I was doing? Hadn't I understood that it was a matter of life and death? That man was a *malakh ha-movess*, an angel of death. He was waiting to finish his work, he would stay there as long as he was allowed to. But I could drive him away if I really wanted to. Unless I was in league with him and was also waiting for him to finish what he had come to do ...

So he went on, interminably. It was pathetic, tedious, unnerving. His eyes, filled with fear and reproach, would not leave mine. I tried to soothe and reassure him; but when he finally fell silent it was not, I felt, because I had succeeded but simply because he was too fatigued to go on. He beckoned me to come closer, and grasped my hand; his touch was hot and dry. 'You must also take care,' he said. 'You mustn't think it'll be different for you. You understand? You won't escape either. When he's finished with me then it'll be your turn.'

'Don't worry,' I interrupted him. 'I understand. You must rest now. Everything will be all right. I'll do what you want me to do.'

He lay on his back, his nose raised towards the ceiling, his mouth pinched beneath it. His hands were on his breast, rising and falling with every breath he took. Once again I sat by the side of the bed until he had sunk into a doze.

Outside the hospital the afternoon air was tepid. Shadows stretched over dusty lawns and dejected beds of flowers. In the road beyond the hospital grounds was a war memorial: an incised concrete slab, surrounded by steps, chains, cast-iron rifles stacked in threes. The unreality of my father's words infected everything around me, everything I thought of. Yet I felt that my eyes had been opened again after too long a lapse. Streets and buildings were nothing more than forms of a common inertness; my thoughts nothing more than forms of delusion. What kind of imbecile, self-indulgent credulity or conceit had been keeping me going between Boaz and Mr Saltzmann these last few weeks? In what way were my superstitious hopes or expectations better founded than my father's fears? He at least had the excuse of having been weakened almost to the point of death by his illness; whereas I had done no more than watch him struggle.

Because my car was parked facing towards town, away from home, I drove in that direction. It was a Saturday afternoon; the shops were closed and the streets were more than usually empty. No one was about in the Market Square, except for a group of youths sitting on their motorbikes, gunning their engines and shouting at one another, going nowhere. I turned to the right: more closed shops, a bridge over some railway lines. A little further on was the fence around an abandoned mine, and then streets of low, iron-roofed houses. A few more minutes, a few more turns, and they were behind me. The town was behind me, though the mine dumps still straggled alongside the road for some distance. I came to the crossing from which the Samarian Road ran off to one side, and I left the main road to join it. It seemed that I was going to the farm.

Why not? Once more I went along the dreary, winding, familiar route. If town had been emptier than usual, the road was busier. Several family parties had chosen to go along it for their Saturday afternoon outings. Now their cars were parked at various unremarkable spots along the road. The adults sat just outside the cars, listening on portable radios to commentaries on the big rugby matches; the children ran about in the veld, jumping on or off the ant heaps, or playing hide-and-seek in the scrub.

By the time I reached the farm I'd left behind the last of these groups. Once through the cattle grid, the road ran straight for a mile or so, then swerved a little to begin the short ascent to the farmhouse and the *koppies* behind. From a distance the house looked no more substantial than a box, with the lines of the *kraals* and outbuildings scratched around it. The huts where Piet and the others lived were out of sight, hidden behind their shelter of thorn bushes.

I pulled up the car in front of the house. No one came to greet me. I didn't expect anyone to come. I hadn't said that I would be paying a visit to the farm that day, so even if the car had been seen approaching along the road, it would have been taken to be someone merely passing through on his way to Platkop or the farms beyond. I sat in the car for a little while, listening to the ticking noises made by the engine as it cooled. Nothing moved about me. I could hear no other sound. Eventually I opened the door and stepped outside.

It was only when I was crossing the bare space between the house and the grove of thorn bushes some distance behind it that I realized why I was there. I had come to tell Boaz that he had failed. He was welcome to stay on the farm or to leave it, as he wished. But I no longer had anything to say to him or any interest in listening to what he had to say to me.

8

The ground between the thorn bushes had been turned into soft sand by the coming and going of the people who lived there. So my footsteps made no sound as I approached. The first that was known of my presence was when one of the yellow, long-tailed dogs which were always hanging around the place got to its feet and ran forward, barking loudly. By then I had already come upon the congregation gathered in front of the hut which Boaz had taken for himself.

About a dozen people were there, apart from Piet and Kagisho and their families. I knew none of the other drab, raggedly dressed, undersized men and women, farm labourers and their wives, who were squatting on the ground. In front of them stood Piet, with a Bible in one hand and in the other a long stick or stave surmounted by a Star of David plaited out of twigs. Next to him, on an iron bedstead, his body covered by a confusion of dirty blankets, lay Boaz. The sight of such a bed dragged out into the open air, exposed to the sunlight, was somehow in itself almost as shocking or unnatural as Boaz's appearance.

He looked very ill indeed, like a dying man. His face was grey, small, annulled, lightless. His lips were parted. He was totally unconscious; the only person there who was unaware that I had come. The others had turned to look at me resentfully, as an intruder, a white enemy; and hopelessly, too, as someone who had the power to stop what they were doing and send them packing, and would probably do so. Only the children, the oval whites of their eyes immense with expectation and pent-up excitement, seemed pleased by the distraction my arrival offered.

203

No one moved or spoke. The sun shone down from a great height on the sand, huddled people, huts of mud and scraps of iron, the unconscious man on the bed. Heavy shadows merged indistinguishably on the sand. The dogs sniffed cautiously at my feet and wagged their curving tails. In the silence a sheep bleated resonantly, with a kind of ferocity of protest contained in the very helplessness and tremulousness of the sound. Until then I hadn't noticed the creature, tethered by a piece of rope around its neck to a thorn tree a few yards away, on one side. It jerked its head, opened its mouth, and again the noise exploded, an astonishingly loud call or yell to come from such a small cavern of flesh and bone. The high, vibrating noise went on for longer than seemed possible, maddening in its stupidity and comprehension alike. Even while the noise rang in my ears, I found myself looking at Piet and he at me: in the look we exchanged I knew, among some other more surprising and important facts, that that clamorous sheep was not his.

I can't say for how long we stared at one another. He was bareheaded; and the unfamiliar prominence of his round, shaven skull made him look like a stranger. He took a deep breath, as if to meet a challenge, raised his stave in the air, and began to speak in a tone I had never heard from him before. He was no longer the businessman *manqué* that I had known, or the patient, slyly submissive underling, or the conscientious shepherd. Or if he was still a shepherd, it was quite another flock, which he was leading to pastures I had never seen. His voice was hectoring and defiant, his gestures bold. He had won back the attention of his audience immediately. One or two of them still glanced anxiously at me from time to time, but even they, like the others, were answering Piet's cries and exhortations with cries of their own, or with phrases that they chanted in unison until Piet silenced them with a single wave of his hand. The little congregation swayed and moaned, the people clutched at the dust with their hands or clapped them together, they sat still and tense when Piet lowered his voice to a whisper. Whenever he turned to the recumbent, motionless figure of the sick man on the bed, opening his arms wide or lifting them high into the air, his audience was utterly silent, as if waiting for the sick man himself to rise and answer the speech breaking continually above him.

I couldn't understand a word of what Piet was saying.

Not a word. He was speaking one of the African languages: to my ears it was composed entirely of clicks, trills, gutturals, deep plosives. Completely cut off from his meanings, I couldn't even tell where one word ended and another began. Yet, as in a dream, I felt that the incomprehensible sounds he was uttering were directed more specifically to me than to anyone else in his audience. The others may have forgotten about me; but I was certain that Piet had not.

As in a dream, too, foreknowledge and knowledge after the event were commingled inextricably in my mind. Each event surprised me as it took place; but once it had happened it seemed to me that it was just what I had been waiting for ever since I had come. Yes, Piet would abruptly bring his speech to an end, at a moment when no one had apparently expected him to do so. Yes, he would point at two men in the congregation, who would get hastily to their feet and go to the tethered sheep. Yes, one of them would grab it by the ears from behind and pull it back, making it rear up momentarily, before the other man knocked its hind legs off the ground. It sat grotesquely upright on its rump, with its forelegs dangling forward, its head pulled back, its throat exposed. Yes, inevitably, Piet would cross the space between himself and the pair struggling with the sheep; he would take a clasp knife from his pocket and open it; he would bring it to the animal's throat, and then, with a deft sweep, do no more than sever the rope.

The maddened animal plunged, screamed, kicked, collapsed, was dragged upright again. Once more it sat in an artificial man-like posture, its thin forelegs held up in front of it with a curiously finicking helplessness, a disgusting daintiness. It showed its even teeth, its tongue, its wide, flat nostrils. Its eyes were rolled back into its dark head. It looked like a shrunken, demented old man; the men kneeling or stooped around it, their faces clenched with absorption, were animalized.

And now?

Yes, of course, once he had done it I had known all along that he would. Piet pointed at me, with the hand in which he held the knife, and at last spoke in a language I could understand.

'You can see how sick Boaz is. This morning he fell down, and since then that is how he's been. It's his heart. So we ask God to take this sacrifice, instead, and to let our teacher live.'

Then he raised his voice, his hand still outstretched. 'Boaz has prayed for you, many days. Now you will pray for him.'

He held out the knife to me. The lamb plunged. I came towards it. Its eye was a yellow blaze of life, crossed by a black, expressionless, oblong pupil.

9

Boaz died the next morning, in the African section of the Lyndhurst General Hospital, to which I had brought him in the car. Piet had been right in his diagnosis. He had succumbed, Dr Friedenberg said, to a 'massive coronary occlusion'. So the sacrifice was in vain.

Yes, I did do what had been asked of me. Under the blade of the knife I felt something soft and thick, then a resilience which suddenly failed, and the knife entered a hollow place behind it, a vacancy. Even while I was doing it I remembered as a child cutting open a tennis ball to see what was inside: the sensations under my hand were much the same. But the cutting of the sheep's throat was followed by a heavy spout of blood, and by cries of exultation from the others that were indistinguishable from cries of grief. Their cries made me lash out in rage with the blade again. It was as though I wanted to punish that wretched beast for dying under my hand.

The others made no objections when I said I would take Boaz with me to hospital in Lyndhurst. Driving back to town, with the sick man awkwardly bundled into the back seat, I remember how consoling I found the emptiness of the countryside around me, its width, its indifference, its hard materiality. It was there, it would last. That was something to be grateful for, I felt then, not resentful of, as I had always been in the past.

I left Lyndhurst for Israel a few weeks later, carrying with me Mr Saltzmann's parting gift of a book containing the daily prayers of the Hebrew liturgy. My father had come home just before I left, though he was still confined to his bed for a month or so. During that time he arranged for a Boer by the name of Klaas Eybers to live on the farm and work it with him, on a profit-sharing basis.

He never again mentioned Boaz to me, and I did not speak of him either. Some years afterwards I learned that Piet had left the farm just after my own departure. He had gone, my father said, into 'the religion business' in one of the African townships around Lyndhurst, and had made a very good thing out of it. He had established his own church. My father had no idea what kind of rites were followed in it, but he did know that the money Piet got from his followers he invested in his ever-growing flock of sheep. He paid a fixed sum per head to continue grazing them on the farm.

LED ASTRAY

Jill Stanlake and Michael Lewin had been living together for four months. Just before meeting Lewin for the first time, at a beginning-of-term party given by one of his friends at the university, Jill had suffered a bitter disappointment. A man in her home town with whom she had been having an affair and whom she had wanted to marry had quite suddenly married someone else. He hadn't even bothered to write Jill to tell her what he had done. So Jill said she was no longer interested in love. But she was still – to her regret, she sometimes said – interested in sex. On that basis she and Lewin had made their arrangement.

They shared a small, shabbily furnished two-room flat, with kitchen and bathroom, on the ground floor of an old converted house in Hornsey. On the two floors above lived a pregnant woman with two children, who had just been abandoned by her husband. In the basement flat there lived another family, whom Jill and Lewin hardly ever saw, but only heard at times, putting out their milk bottles or emptying rubbish into the bin in the side alley of the house. The furtive, subterranean, anonymous life of that family added to the privacy of the young couple rather than detracted from it, and the misfortunes of the pregnant woman made it unlikely that she would be either prying or disapproving. So once they were in their flat, the two of them could do as they liked; their parents were far away, in Bristol and Leeds, and neither set knew of their arrangement. The house as a whole was a run-down, ramshackle place, with peeling stucco frames around its windows, all its brickwork much in need of repointing, and a sodden little garden at the back, where a few clothes lines were strung slackly between two brick walls. From the window of the bedroom Jill and Lewin shared, everything in view was dark and rectilinear – so many cubes bricked in and roofed over for people to live in, so many left open for dispirited shrubs and lawns to grow in, for other clothes lines to hang across.

Their affair was something that Lewin intended one day to look back on with pleasure, gratitude and amusement. He often gave himself pleasure now by anticipating his emotions then. He doubted that the affair would come to an end as little as he doubted that he would one day be successful. He was a research student in modern history at King's College, London, having just come down from Oxford, and was supposed to be working for his PhD on a grant he had received, but he did not intend making an academic career for himself. He was attracted by the idea of going into television, or into journalism of the superior kind. If he had had money, he might have gone to the Bar. He was, anyway, on the lookout for openings, and was sure he would find one, eventually. He claimed to despise failure, and, indeed, looked down on Jill because she had failed to marry the man she wanted to marry and had accepted as a lover someone (himself) who had told her that he didn't love her.

That was just one of the reasons he didn't even want to consider the possibility of marrying Jill. Other reasons were his youth, his poverty, the intensity of his ambitions, his uncertainty as to how he should realize them, the distress he knew his parents would feel if he were to marry a Gentile girl, and, not least, his desire simply to be a man who had had a few affairs before he finally settled down. His affair with Jill was his first; he had never actually lived with anyone before. But he had had some rather hurried, harried experiences in the past, and he flattered himself that women found him attractive. He was sturdily built and fair-haired; his face was broad, and he had greenish eyes set well apart from one another, wide cheekbones, an upturned nose, and a skin that was almost coarse in texture, though not unpleasantly so. Someone had once told Lewin, whose grandparents had come from Odessa, that he had the face of a Russian peasant. Lewin had admitted that this was probably true; but, he had added, with a characteristic sardonic slant of his pale eyebrows and a pout of his thick strong lips, though he might look like a peasant, his mind was 'all Jew'.

Jill had thought his answer vulgar. They had subsequently had an argument about it, in which Lewin had accused her of being that kind of cowardly 'liberal' who would like to improve the world by wiping out all of the distinctions and differences that make it an interesting place to live in. But they argued rarely. In fact, they lived together very placidly and both got deep pleasure from the variety and domesticity of their lovemaking. Nothing in the previous experience of either, they both said, had been anything like it. And their pleasures were made keener by the season – the coldness and darkness outside the flat, with frost gripping every unevenness of the mud of the back garden and making a kind of glittering rock out of it, with electric lights burning inside at three in the afternoon, gas fires throwing too small an area of heat around them, and draughts blowing under ill-fitting doors. Living 'in sin' with Jill, Lewin felt himself to be, in many ways, more innocent than ever before, certainly more innocent than in his ignorant, curious adolescence, or his itching, aggressive Oxford days. Yet at the same time he was often filled with an enormous, absurd pride at their lovemaking, as if he were the first man in the world ever to have done with a woman what he did with Jill, as if he had invented passion single-handed, and was thus nothing less than a benefactor to the entire human race.

Jill was a tall straight-backed girl; a secret chocolate-eater, a hoarder of string, a wrapper of parcels, a conscientious darner, an earnest essay-marker (she had just started working as an English teacher at a girls' grammar school when Lewin met her), a tidier of drawers. She was not in the least slatternly, and this was one of the things Lewin most liked about her. She spoke little, and then only in rather abrupt sentences, her words colder and more off-hand than her low voice. In repose, the set of her mouth, under a tiny upper lip, was glum but game. That suggestion of effort, of anxiety, of fear, behind her watchfulness and shy smile was what had first drawn Lewin's attention to her.

Since then he had learned that she nourished large, fierce grievances against society (with its 'double standards'), against her parents, against all churches and clergymen, most politicians, and the headmistress of the school where she taught. She declared herself to be a rebel and a feminist with a vehemence that Lewin found rather irritatingly old-fashioned, and she had once surprised him by saying that because she was a woman she knew what it was like to be a Jew, a member of an oppressed minority. Often the ferocity of her assertions amused him. It consorted so oddly with her flying hair and anxious blue eyes, her delight in chocolates and displays in shop windows, her terror of dogs and angry bus conductors, the neatness and conscientiousness with which she did her work. Having spoken briefly, once, about the man who had treated her so shabbily, she did not refer to him again, and Lewin did not ask her about him. It was none of his business. Ultimately, what she did with her life was none of his business. That was their arrangement.

One Saturday morning, Lewin was studying in the living room of the flat; Jill had gone off to do the weekend shopping. The table where Lewin sat faced the window. It was a grey, cold, windy day, and every now and again flurries of snow or sleet whirled about outside – dark in the air, white when they fell on the road or the window sill, where they soon melted. At intervals, an overcoated man or woman hurried down the pavement or a car passed, but most of the time the street was empty. A few lights were on in the houses across the street. Lewin glanced up occasionally, hardly seeing what was in front of him. He was absorbed in what he was reading, conscious of little but the printed words of the book, the vague shapes of the walls of the room, the hiss of the gas fire, the habitual posture of his own body over the table.

When he became aware of the sound, he seemed to have been hearing it for some time without really noticing it. Yet it was so strange a noise that once he was aware of it he could hardly believe that it had registered itself simply as something 'outside', to be ignored, like the hiss of a car down the wet street or the faint vibration of the window every time a gust of snow was blown against it. He looked up from his book, seeing clearly, with an effect of suddenness, the black lines of the kerb on the other side of the street, and the steps leading to the houses beyond. There was a faint frown between his brows; he was waiting for the noise to come again. What on earth had it been? Where had it come from? Above? Below? Out on the street? But, at the moment, nothing moved in the street and there was no sound within the building. Had he imagined it?

Then it came again and again, much more loudly than before, and growing louder still with every repetition. Now Lewin thought he recognized it, and for a fleeting moment his mind accepted the recognition, before rejecting it violently; it was so absurd, so grotesque. He had thought the noise to be the mooing of a cow. A cow in Maher Street, Hornsey! A cow in the house! For he was sure now that the noise did come from within the house; it was too close to have come from anywhere else. Persistently, regularly, still growing in volume, the noise went on – a great, deep lowing or bellowing.

Was it some kind of noise from a radio or television set? But there was unmistakably an animal-like note within it, a particular vibration of chords that only lungs and a mouth of some kind could have produced. The vibration seemed to penetrate right through Lewin's body, which responded with a protest that was also, unwillingly, a kind of sympathy. Whatever was uttering the sound had no more control or consciousness than a beast, and was giving voice as an animal might – blindly, knowing no motive or impulsion other than the sheer pain of its existence in the world. The bellowing went on, with a slow, delayed rhythm, and then, as abruptly as before, stopped.

Lewin was now determined to find out what was wrong. He went out of the flat, closing the door behind him, and into the hall. It was dark there; the only light came through the small panes of coloured glass in the top half of the front door. He stood there for a moment, hesitating. The front door swung open. Jill stood on the step. Each of them was startled to see the other. In one gloved hand she held a shopping bag.

'Michael! Are you going out?' She had begun to smile, but the expression on his face checked her. 'What's the matter?'

'There's something funny going on. I think it's upstairs. Listen!'

Jill stood on the step, her coat buttoned to her neck, her face turned upwards. There were a few gleaming drops of moisture in her hair, and her soft cheeks were bruised by the cold. Lewin reached out and took the shopping bag from her.

She stepped into the hall. 'There's nothing,' she said. 'You're imagining things.'

'No, I'm not.'

Even as he spoke, the noise – the bellow or groan – came again. Jill's face went quite still, the look upon it simply locked for a moment. When she spoke her features seemed to shudder into life with her words.

'She must be having her baby!' she cried.

'No!'

'I'm sure.'

'God, what a frightful noise.'

'She might be wanting help. Have you tried the door?' She pushed at the door that led upstairs. It opened on a flight of linoleum-covered stairs, down which, even more clearly than before, there came yet another immense groan, a heave of sound.

'Shall I come, too?' he asked.

But Jill was already halfway up the stairs and did not reply. So Lewin put down the shopping bag and followed her.

The landing upstairs had been made into a narrow hall, and from it one door opened on a kitchen, another on a living room. Both doors were ajar, and each showed a different kind of disorder within. Overhead, on the floor above, Lewin heard footsteps and voices – Jill's and someone else's. Then Jill called him, her voice overborne by another groan, and he ran up the next flight of stairs. There he found an even narrower landing, and again two doors opening from it. Through one, Lewin glimpsed a big double bed, with a mound rising up in the middle of it, and the white oval of the woman's face beyond the mound. The dim, small face seemed to have no relation to the shape below it or to the sounds that were coming from it. Out of the other room Jill emerged, with a child holding each hand.

'Michael, take the children downstairs. Take them to our flat. They're absolutely terrified.'

'What's happening?

'She's having her baby. I told you. She's phoned for the midwife; she should be here any minute. And her sister's coming from Ilford – she phoned her, too. And then the contractions really started, so she crawled into bed. I wish she'd told me – look at these poor kids!'

The children stared at him with large eyes: two blue, two brown. Lewin wanted to smile at them, but could not do it.

'Go on,' Jill said. 'Don't just stand there. Take them down. I'll come when I can.'

'What are you going to do?'

'Nothing, I hope. I'll just stay here until the midwife comes. I can't leave her alone.' She spoke hurriedly and softly, almost whispering. 'God, I hope the baby doesn't come first – I haven't the faintest idea what to do.'

'You're supposed to boil water,' Lewin said, and stifled an impulse to giggle stupidly. 'That's what they always do in the pictures.'

Jill did not answer. He felt her eyes rest gravely on him; then she was gone. Lewin saw her in the woman's bedroom, standing at the side of the bed. She bent over and held the woman's hand. The gesture disturbed Lewin in its curious intimacy. He felt himself excluded: he did not know what he was doing there. The woman uttered another profound groan. The most startling thing about it to Lewin was that she did not seem to move when she made the noise. He would have thought that only a contraction or spasm of her entire body could possibly have produced so deep and loud a sound. The woman lay quite still. Lewin fled, taking with him the two children; they came obediently, silently, rigidly, when he held out his hands to them.

Though the woman's groans still vibrated through the house, and though he had the two children with him, it was a relief to Lewin to find himself back in the living room of the flat, with the gas fire still burning and his book still open on the table. He looked at the children. The younger was staring curiously around the room; the elder had just turned her head away and was gazing at the books on the low bookshelf against the wall. The fixity with which the child looked at the backs of these large, greyish books, meaningless to her, was even more expressive of misery than her pallor or the size of her eyes in her face. The two girls were dressed in tiny skirts and jerseys, of an identical pattern and colour, and their hair was tied with ribbons in neat ponytails. Lost, dry-eyed, they stood together in the middle of the room.

It seemed to Lewin years since he had last spoken to a child. What kind of thing did one say to them? How was he to distract them from what was happening overhead? Did they know what was happening? Ought he to say something about it? 'Your mummy will soon be better,' he said.

The older girl's head was still turned aside; her lip trembled in response to his words. But the younger said loudly, 'My mummy's going to get us a little baby.'

'That's right. You'll like that, won't you. What's your name?'

'Jenny,' the child whispered, suddenly as coy as she had been bold a moment before. She swayed slightly from side to side on her plump legs.

'And yours?'

But the other did not reply, did not even look at him.

'Her name is Mary,' her sister said.

'Jenny and Mary. What very nice names.'

Upstairs, at regular intervals, their mother was still uttering her intolerable, gross moans. The noise subdued Lewin and infuriated him at the same time. He wanted to shout at her to shut up, for God's sake! When was the midwife coming?

'Would you like something to eat?' he asked the children. 'I've got some nice biscuits for you. Come and see; they're in the kitchen.'

He took them into the kitchen, sat them at the table, and gave each of them a cup of milk and two biscuits. Mary, the older child, held both her biscuits in one small hand, but did not eat them. She sat there for a few minutes, while her sister ate and drank and played with the crumbs that dropped on the table. Then the older girl climbed quietly off her chair and said, 'I must go back to my mummy now.'

'No, you mustn't. Your mummy's very busy.'

They confronted one another, the child's legs planted stiffly on the floor, her neck and shoulders rigid, the muscles of her face seeming to strain away from each individual, diminutive feature, exposing them all equally, simultaneously. Her stiffness and completeness surprised Lewin – she was another person, another full life. One day she would groan in childbirth, too.

Then the girl's face collapsed, and she began to sob with such inconsolable shudders for breath between each cry that Lewin felt she was not merely beyond any comfort he could bring to her but was even beyond knowing anything of his presence in the room. Her sister cried, too, but more out of sympathy with the other's tears than out of a similar frenzy. Lewin could not leave them, because he was afraid the older girl would bolt upstairs the moment he turned his back, but he could not approach her, either. He just stood there. Eventually she retreated from him and stood with her head against the sink cabinet, her back to him, her shoulders shaking. They were standing like that when Jill came in.

'Thank goodness you've come,' Lewin said. 'I can't deal with them.'

'It doesn't look like it, does it?'

'All right, you do better!' he shouted, enraged by the unfairness of the remark. He had been doing his best. And what a sordid, squalid mess it all was anyway! What did it have to do with him? The flat, the house, the street, the sombre, peeling neighbourhood all seemed like a prison to him – a place in which he had been trapped and where he was forced to witness things happening to people for whom he was in no way

217

responsible. What was he doing here? Jill seemed a stranger to him. He felt he was a stranger to himself.

The midwife and a nurse came, followed by a doctor, who stayed for ten minutes and then left. Everything was apparently in order. Jill gave the little girls lunch, she took them for a walk to a nearby park, she brought them back to the flat and played games with them on the floor of the living room, using toys she had fetched from their room upstairs, she saw to it that each of them went to the lavatory.

She was particularly attentive to the older girl, who never really settled down, who remained tense, quick to start to her feet and ask if she could go back to her mummy now, whose laughter during the games had a false, anxious shrillness. Lewin watched Jill, who hardly seemed aware of him, she was so busy. His feeling of oppression and estrangement so weighed on him that eventually he developed a headache, and went out for a walk on his own, to clear his head.

He walked for a long time, for miles, through the unending coil of streets. But wherever he went he heard in his inner ear the groans of the woman upstairs; he saw Jill's small face, absorbed in the children, or with the strange locked expression that had come upon it when she had first heard the woman's groans. When the early dusk came down, Lewin found himself in a park, standing on a humped ornamental bridge over a little lake. The cars that passed on the road alongside the park already had their lights on. Behind Lewin, at one end of the lake, there was a long slope of lawn; at the other end was a grove of black trees. No one was about. A few isolated flakes of snow drifted downwards, without haste, from the one-coloured sky. On the lake a duck sailed towards him, drawing behind it an arrow-shaped pattern of ripples in the water. The ripples gleamed with a faint wavering silver that was lost as they widened on both sides. The duck passed under the bridge, and in the distance a bell rang. He had to be getting home. A melancholy gentleness of mood that he did not understand but could not resist had fallen upon him. In spite of the cold that gripped his ankles, he lingered there, until the bell rang again.

He found, when he got back to the flat, that the baby – a little boy – had been born, and that the delivery had been normal; that the aunt of the little girls had finally come and taken them away with her to Ilford; that another woman, a Health Service 'home help', had moved into the flat and would be staying there for a fortnight, until the mother was on her feet again; and that a message about the birth of the child had been sent to the father, who had so far made no response to it. So the crisis upstairs was over, for the time being at least, and the privacy of their flat was restored to Jill and Lewin.

Jill had been sitting on a couch in the dark, with the fire on. She had not stood up, or moved, or greeted him, when he came in. She answered his questions about what had happened while he was away, and then they sat in silence, Lewin in a chair near her, still in his overcoat, with his scarf around his neck. Jill had her legs drawn up under her. She looked tousled and weary. Her head, resting on one hand, drooped under the weight of her thick hair, and the corners of her mouth drooped too.

'Is something wrong?' Lewin asked.

Jill did not answer him.

'You're unhappy,' he said. 'Why?'

She spoke after a pause, without looking up. 'Because we must do something.'

'Do something? What do you mean?'

'I mean, I can't live with you – like this – any longer.'

'Why not?' He tried to laugh. Yet he realized that he had been expecting her to say something of that kind. He almost felt relieved that she had done so. For if she had not, he might have been forced to speak, and he did not know what he wanted to say. All he knew was that ever since he and Jill had stood together and heard the woman's groans he had felt a pressure upon himself, upon them both, that had been impelling them towards this moment in the shabby, familiar room. Even before she answered his question, he was staring about it, at every ugly, hired item they had lived with and thought of as their own.

Jill raised her head and looked at him. Her face was pale. Only the cheek that had been resting against her hand showed the faintest colour. 'Because I love you. And because I want to have a baby, too. I want to have your baby. Please don't leave me, Michael.' Her voice shook a little on the last few words. She closed her eyes, too late to halt the tears that crept slowly under her eyelids and ran down her cheeks.

'I love you, too.' The words were wrenched out of his chest, leaving a hollow that was filled instantly with a hot flux of emotions he could not have named – regrets, fears, exultations, incredulities. One ironic point of his consciousness flickered brightly, signalling to him that if he was to leave her, he would have to do it now, tonight. Their arrangement was at an end.

But he did not move, nor did she, until they heard a queer, cracked whimpering yell from upstairs. Jill shivered and rose, and came to his chair, kneeling beside it. They were shy of touching one another. Suddenly they both laughed, nervously and excitedly. Their hands met, and only then their eyes. Each saw in the other's the recognition that it was not going to be easy for them.

AFTERWORD

The first story in this collection was published in 1953; the last in 1968. They are presented here in chronological order. I have taken the opportunity to excise from them many superfluities and ineptitudes; nothing, however, has been added. The book includes everything I would wish to keep from two earlier volumes, *A Long Way from London* and *Beggar My Neighbour*, which are both out of print. The last four stories have not previously been collected in England.

Only 'The Box' and 'A Day in the Country' were written while I was still living in South Africa; they are also the only two which stick closely throughout to my memory of the events they describe. In every other case I can remember quite vividly the person, or incident, or set of circumstances which, years later, was to suggest the story. Such a memory would suddenly turn in its sleep and show how much life there was still in it. Then came a time for curiosity, speculation, invention, the righting or the aggravation of old wrongs, a playful or malicious juxtaposition of quite different people and incidents upon those recollected, a readiness at all stages to subject the results to rough handling, to sudden reversals and abridgements. To what end? Surprise, chiefly. Not in order to trick the reader; but rather in the hope that if I managed to surprise myself, there was a chance that the completed tale would be truly self-sufficient. It would not collapse the moment

I turned my back on it; it would not need any foreword or afterword from me.

Life itself, however, has uttered its own afterwords to some of these stories; it has presented them with sequels more melodramatic or pathetic than any I might have dared to invent. For instance, a couple of years after the publication of 'A Day in the Country', the original of the young, aggressive, thick-armed Boer who appears in it was shot dead on a railway platform by the husband of a woman he was having an affair with ... The farm across which Boaz and the narrator wander in 'Through the Wilderness', picking up small, shining stones, looking at them and throwing them away – that farm turned out to be the site of a diamond- strike worth millions of pounds, and is now the scene of large-scale mining operations ... The man upon whom the character of Harry Grossman in 'The Zulu and the Zeide' was based became, in due course, very old and difficult to cope with, senile indeed. So his children hired an African male servant to look after him, as I write of him doing for his father. But because times had changed and the family had prospered, these two did not wander about on foot, as my characters do, but instead drove about in a car, with the African at the wheel. One of their favourite drives was to 'Israel', which the old man had developed an inordinate desire to visit before his life ended. They would drive to a spot in the empty countryside around Johannesburg; the driver would point at the veld ahead of them and say, 'There's Israel,' and his employer would sit Moses-like in the seat of his car, looking out upon the promised land ...

Readers of another story, 'The Example of Lipi Lippmann', written long before I had heard of this, may recognise something familiar in the situation.

But enough. If I go on I shall be accused of romancing again, or of bewailing missed opportunities. I wish to do neither. The chances these stories took are now entirely their own.

Of the previously uncollected stories, 'Led Astray' was first published in *The New Yorker*; 'Sonia' and 'Through the Wilderness' in *Commentary*; and 'Another Day' in *The Atlantic Monthly*. 'Another Day' and 'Through the Wilderness' were reprinted in *Penguin Modern Stories No. 6*.

Dan Jacobson

The Confessions of Josef Baisz

Josef Baisz is as remarkable a creation as the imaginary country, Sarmeda, in which he lives. Throughout his career – whether as soldier, scholar, husband, murderer or kidnapper – he is driven by the overwhelming urge to subvert and destroy. A man of peculiar genius, this desire spurs him on to 'greater' things until he finally arrives at the inevitable and yet crushingly unexpected denouement of the tale which he himself narrates.

The Evidence of Love

Kenneth Makeer – intelligent, South African and black – travels to London to study law where he meets a fellow South African – a white girl – whom he eventually marries. Yet mixed marriages are outlawed in the Union, and so when they return home they come face to face with racial intolerance and hatred at its most brutal.

This is a passionate, harrowing and dramatic story which hurtles towards its ugly and untimely conclusion.

'It is scrupulously well written. It is very much the sort of novel that counts' *Guardian*

'An admirable writer has written another admirable book' *Spectator*

DAN JACOBSON

HER STORY

Celia Dinan died some two hundred years ago – back in the twenty-first century. As her life is rediscovered it becomes apparent that she is the author of a powerful and passionate tale – a tale which only she could have written but which 'everywoman' will painfully acknowledge as her own.

THE PRICE OF DIAMONDS

Lyndhurst, South Africa, is a declining diamond-mining town, much like Kimberley, where the author of the novel grew up. As long-term business partners and friends, Mr Fink and Mr Gottlieb find themselves tempted away from the straight and narrow towards the devious ways of trading illicit diamonds. In this compassionate and humorous novel, Jacobson reveals the serious themes hidden beneath the comic life of his characters.

DAN JACOBSON

THE TRAP AND A DANCE IN THE SUN

The Trap and *A Dance in the Sun* bring together Jacobson's initial two novels – stories of racial confrontation and social injustice on the South African veld. In *The Trap,* relations between the white farmers and their black workers are brought on to a sinister and harrowing conclusion whilst *A Dance in the Sun* sees two young innocent bystanders becoming embroiled in a long-standing family saga. These stories have retained their freshness and their power to move the reader.

'This author is stylish, he tells everything in simple words, but his undertones are subtle…it is quite masterly' *Observer*

THE WONDER-WORKER

As events switch between London and Switzerland, Jacobson introduces us to a host of vivid and extraordinary characters. Most notable amongst these is London-born Timothy Fogel, a child with the wilful belief that he has been endowed with special powers. As events unfold it becomes apparent that this belief has cataclysmic implications for all involved. *The Wonder-Worker* is a remarkable and evocative novel about obsession, passion and the extraordinary power of the human imagination.

OTHER TITLES BY DAN JACOBSON AVAILABLE DIRECT FROM HOUSE OF STRATUS

Quantity		£	$(US)	$(CAN)	€
☐	THE BEGINNERS	7.99	12.99	19.95	13.00
☐	THE CONFESSIONS OF JOSEF BAISZ	7.99	12.99	19.95	13.00
☐	THE EVIDENCE OF LOVE	7.99	12.99	19.95	13.00
☐	HER STORY	7.99	12.99	19.95	13.00
☐	THE PRICE OF DIAMONDS	7.99	12.99	19.95	13.00
☐	THE RAPE OF TAMAR	7.99	12.99	19.95	13.00
☐	THE STORY OF THE STORIES	7.99	12.99	19.95	13.00
☐	THE TRAP AND A DANCE IN THE SUN	7.99	12.99	19.95	13.00
☐	THE WONDER-WORKER	7.99	12.99	19.95	13.00

ALL HOUSE OF STRATUS BOOKS ARE AVAILABLE FROM GOOD BOOKSHOPS OR DIRECT FROM THE PUBLISHER:

Internet: www.houseofstratus.com including author interviews, reviews, features.

Email: sales@houseofstratus.com please quote author, title, and credit card details.

Hotline: UK ONLY: 0800 169 1780, please quote author, title and credit card details.
INTERNATIONAL: +44 (0) 20 7494 6400, please quote author, title, and credit card details.

Send to: House of Stratus Sales Department
24c Old Burlington Street
London
W1X 1RL
UK

Please allow for postage costs charged per order plus an amount per book as set out in the tables below:

	£(Sterling)	$(US)	$(CAN)	€(Euros)
Cost per order				
UK	2.00	3.00	4.50	3.30
Europe	3.00	4.50	6.75	5.00
North America	3.00	4.50	6.75	5.00
Rest of World	3.00	4.50	6.75	5.00
Additional cost per book				
UK	0.50	0.75	1.15	0.85
Europe	1.00	1.50	2.30	1.70
North America	2.00	3.00	4.60	3.40
Rest of World	2.50	3.75	5.75	4.25

PLEASE SEND CHEQUE, POSTAL ORDER (STERLING ONLY), EUROCHEQUE, OR INTERNATIONAL MONEY ORDER (PLEASE CIRCLE METHOD OF PAYMENT YOU WISH TO USE)
MAKE PAYABLE TO: STRATUS HOLDINGS plc

Cost of book(s): _____   Example: 3 x books at £6.99 each: £20.97

Cost of order: _____   Example: £2.00 (Delivery to UK address)

Additional cost per book: _____   Example: 3 x £0.50: £1.50

Order total including postage: _____   Example: £24.47

Please tick currency you wish to use and add total amount of order:

☐ £ (Sterling)   ☐ $ (US)   ☐ $ (CAN)   ☐ € (EUROS)

VISA, MASTERCARD, SWITCH, AMEX, SOLO, JCB:

☐ ☐ ☐ ☐ ☐ ☐ ☐ ☐ ☐ ☐ ☐ ☐ ☐ ☐ ☐ ☐ ☐ ☐ ☐ ☐

Issue number (Switch only):

☐ ☐ ☐

Start Date: Expiry Date:

☐☐ / ☐☐   ☐☐ / ☐☐

Signature: _____

NAME: _____

ADDRESS: _____

_____

POSTCODE: _____

Please allow 28 days for delivery.

Prices subject to change without notice.
Please tick box if you do not wish to receive any additional information. ☐

House of Stratus publishes many other titles in this genre; please check our website (**www.houseofstratus.com**) for more details.